As the year draws to a close and the season of sharing
and celebration begins, it's time for

Friends, Families, Lovers

Let these gifted and popular authors—Kathleen Eagle,
Sandra Kitt and Ruth Jean Dale—draw you into their
stories. Let them draw you into the circle of love....

About the Authors

KATHLEEN EAGLE has published more than twenty romance novels, both historical and contemporary. This award-winning author set aside a seventeen-year teaching career on a North Dakota Indian reservation to become a full-time fiction writer. She has also taught university-level English and is a frequent speaker at writers' conferences and workshops. Kathleen now lives in Minnesota with her family. Her husband, Clyde, is a Minneapolis teacher whose Lakota Sioux heritage has inspired many of her stories.

SANDRA KITT has been writing for the Harlequin American series since its beginning. Besides being a well-known and highly regarded author, Sandra also maintains a demanding career as a librarian with the American Museum of Natural History. *And* she's a graphic designer and printmaker whose work has appeared on UNICEF greeting cards. Sandra and her husband live in New York City.

RUTH JEAN DALE is rapidly gaining a reputation for her humorous yet moving stories. She writes primarily for the Harlequin Romance and Harlequin Temptation series; her "Taggarts of Texas" miniseries includes two Romance titles, a Temptation and a Harlequin Historical Romance. Ruth Jean spent twenty-five years as a newspaper writer and editor. Her husband is a former Marine captain who went on to a second career—also in newspapers. Now, two of their four daughters work as writers. Ruth Jean Dale has lived all over the U.S. and, with her husband, recently moved to Colorado.

Friends, Families, Lovers

Kathleen Eagle • Sandra Kitt
Ruth Jean Dale

Harlequin Books

TORONTO • NEW YORK • LONDON
AMSTERDAM • PARIS • SYDNEY • HAMBURG
STOCKHOLM • ATHENS • TOKYO • MILAN
MADRID • WARSAW • BUDAPEST • AUCKLAND

HARLEQUIN BOOKS

FRIENDS, FAMILIES, LOVERS
Copyright © 1993 by Harlequin Enterprises Limited

ISBN 0-373-83260-5

FRIENDS, FAMILIES, LOVERS 1993 first printing
October 1993

The publisher acknowledges the copyright holders of
the individual works as follows:

THE SHARING SPOON
Copyright © 1993 by Kathleen Eagle

LOVE IS THANKS ENOUGH
Copyright © 1993 by Sandra Kitt

THE MORE THE MERRIER
Copyright © 1993 by Betty Duran

CONTENTS

THE SHARING SPOON
Kathleen Eagle

For Mr. Eagle and his students at the
Four Winds School,
with love from Mrs. Eagle

Prologue

IN HIS MIND Kyle Bear Soldier turned the brown brick high-rise complex into South Dakota buttes. He'd gone back home a thousand times in the twelve months since he'd moved to Minneapolis, but only one of those trips had been physical. In July, when he'd been desperate for South Dakota skies and Lakota Sioux renewal, he'd gone home for the Sun Dance. It was September now, almost time for school to start, and his daily run was a good time to take himself back mentally, over the tops of the tall buildings, beyond the trees and back home.

The city was a good place to find employment. There was plenty of excitement, all kinds of amusement and crowds of people—more people in a few square miles than could be found, living or dead, in the whole expanse of his home state. Most of the time he could live with that. There was a lot of asphalt, tons of concrete, but there were a good number of parks, as well, and ten miles outside the city a guy could find peace beside a lake or a stretch of open field.

But there wasn't a butte in sight, and there were too many shade trees to suit Kyle. Pine trees were fine, but those big leafy shade trees made it hard to see out, hard to breathe. And winter, which would be coming on soon, might not have been quite as mean as it was in South Dakota, but day after day, month after month, it was one hell of a lot of gray and white.

There was a community of his people here—a community within a community—and Kyle had come to the Twin Cities to be part of it. Not only were there Lakota people from North and South Dakota, but there were East River Sioux—the Dakota people—and there were Minnesota Chippewa, who preferred to be called by their own name, which was Ojibwa. In lesser numbers there were Native Americans from other parts of the country, all come to the city to find a new life. Sometimes, as in Kyle's case, they actually found work. And like Kyle, they all got homesick. They yearned for the land that had given their ancestors sustenance, places where few man-made structures rose above the ground floor. Their roots were on Indian reservations, places generally known as "God's country."

And God's country it was—God's and what was left of the creatures He'd designated to be the land's native inhabitants. Jobs were scarce in God's country. There was little money there, and the food on the hoof was, for the most part, claimed by somebody other than God these days.

"How's it goin', Kyle?"

He turned and slowed down to offer Tony Plentykill a handshake. "Good." Tony, a man half a head shorter than Kyle, was wearing a new shirt. He'd forgotten to take the little round inspector's sticker off the pocket, so Kyle did it for him. "Where you headed?"

"Feed." Tony jerked his chin to indicate the direction. "Over to the church. Then there's a doings over at the school gym. Two drums," he said, wielding an imaginary drumbeater in one hand. "Better get something to eat so you can *really* sing one." He cupped the other hand behind his ear and grimaced, as though he were getting into a song.

"I'll be there. The kids have been bugging me to put on the bear face again. That's what I'm supposed to look like when I dance."

Tony gave a little yelp, punched Kyle's arm and tapped one tennis shoe against the pavement. For a minute Kyle thought the man was going to start grass-dancing right there on the street.

He laughed and returned Tony's punch. "I can feel that drumbeat already. I'll be there."

Chapter One

CYNTHIA BOYER had learned her civic and social responsibilties at her mother's knee. Those who were privileged had their obligations. Of late, Cynthia hadn't felt very privileged, but she thrived on responsibility, and it was about all that made sense anymore.

As a new teacher at All Nations Elementary School in Minneapolis, she had decided to focus her attention on the needs of her students' neighborhood, to serve as she'd always served, twice a month, with her hands as well as her checkbook. It was the "hands" part that always drove her mother's eyebrow into an arch of displeasure, but it was Cynthia's way of going Mother one better.

Her mother didn't understand why she'd taken a teaching position, either, but then, Mother hadn't been childless, had never experienced a frigidly civilized, no-fault divorce, and had undoubtedly never felt hollow inside. Cynthia didn't need a salary, but she desperately needed meaningful work. When school-board member Karen Grasso had mentioned the vacancy at All Nations, Cynthia knew she had found that work. Karen had been her friend forever, and she knew Cynthia better than anyone did.

She hadn't met her students yet. She'd been interviewed by the school principal, two parents and someone from the central administration. They'd all asked her how she felt about working in the neighborhood. The Phillips neighborhood was a part of Minneapolis she had only driven through, and not often, but now she would be driving *to* it every day. Did that scare her? she'd been asked. Not at all, she'd answered. They'd smiled and nodded and offered her the job.

And so, on the evening before her first staff meeting of her first day as a teacher at All Nations, Cynthia had come to St. Jude's church basement as one of the volunteers who would help serve a free meal to the needy as part of the Loaves and Fishes program.

Linda Kopp ran the kitchen. The church paid her to see that all the serving spoons found their way back into the right drawers, that the health-department codes were followed, and that the teams of volunteers who came from all over the Twin Cities were able to put a meal together on schedule.

"Guests come through the line, but they don't pick up the trays," Linda instructed. The kitchen crew had already done most of their work, but they popped their heads through the serving window to lend an ear while the serving team gathered around the long spread of steaming pans and stacks of trays.

"Trays are handed to the guests after we fill them. If there's enough left for seconds, we have to use clean trays. They can't bring dirty trays back up for refills. Plastic gloves are required for volunteers." She pointed toward the dispenser box, and there was at least one disgruntled groan. "These are all health-department regulations, you know."

"Of course," the woman standing next to Cynthia mumbled, and she took it upon herself to pull out several of the disposable gloves and distribute them. She had introduced herself rather brusquely as Marge Gross. "Aprons are, too. Do you have aprons?"

The aprons, too, were disposable. Cynthia felt as though she were preparing to operate on the green beans. She'd done a lot of volunteer work, but this was her first Loaves and Fishes experience, and she got the feeling everyone around her was gearing up for a race. She wondered who had the starter's gun and where the starting block was. At the very least she wanted to be in the right place.

"Here they come," someone called from the back of the huge parish basement.

"You can do peaches," Marge said as she edged Cynthia away from the beans. Peaches were fine, she thought absently as she watched the crowd pour in. They came in all shapes, sizes, genders and colors, but there was a preponderance of Native Americans, and many of them were children. Undoubtedly some of them were those she would spend the next nine months teaching about the visual arts.

The sound of voices rolled over the serving table. Apparently the people were hungry, for the line moved quickly, with each person's eyes following the progress of a tray from hand to hand on the servers' side of the table. Hungry people, Cynthia thought as she strained the juice from a spoonful of canned peaches and plopped them on a tray. But they didn't look particularly miserable or downtrodden. Mothers were trying to keep their kids in line; friends were chatting, and youngsters were jostling for position. They looked like people attending a potluck supper.

But this wasn't potluck. This was charity, and these were poor people, and Cynthia was performing a service.

The man who faced her across the table looked the part. His bulbous red nose and puffy eyes branded him as readily as his tattered trench coat, which struck Cynthia as odd apparel for such a warm evening. He scanned the table. "Spaghetti, huh?"

"I haven't tried it, but I'm sure it's tasty," Cynthia said as she dished up more peaches.

"If it isn't, I know how to really heat things up."

The remark almost slid past Cynthia but she stiffened when he slipped his hand inside his coat. It happened so quickly that she didn't have time to get her vocal cords working and warn people to hit the deck.

Louisiana hot sauce. A sly twinkle nearly displaced the weariness in the man's face when he showed it to her.

"Yes, I . . ." Cynthia managed a wan smile as the tension eased from her shoulders. "I guess that would do it."

"Don't hold up the line," Marge warned.

The hot sauce disappeared as the man eyed Cynthia, placing a grubby finger to his lips as a signal that he'd shared a secret with her.

Linda Kopp slid behind Cynthia and touched her shoulder. "We need another beverage-cart handler. George can handle this end of the table," she said, gesturing to the man who was handling trays and utensils.

Cynthia was assigned to a heavy-duty kitchen cart containing insulated carafes, pitchers, milk cartons, cups and condiments. She poured as fast as she could, but the requests came faster. Her hands were sweating inside the plastic gloves, and hair was sticking to her forehead. Two coffees. Five lemonades. Three milks. Four of each. She didn't have enough hands.

"Kyle wants more lemonade."

Cynthia glanced down at a bright-eyed girl who'd just lost her two front teeth. Her pigtails were banded in bows of red yarn, and she offered up a cup and the smile of one who'd been specially chosen for an errand. Cynthia refilled the cup and watched the child carry it toward the end of the table. She expected the child to deliver the glass to the small boy whose chin was barely table level but, instead, she handed it to one of the men.

He thanked the girl, then flashed Cynthia a winning smile before turning back to his conversation with two older men and a teenage boy. The dark-eyed smile stunned her just as effectively as the man in line had, but the shock waves went much deeper. Kyle whoever-he-was was, in a word, a knockout.

The word could not have been her own, Cynthia told herself. It must have been something she'd read recently. There was a blob of sweat in the middle of his blue T-shirt, and he wore a brow band. He'd obviously been running. He was a *jock,* for heaven's sake. Not her type at all.

And able-bodied as all get-out. Why did he expect to be waited on, and why wasn't he out working to pay for his supper?

With a mental "harrumph" Cynthia pulled her thoughts away from the man and continued to fill beverage requests without risking another glance toward the end of his table. But soon the little girl was back.

"Kyle wants coffee."

"The coffee's very hot," Cynthia cautioned as she handed a cup of milk to another small customer. "I don't want you to burn yourself."

"I can carry it. I always get coffee."

"Not for yourself, I hope."

"If I want some, I do." The child waited a few seconds before patiently repeating herself. "Kyle wants coffee."

Cynthia filled the cup and looked his way again. He was studying her, waiting. She smiled pointedly for the helpful child. Not for the man. Did he think he was patronizing a restaurant here? The little girl carried the cup away carefully, and Cynthia went back to her work.

"I forgot. Kyle wants sugar."

Cynthia glanced up from the stream of milk she was pouring for another child. It was the same obliging little girl, same large chocolate-drop eyes. Handsome is as handsome does, Cynthia thought, and Kyle's behavior surely let him out.

"Have you eaten?"

"My mom's in line for us." The little girl cocked her head to one side. "You new?"

"No, I didn't know, but I'm—"

"I mean *new*. A new volunteer. I haven't seen you here."

"Oh. Yes." Cynthia smiled, rejecting the inclination to ask whether she came often. "Where do you go to school?"

"All Nations," the girl said, standing steadfast when an older girl tried to edge her away from the beverage cart. "The *almost* new school."

The older girl's request for lemonade registered with Cynthia, and she set about filling a cup. "I'm going to be a teacher there this year."

"You?" The little girl watched the lemonade change hands. "What grade?"

"Art," Cynthia said.

"Oh, yeah. The last guy quit after somebody sort of doctored up the coffee in his thermos bottle. Can I have the sugar?"

"How about some lemonade? Then I'll just move over that way." She shook a cup loose from the stack as she pushed the cart between the row of chairs. It was time she put an end to this go-fetch routine. "What can I..." She thought better of saying "do for you?" and said, instead, "...offer you gentlemen? Someone needed sugar?"

"Kyle did," the little girl insisted. "C'mon, Kyle. My mom's up to the front. I'll let you cut in line."

The man turned and offered the child a smile. "No, that's okay."

He was a guest, Cynthia reminded herself when he lifted his dark eyes to meet hers. She couldn't quite remember why she'd taken up the cool pitcher in one hand and a paper cup in the other. "You should get something to eat," she said to the girl.

"Sugar would be good." He snatched at the tip of one perky pigtail. "Then we'll see if Lee Ann leaves me anything." The little girl giggled and whipped her pigtails with a quick shake of her head. "Go on up there and help your mother, Lee Ann. Hurry up, now."

A tall, gangly young man shoved his empty cup Cynthia's way. "Coffee," he ordered, and when she took the cup, he scowled at her hand. His glasses were held together with adhesive tape at both temples, and he seemed to need to squint to focus. "Do you have a hole in your gloves?"

Cynthia examined her left palm, then turned her hand over, searching as she might for a run in her stocking. "I don't think so."

The tall man peered into her eyes, sober as a judge. "How'd you get your hands in them, then?"

The man named Kyle was laughing along with the rest of the annoying men at his table. Lee Ann had skipped off to join her mother, and Cynthia smiled tightly. She had fallen headfirst for that one. Bristling a little, she moved her beverage cart along and continued to do her job. She knew Kyle was watching her, and so she deliberately ignored him. She had enough to do.

The room was hot, and the crowd kept her pouring in more ways than one. The only way to keep the sweat from dripping off her brow and into the lemonade was to wipe it with her sleeve. Her hands felt so clammy she wished she *did* have holes in her gloves.

A toddler appeared at her elbow with two chocolate cookies. "Milk would be good with those," Cynthia said.

The child put one of the cookies on the corner of her cart, then tipped his head back and waited for a sign of acceptance. Cynthia thanked him, and he shoved the second cookie into his mouth and disappeared under the table.

"Aren't you going to eat your cookie?" Kyle asked as he approached the cart, cup in hand. "The kids are up there clamoring for the last of them, and that little guy gave you one to eat. That's his gift."

Cynthia glanced at Kyle, then at the cookie. No one was clamoring for anything to drink at the moment. She had the feeling this was some sort of test, just like the glove joke. She picked up the cookie with plastic-covered fingers and opened her mouth to take a bite.

"'Course, *I* didn't get any."

She glanced up. "No dinner at all?"

"They ran out."

The hall was clearing out now, and he was right. Cookies were the item most in demand at the serving table. The rest was being cleared away. Spontaneously she offered him the bit of food she held. He put his hand around hers, steadied the cookie and took a bite. "Thanks."

"That's all right. I had supper before I came."

"Figures." He took a swallow of coffee, then shrugged dejectedly. "Guess I'll have to go looking somewhere else."

"There must be something left," she said quickly. "I think there's milk. Green beans, I'm sure."

"I'm like the kids. I hate green beans just naked like that."

He gave her a boyish smile, and she thought, *Picky,* but said, "Naked?"

"I like them better *in* something. Like soup, or a hot dish."

Maybe "picky" wasn't the right word. "But one cookie isn't enough."

"Next time I'll get in line right away." He backed away smiling. "Thanks for sharing a bite with me. Better than nothing, right?"

"I could—"

"Make supper for me?" He obviously enjoyed the look of shock that registered on her face. "Just kidding. See you around." And he left without giving her a backward glance.

Around where?

He looked awfully good in those running shorts.

Make supper for him?

Around where?

Chapter Two

THE ANSWER—around All Nations Elementary School—came the next day when Kyle arrived ten minutes late for the first faculty meeting. He was dressed in blue jeans and a striped summer shirt, which Cynthia would have considered too casual for a day of professional meetings if she hadn't been the only professional in the room who was professionally dressed.

While he was making his way to an empty chair and offering a handshake here, a nod there, Cynthia found herself squirming a little. She was sure he was the same man—the one who'd been sitting at the table with the rest of the guests while she'd been serving, doing her civic duty. She remembered exactly what she'd thought, and she was doing her best to remember anything she said that might embarrass her now. The last thing she wanted to do was offend anyone, and this man, this—

"Kyle Bear Soldier," principal Darlene Toule announced with a teasing flourish. "Still running on Indian time."

Kyle took a seat toward the front of the sixth-grade classroom, where most of the empty seats were. "Left my running shoes at home this morning. That's why I'm late, see. But I got myself all dressed up for the first big meeting of the year."

He hadn't missed much, Cynthia thought. They hadn't gotten down to business yet. So far there'd been just a few introductions and lots of welcome-back greetings. She wanted to be part of this group, and she was anxious for the new-kid-on-the-block feeling to wear off. With Cynthia, it always took time. She had introduced herself to Lily Moore, the elderly Indian woman who was sitting next to her, and their brief conversation had been a start.

"This is Kyle's second year with us," Darlene continued from her place of authority at the head of the class. "We recruited him from South Dakota to teach fifth grade."

"He's one of those West River Sioux," Lily related behind the screen of her hand. "They speak L, and we speak D. I'm East River Sioux." Lily seemed to chuckle, but no sound came. Her ample breasts bounced gently. "The other difference is they're ornery and we're not."

Cynthia nodded solemnly, wondering what river the woman was talking about. She knew nothing about L and D, but since Darlene was moving on with the introductions, this was not the time to ask. She wasn't sure how she should interpret the twinkle in Lily's eye.

Darlene introduced the Indian language teachers. Marty Blue, representing the dominant tribe in Minnesota, taught the Ojibwa language, while his wife, Patty, another South Dakotan "from a little town west of the Missouri River," taught the Lakota language. Lily Moore was not a certified teacher, but she contributed to the language program as a native Dakota speaker. And Cynthia felt somewhat enlightened about the river separating two letters—those living on the west side spoke Lakota, those on the east, Dakota.

The reference to the language program prompted Darlene to mention the experimental nature of the program at All Nations. It was that aspect that most interested Cynthia. She knew a lot about Native American art, but little—with the exception of her artist friends—about the people. She knew all the sad statistics, the dreaded high numbers in illness, infant mortality, alcohol dependency, unemployment and school dropouts. It was this last statistic that All Nations was intended to change.

"We've gotten some criticism since we opened last year," Darlene admitted. "This is a public school, and we have to abide by desegregation laws, but we're having a little trouble achieving racial balance."

"The Bureau of Indian Affairs never worried about that," someone in the back of the room commented. "I went to a BIA school. Didn't see the government recruiting anyone for racial balance."

"Well, that's federal, and this is state." Darlene folded her arms across her chest, ostensibly taking a stand. She was a small middle-aged woman of mixed blood for whom taking a stand was clearly not a new experience. "We just have to build such a great program here that non-Indians will flock in and sign up. With this city's magnet school system and open-enrollment policy, we have to be competitive, because parents can shop around."

"We've got Indian kids on the waiting list," Lily reminded her.

"I know, but we can't take any more until we can recruit more non-Indians." There was some grumbling in the ranks, but Darlene lifted a hand to pacify them. "The road isn't always smooth, but I think we have to come together somehow. Our school is called All Nations, and we really want all nations. We have a lot to teach all our students." She looked from one to the other, a gesture that recalled her own teaching days. "We Indian people have good things to share."

"We Lakota end our prayers with *mitakuye oyasin.* All my relatives, which means all nations, all races, all species, even the four-legged ones," Kyle said.

Cynthia was secretly impressed, at once eager and uneasy about coming face-to-face with this man again. He turned in his chair and craned his neck, and she thought, *Oh, dear, not now.* Her pulse fluttered wildly as she escaped his notice. He connected with the Ojibwa language teacher, Marty Blue. "So when Chippewa people come to our sweats, they usually just say, 'All my rabbits.'"

When the chuckles and groans subsided, Marty shot back, "We say, 'All my rabbits got chased away by those damn Sioux puppies.'"

The laughter increased, and Darlene, laughing too, shook her head. "I'd better introduce you to some of our new teachers, who are sitting here laughing just out of politeness and trying to figure out what to make of you guys." She directed her explanation Cynthia's way. "Kyle is Sioux—*Lakota,* pardon me. And Marty is Chippewa—*Ojibwa,* pardon me. Long time ago they used to crack each other over the head with war clubs. Now they just crack sick jokes, mostly about rabbits and puppies.''

"Gets 'em in the gut every time," Kyle chimed in. "These guys know a hundred ways to cook rabbit."

"But they've only got one recipe for puppy soup. No imagination, those Sioux."

"You guys just gave me a great fund-raising idea," Darlene said. "The All Nations Elementary School Recipe Book, compiled by—" she presented each with a flourish of the hand "—Kyle Bear Soldier and Marty Blue."

"What's that recipe for Chippewa-chip cookies, Marty?" Kyle's taunt brought out a few more groans, but the uninitiated were not to hear the punch line this day.

"I don't want my new teachers skipping the coffee break just because we're serving cookies, you guys, so let's get on with the introductions," Darlene said. "Cynthia Boyer is our new art teacher, and she's a personal friend of more Native American artists than she could shake a stick at, if she were into shaking sticks at Indians."

"Which I'm not," Cynthia said quickly. Several heads turned, and she could feel her face flushing as she told herself, *It was a joke, Cynthia.* "I mean, I'm not...I mean, I *am* a connoisseur of Native American art, and I do know...because I have studied..."

Darlene smiled. "You know a lot about art, and you're going to be good for our kids. We're glad to have you."

"Thank you. It's very exciting for me to be here."

The meeting continued in the same low-key vein, information mixed with humor. Cynthia took notes whenever schedules or procedures came up. She gave herself permission to be comfortable with the casual atmosphere, and she knew she'd actually be able to do that once she'd dealt with the moment that was bound to come when the meeting was over.

When it came, he kept it light.

"Got any cookies on you?" Most of the staff had left the room, and Kyle had obviously hung back, waiting to deliver this line. "I missed breakfast."

"I guess I'm a little unprepared," she confessed as she tucked her notebook under her arm, squared her shoulders and returned his smile.

"I think you're a lot surprised to find I'm gainfully employed, as they say. Welcome to All Nations, Cynthia." He offered his hand.

"Thank you."

"Hey, listen." The handshake ended abruptly as he shoved his hands into the pockets of his jeans. " 'Nothing's good or bad, but thinking makes it so.' That's one of my favorite lines from ol' Will Shakespeare, and you don't have to be worried about whatever you were thinking last night. You'll get over it. All Nations will help you get over it."

"Really?" Together they headed for the classroom door. "What was I thinking, other than that you were there for the meal?"

"That I was there for a *free* meal, and you felt sorry for me." She looked up, and his knowing smile surprised her. "All Nations can help you get over that, too, if you stick around long enough. But you'll have to pay some dues first."

"I don't mind paying dues. In fact, I expect to."

"Trouble is, you can't pay them with U.S. coin."

"What'll it take, then?"

"I s'pose puppies are out of the question." He stopped in the doorway and turned, blocking her exit, waiting. She wasn't sure whether to laugh or be appalled. It was a strange sense of humor these people had. Puppies, indeed. He offered that infectious smile. "Cookies, maybe. We like sugar."

"I noticed."

"Then you'll do fine. Where do you live?"

"I just moved. I grew up in Wayzata, but I just bought a condo in the Lake District. I thought it would be good to become part of the city now that I'm working." He raised an eyebrow. "*Here.* I mean, now that I have a job in the city, I want to be involved with city life. *Personally* involved. You know what I mean."

"Sure." He seemed to be looking through her eyes and into her head, gauging her most subtle response, particularly to the news "I live on Portland Avenue, just a few blocks from here."

"That's convenient. In good weather, you don't even have to bother about taking your car out of the garage."

He laughed. "I don't have to worry about it in bad weather, either."

"Ah, so you're one of those die-hard joggers. I admire that."

"I admire someone who's willing to venture out of the suburbs and put her life on the line in the Lake District." The Lake District was definitely high-rent, and his sarcasm, however gentle, came as a surprise after all his good-natured teasing. "And to park her car here in the lot."

"They told me the parking lot had security." Again he raised an eyebrow. "It does, doesn't it?"

"It does." He leaned against the door frame, studying her. "Do you? You look secure enough not to need this job, which isn't going to be easy. You know that."

"I know." Needing pay and needing work were two different things in Cynthia's book. "But I *want* this job. And I want to do well. Even though I'm not First Nation, I've always admired your art."

"First Nation?" He chuckled. "Is that the latest? I think I was Native American last year."

"Is that preferable? I mean, I know you don't like—"

"I prefer Lakota over 'them damn dog-eatin' Sioux,' but you guys keep on changing your politically correct terms on me. I can't keep up. As for my art, I can't even draw a decent stick figure. Some of these kids are really good at it, and some of them are like me."

"But you have a heritage in the visual arts that's admired the world over. I'm..." Not an expert, she told herself. Don't claim that. And she certainly wouldn't admit to being an avid collector, because that would only underline the high-rent label. "...quite knowledgeable in that area."

"Good. Make up for what Andy Rooney said—that there's no such thing as Indian art, that our religion is superstition, and whatever the hell else he thought might amuse the public." He wandered over to the chalkboard and picked up a first-day, first-assignment piece of chalk. As he talked, he sketched a stick man. "It takes another white person to dispel the white lies. Tell the kids that people like you realize there's great Indian art. And that theirs isn't half-bad, either."

"Hmm," Cynthia said, considering his drawing. "Speaking of half-bad..." She took a step closer and experimented with a teaching strategy. "What would you think about adding a face? Would you do that for me?"

He played along. "In a million years you couldn't get me to draw a face. I can't draw."

"But you just drew," she coaxed. "How about a face that shows you how you feel right now?"

He wagged the chalk at her and grinned. "Nice try, teacher, but you ain't gettin' nothin' out of me *that* easy. You've gotta work a lot harder for that one."

"Well, then, draw my face." She responded to his wary scoff by touching his arm. "Go ahead, draw what you see. Just the expression."

"You're really stickin' your neck out now." His eyes narrowed. "That's an open invitation, right? You'll take what you get?"

"Anything."

"Brave lady," he said. He studied her for a moment, then touched the chalk to the board again.

"Those are very big eyes," she said after a moment.

"They're wide open. A little bit scared." He was getting into it now. "This is a nice mouth. Not mean."

"I can see that. You're doing very well."

"It's a mouth that would say kind things. And it would taste good." He glanced up, challenging her with a mischievous male look. "You're not married, right?"

"How did you know?"

"Because you said *you* bought the condo. Not *we*." He added another feature to his drawing. "This is an ear that listens closely, even to the smallest voice, or maybe especially to the smaller ones. The ones who get pushed aside in the lemonade line. You'll need this ear." The chalk squeaked as he drew. "And here's the other one. It's a little bit lower than the one on the other side."

"Hmm," Cynthia said, evaluating again. "You have a keen eye."

"I like what I see, too. I just can't draw it very well." He tapped the tip of the chalk against the ear he'd just drawn. "See, this is the one I think might be just a little bit more sensitive to touch. Like warm air, or maybe a moist, um—" his voice took on a quiet mellifluous tone, and he lifted one shoulder "—puppy's nose or something. You know, if one jumped in your lap and started licking your ear. Then these eyes would close," he said, putting in a series of crescent shapes, "and this mouth would turn up at the corners and smile." He turned to her. "Just like that."

"My eyes are still wide open."

"Nobody's licking your ear, though. I'd give it a shot, just to prove my point, but it's not a good time."

He offered her the chalk. "Now you draw me. Whatever you see."

Their fingers brushed as she took the chalk in hand. It was as though static electricity had caused a crackle, and they exchanged wary glances. She shook off the wobbly feeling as she set to work.

"Ve-ry good," he drawled. Too easily, she thought. Far too glib, this man. "Do I have that much hair? Aw, c'mon, you're making me look a little too cocky with that—"

"You *are* a little too cocky. You've got a certain look in your eyes, but I can't capture it with this chalk."

"Here, I'll show you what it is."

Kyle took the chalk from her and had his say. Spring-loaded, his cartoon eyes popped out of his cartoon head and bounced toward his own drawing of Cynthia.

"That's it!" she exclaimed, delighted. "That's it. You should be an animator."

"I am." He smiled, delighted, too. "You should see your face now."

"You're a very good teacher, aren't you?"

He set the chalk down and brushed the dust from his fingers. "I have my good days."

"I'm a little scared," she confessed with a sigh. "I'm long on content and theory, but a little short on classroom experience."

"Your theory worked on me. First time a woman ever got me to draw her a picture." She decided not to ask how many had tried, and he smiled knowingly. "I don't want you to think I'm always this easy. The kids here aren't, either. But we're not impossible.''

NOT IMPOSSIBLE. During the first week of school Cynthia reminded herself of those words over and over again. It was not impossible to hold a third grader's attention longer than three minutes at a time. She simply hadn't figured out a way to do it yet. It was not impossible to keep the fourth-grade boys from making projectiles out of modeling clay and bombarding each other from across the room. It was not impossible to get through a whole class without having half the paint spilled on the carpet and half the art paper turned into airplanes. But maybe she wasn't up to the challenge.

Each class was scheduled for the art room twice a week. Teachers dropped off their kids and reported back at the end of the period to escort the students back to their regular classrooms. But changing classes, like everything else, wasn't running smoothly for Cynthia. She was standing outside her door, thinking the kids' noise was no worse with her outside than it had been when she was standing over them, when Kyle came down the hall with his students, more or less in single file.

''What's wrong?''

''Miss Tetley hasn't come for her class yet, so I have no place to put *your* class, and I need a few minutes to clean up the mess and—'' she sighed as she waved her hand over her head ''—collect my thoughts.''

''What we do is we get Miss Tetley's class to clean up after themselves.''

"Yes, I've—" she was trying not to sound as totally defeated as she felt "—tried that."

"You people take a seat on the floor here and keep your hands to yourselves," he told his kids. One by one, they slid their backs down the wall and settled on the floor. "Because if you don't, I might not feel like playing basketball at recess like we planned. Cynthia's going to tell you something about some famous artists—"

"Ms. Boyer," Cynthia insisted wearily.

"About *Ms.* Boyer, plus some other famous artists, while I show some fourth graders how to clean up in a hurry."

"Way to go, Kyle," one of his bunch cheered.

"James, we don't call our teachers by their first names," Cynthia said.

"You're Ms. Boyer," came the correction. "I'm Kyle. I like to keep it simple."

She stood guard in the hallway with his comparatively well-behaved class. All she heard him say after he entered her room was, "If you guys don't want to see me get angry, you'll get this mess picked up. *Now!*"

She had tried words to that effect, but the "now" part hadn't sounded quite so forceful. Jennifer Tetley came scurrying around the corner as though she'd heard it, too, and she waved one hand excitedly, patting her chest with the other to prove how she'd worn herself out hurrying. She gasped out bits of excuses and apologies for being late.

"Paper jammed in the copier...phone call...ran into Marty on my way down to—"

"Mr. Bear Soldier's class is waiting for their—"

"*Kyle's* class," four of the children sitting on the floor chimed in unison.

"And I'm cutting into their time, I know," said Jennifer, "and I'm sor—" Kyle stepped back into the hallway. The room was quiet, and the two women exchanged looks of surprise. "What did you do to them?" Jennifer asked.

"Intimidated them nicely. You owe me, Jennifer."

"I realize that." She smiled sweetly. "And I will definitely make it up to you."

"You bet you will. Three minutes for every one, that's what I charge." Her students poured out, and his filed in under his supervision. "Hey, keep your shirt on, Tom. You know where to sit. Remember that basketball game."

"Yeah, bean brain," one of the boys chided. "Don't get him mad."

"What happens when you get mad?" asked Cynthia.

"It's not pleasant," Kyle assured her. "Just plain not pleasant."

"I see." He gave her a sly wink, then turned and headed down the hall, leaving her feeling a little bereft as she closed the door. "You wouldn't want to get me mad, either," she said as she turned to the class. Most of them were seated, and there were a few quiet titters. Tom Gorneau snatched a ruler off the table and playfully slapped the top of Shelley White Lightning's head with it. Shelley yelped as Cynthia moved to her desk with a sigh. So much for her power of intimidation. She wondered who she could get to trade her just one minute of tranquillity for every three of the kind of chaos she'd endured in the first five days of school.

On the bright side, she had only 165 to go.

Chapter Three

AFTER THE SECOND WEEK of school, Cynthia was ready to quit. She didn't need the paycheck, and she certainly didn't need the headache she took home with her every night. The students had wonderful potential and she had wonderful ideas, but she couldn't seem to get those two pluses to add up right. She had posted her list of rules, and she referred to them often. No one paid much attention. She wanted to spend more time teaching and less time handling crises, but her classroom was in crisis much of the time.

At the end of the second Friday there was another mess to clean up. Cynthia peeled a blob of rubber glue off one of the tables and looked to her bulletin board for encouragement. Five finished pencil sketches out of a class of eighteen. She had taken the sixth graders outside to use the intersection and the buildings around the school for a lesson in perspective. She'd lost two girls, who had crossed the street and kept on walking in defiance of Cynthia's vehement protests. Meanwhile, one of the boys had scribbled on another one's paper, and two others had decided to play hackey-sack. Cynthia supposed she was lucky to have gotten five drawings out of the deal.

"Got some time on your hands?"

"More like glue," Cynthia replied as she scraped the remnants into the trash can. Kyle had taken to checking in on her at the end of each day, and the sound of his voice had become a balm, as well as a signal that the day was over and she'd survived.

"Things getting pretty sticky, are they?" She started to nod, but his calm smile annoyed her. Instead, while he perused her bulletin board, she went on with her cleaning, carrying on as if this were just another day at the end of just another week. "Some of us are getting together at Big Jim's for the TGIF blue-plate special. Care to join us?"

"I can't." The abrupt refusal sounded ungracious to her own ears, and she hastened to soften it. "Thank you, but I really can't."

"Somebody waiting for you?"

"No." He looked skeptical. "No, there's no one waiting. I have this mess to clean up, and I have lessons to prepare, and I have..." She was floundering now, partly because she wanted to go with him and be part of the group. She gestured vaguely. "I have tropical fish. You know, they have to be fed."

"Tropical fish, huh?" He smiled. "That's a good one."

She turned and moved toward the window, where she could get a look at the courtyard below. A chipmunk scampered the length of a stone retaining wall and disappeared into a clump of spent daylilies. "And I think I have a letter of resignation to write."

"After two weeks?"

"I'm no good at this. They need someone who can..." She'd expelled too many disconsolate sighs of late, regretted too many outbursts, lost too much ground. She wanted to get with the program, say the right words, tell the right jokes, but she couldn't seem to think fast enough. "They need someone else."

"They'll have a hard time finding someone else now." She lifted her hand to her temple as he closed in behind her. "Headache?"

"Every day. And I'm not usually prone to head-aches."

He put his hand on her shoulder. "Take some aspirin and then come with me."

"That sounds ominous." But alluring, like the warmth of his hand.

"Maybe it is. I want you to meet some people. I've got a couple of ideas I want to bounce off you," he said, taking both her shoulders in his hands and turning her to face him. "I've got a problem and I need your advice." She shook her head slowly, inviting him to try again. "Okay. I need a ride, how's that? I don't have a car. But the rest was all true," he added quickly.

"Everyone else has left?"

"Blew out of here with the last bell."

"Okay," she said, secretly glad he'd come up with a compelling inducement. "One blue-plate special with a side of aspirin. I've never been to Big Jim's, but I've heard it's a very interesting place."

"Almost as interesting as All Nations," he assured her. With a look, she questioned the likelihood. *"Almost."*

BIG JIM'S WAS an old-fashioned downtown diner that specialized in hearty American meat-and-potato meals. The owner, Mavis Chin, had left Southeast Asia and come to the States in the hope of locating her

American father. Instead, she located the perfect site for the business that would make the best use of her skills. Shrewd businesswoman that she was, she resolved to serve American-style meals at recession-style prices, and the place was always packed. Diners conversed in the multitude of tongues that reflected the diversity of inner city America, but when they ordered, it was in the language of chicken-fried steak with home-style potatoes.

For many of the teachers from All Nations—mostly those who were single—the Friday-night special was a regular weekly break from quick-stop fast food and microwaved diet entrées from the freezer. They occupied their usual territory—three booths and two tables toward the back. Whenever anyone had a date, it was an unspoken rule that they got the corner booth. Rumor had it that it was only a matter of time before Kyle Bear Soldier would occupy that booth with Cynthia Boyer.

When the two walked in together, the high fives from Marty Blue and Pete Stoker acknowledged Kyle's quick work. He knew they'd been betting on him, and the shy side of a month would have been commendable in their eyes. But the lady was the serious type. She was trying too hard. Another two weeks and she would be gone. Maybe she didn't really belong here. Maybe she wasn't a survivor, in which case she would leave sooner or later. But Kyle had decided to do what he could to make it later, and for that he'd been rewarded with those "nice goin'" gestures from his male colleagues.

As for the women, Jennifer Tetley gave Cynthia the once-over, and Patty Blue warned her to "stay away from the combination plate if you're wearing a girdle."

Kyle glanced at Cynthia. There was a hint of added pink in her cheeks, but her delicate laugh covered for her nicely. Sober shoptalk came fairly easily to her. When people started joking around, she listened, bright-eyed and pretty as a princess in a child's picture book. She would join in eventually, he told himself. He had to give her time.

"Hard week, Cynthia?" Pete asked.

"About as hard as it was for the rest of us this time last year, when we were all new," Kyle supplied as he directed Cynthia toward the corner booth. "Remember?"

"Things are going a hell of a lot better than they were this time last year," someone else muttered.

Marty added, "It took a year for you Sioux to get with the Ojibwa program."

Kyle laughed as he handed Cynthia one of the menus from the slot behind the napkin box. "It took a year for you Chippewa to let us have something besides rabbit for school lunch."

"I was kinda gettin' to like that cottontail stew," Pete put in. "You ought to put it on the menu, Mama Chin."

"Home-style American cooking." Mavis herself delivered the water to the tables, keeping her customary high profile. "That's my specialty."

"You've got spaghetti on here." Kyle perused the laminated menu.

"Minneapolis spaghetti only. Chunky style."

"Patty'll show you how to make chunky rabbit stew, Minneapolis-style." He winked at Cynthia over the top of the menu, just to let her know they were teammates in this game. "Well, Minnesota-style, anyway. Those Chippewa wives, they know how to keep a guy's weight up. Right, Marty?"

Marty patted his bowling-ball belly and grinned at his wife. "Damn right."

When the iced tea and hot coffee came, Pete Stoker raised his glass. "Here's to a year of survival."

"Here's to four hundred years of survival, and to us finally getting to be part of the public-school system," Kyle said. Cynthia touched her water glass to his coffee mug, and he appreciated her willingness to get into the spirit of things. "I don't know if you remember, but this time last year we were taking a lot of heat—in the press and elsewhere."

"I remember. That's what first caught my interest about the school."

"We were just starting out," Marty put in. He leaned across and offered a sample of the deep-fried battered onion rings he'd ordered as an appetizer. Cynthia took one as he elaborated. "New school, new concept, and half the educational community hoping we'd fall on our faces."

"Yeah, but the other half wanted to see us make it." Kyle shook off the onion-ring offer. "And we are making it. Hell, if I'm making it here, it should be easy for you natives."

"You've lasted one whole year in the city, cowboy," Patty said. "Congratulations."

When the food was served, people settled into quieter conversations at their own tables, along with serious eating.

"Do you miss South Dakota?" Cynthia asked. She watched Kyle sprinkle his baked potato generously with black pepper.

"I miss it so damn bad sometimes I feel like packing up in the middle of the night and hitching a ride on a westbound rig." He offered the shaker. She shook her head. "I generally get over the urge by sunup."

"What do you miss most?"

"The big sky." He studied the crust on the hot breast of fried chicken he balanced gingerly over his plate. "The buttes. The scraggly ol' buffalo grass. The sound of the wind. It doesn't sound the same here, you know."

"I guess I thought wind was wind."

"Just like mashed potatoes are mashed potatoes?" He eyed the white mound in her plate and wondered how much of that she would eat. So far she was just playing with it. Hadn't even spiced it up. "Urban cowboys aren't anything like real cowboys, and urban Indians... well, the two words just don't go together naturally."

"I remember once when I was a little girl, downtown shopping with my mother, we saw a group of, um—" She seemed intent upon drawing furrows in the potatoes with her fork, but he could almost hear her flipping through her mental file of correct terms "—Native Americans. I mean, I don't know what tribe they were affiliated with, but I saw that two of the men wore braids, and I asked my mother if they were *real* Indians."

"What did she say?"

"I believe she said, 'Not the kind in the movies. They're not savage.'"

Kyle laughed. He sank his teeth into his chicken, taking pleasure in its juiciness and her honesty.

"But, you know, that confused me," she said. "It left me wondering what a 'real Indian' was."

"So you took this job to find out?"

"I know a number of Native American artists. I know lots of people who are... you know." She shrugged. "Lots of people."

"Lots of real Indians?" He figured he could push her a little now without losing his advantage. He lowered his voice. "How well would you like to get to know me?"

"Better than I do now," she told him. The look she gave him added that getting to know him would be a prerequisite to *knowing* him.

"Fair enough." He set the chicken back on his plate and leaned a little closer. "I'm going to tell you a secret." Her eyes said she was ready. "Since I left home, I get to wondering sometimes whether I'm still real."

"A real Indian, you mean?"

"I'm going to a sweat this weekend just to make sure."

"What kind of sweating are you into, besides jogging to work?"

"I don't jog to work." He sat back, smiling. Those big blue childlike eyes of hers were so much fun to talk to. "If I did, I'd be sweaty for the rest of the day. And while our job isn't exactly what you'd call 'no sweat,' you don't want to start the day out that way." She nodded in guileless agreement. "I'd rather sweat at night. Wouldn't you?"

"Strictly speaking, I'm not much of a sweater."

"I caught you at it today. After school was out, when the world was coming down pretty hard on you, and you were ready to quit. Instead, you came with me." She refused to meet his eyes, and he knew she was embarrassed to think she'd tipped her hand his way, or anybody's way, in a moment of frustration. She would have preferred to keep all her frustration to herself. "This is better, isn't it?"

"I know two weeks isn't much, but I'm not accomplishing anything in the classroom," she confided almost in a whisper. "Not a thing."

"I saw five good drawings on your bulletin board. If you stay, next week there'll be more. If you leave, there won't."

"How many more will there be?"

"In a week, maybe ten. Maybe just one. But you've got five right now. Five good pieces."

"Don't say 'easy,'" she warned. "They weren't five easy pieces."

"Nobody said it would be easy."

She nodded again, and he felt a little guilty about minimizing her difficulties. He'd had his share, too, and he would have gladly taken on hers if there had been a way to do so, simply because those eyes were so big and needy. He was sure she didn't realize what clear windows they were to her soul. Looking in on her each afternoon had been his way of offering support.

In the end, he knew it was up to her. She didn't need this job the way he did. But she damn sure needed something, or some*one*.

"A sweat is a purification experience. The Lakota call it *inipi*. One of the teachers who lives out of town has a sweat lodge on his property. You get about six, eight guys, and go into this dark little wigwam type thing," he explained, making the shape with his hands. "You heat a bunch of rocks in a fire outside. Now, the Lakota bring those rocks in a few at a time, but the Chippewa, they just wanna get things steamed up in a hurry, so they put the whole pile in at once."

"Ojibwa," Cynthia corrected with a smile.

"Ojibwa," he confirmed. She was adding to her file of proper terms, and he didn't mind helping out. "Anyway, you sprinkle water on the rocks, make steam, make sweat..." He smiled playfully. "Lots and lots of sweat. Good for the soul. And you share some thoughts, some hopes, some concerns. You pray together, basically."

"Pray while you're doing all this sweating?"

"Sometimes you're just praying for a little cool air." Her soft smile drew out his confidences. "Sometimes you're just praying for the strength to stick it out a little longer. To stand the heat a little longer." He paused, studying those pretty eyes. "What made you come to All Nations to teach, Cynthia?"

"I thought I could do some good."

"And you've decided you can't?"

"I could if the kids would settle down and pay attention." She sampled her meat loaf. "Obviously they do that for you."

"Sometimes they do, sometimes they don't. I'm doing better than I was a year ago. And I've done a lot of praying for the strength to stand the heat a little longer." She looked at him skeptically. "I lose them, too," he assured her. "I lose their attention. Sometimes a kid just ups and walks out."

"That's happened to me."

He nodded. The news of such incidents always got around. "They come back. Some of these kids have it rough. You know that, don't you? That school is a safe haven for many of our kids. There's not a lot of money in this neighborhood. A lot of unemployment, too much alcohol, drugs anywhere you care to look."

"I know." She toyed with another bit of meat loaf, spearing it, dipping it in gravy that had to be cold by now. "It made me sad to see all those people coming to the church just to find a decent meal. I haven't been back since."

"Why not?"

"I don't want to embarrass anyone."

"I wasn't embarrassed. Were you embarrassed?" She was still playing with that meat loaf and avoiding his eyes. "You were, weren't you? Cynthia, people coming together to share a meal is not a sad thing."

"At least they're getting something to eat. I know. But to be obliged to accept that kind of charity simply because our society—"

"Ours?"

"Mine, then," she amended.

"Society girl." He shook his head, chuckling. She stared at him, letting him know she was serious. "You *don't* know, Cynthia," he said indulgently. He knew she would have objected to being patronized if she'd thought he was in a position to patronize her. In her world, an Indian man could hardly be a patron, which might have angered him if he could think of one good reason he might ever aspire to such a stupid role. Given time, she would come to realize these things. Given time, she might even come to value them.

"If people without money embarrass you, you've come to the wrong place," he instructed patiently.

"It's not that poverty em—"

"Well, poverty's another issue. There's more than one kind of poverty." He slid his hand over hers. "Stick with us a while longer. Let us show you the difference between charity and sharing." She started to object again, but he persisted. "I know you came to teach. All Nations needs good teachers *from* all nations, and I sure think you've got the makings. But if you learn nothing else from us while you're teaching, learn what 'Indian giving' really means."

AFTER THEY LEFT Big Jim's, Kyle directed Cynthia to an address not far from the school, but it wasn't his home address. Despite the fact that she knew the neighborhood, somehow he wasn't quite ready to show her where he lived. He took her, instead, to a small strip mall, where shops that had fallen into disrepair were now being renovated by community crews, people who had elbow grease to invest rather than dollars. He was pleased to see the spotlight over the new sign above the shop in the middle, which read, "Expressions of the Four Winds."

"There's someone I want you to meet," he told Cynthia.

She peered through the windshield. "Is it open?"

"Doesn't matter. She's always here at least an hour after closing time." He couldn't see Cynthia's face clearly in the shadows, but he thought he detected a bit of neck stiffening over in the driver's seat. "My sister-in-law. She's working real hard to get this place back on its feet."

Delia Bear Soldier was working very hard indeed, and Kyle was proud of his brother's wife. Because of her experience in a South Dakota gift shop, she'd been hired to work for the neighborhood arts and crafts co-op, and she'd been putting in long hours. The shop was intended to provide a marketplace for Native American jewelry and art. There were many such shops in Phoenix and Denver. The people of the Phillips neighborhood had decided they ought to have one, too.

After the two women shook hands, Cynthia perused the glass cases containing turquoise and silver jewelry, wondering whether she was expected to make some comment, since she'd been an art buyer, too. *Comment,* she reminded herself. She was learning to reserve judgment, and she got the feeling it was too soon to make any recommendations that might occur to her. Delia was watching, waiting to see what she would do. She wanted to say the right thing—if she could just figure out what that was.

An exquisite squash-blossom necklace caught her eye. "Are these made by local people?" Cynthia wondered.

"That's Navaho," Delia replied as she lifted a whimpering toddler into her arms. "We're taking some things on consignment from New Mexico and Arizona. Directly from the artists. No middle man. Trying to open up the market in this part of the country."

"It's a wonderful idea. You have some beautiful pieces here." She glanced up from the display case and found that Delia, bouncing the baby to quiet him, had taken a step closer. "I used to buy Indian-made jewelry for several galleries," Cynthia said. Then she turned to Kyle, who offered no hint as to whether she was taking the right tack. Elbows on the counter, chin in hands, he was studying a display of beaded cigarette lighters that Cynthia would have said did not belong in a shop with fine jewelry. But she reminded herself that she had not been asked.

"They were located in a different kind of neighborhood, right?" Delia asked pointedly. "Our prices are reasonable here, and the artists are going to be getting a better return for their work. If we can get the word out, we think people will come to our shop, located in *our* neighborhood." She pointed to the quill and bead earrings. "These were made by local crafters," she said. "And the quilts."

"They're beautiful. And the baskets." Cynthia admired a large duck woven from split willow. "I'm more familiar with Papago and Apache basketry, but this is Cree, isn't it?"

"She passes the basket test," Delia told Kyle, and he chuckled.

Cynthia wasn't sure what was funny about it, since she figured it might have been the first test she'd passed in weeks.

"How do you like teaching at All Nations?" Delia asked.

"I think I may become a basket *case,*" Cynthia admitted readily. "I've been out of the classroom for a long time. I'm trying to get a handle on the discipline end of it, but I'm afraid I'm not doing very well."

"These kids can be a handful for any of us," Kyle offered. "Cynthia has some great ideas. She's gonna do fine."

"If you have trouble with any Bear Soldier kids, you tell me about it," Delia said.

Cynthia started to thank her, but the baby in Delia's arms was reaching for Kyle, and it surprised her to see him take the little boy into his arms with practiced ease. The men who had been part of her life so far—her father and her former husband—had scrupulously ignored small children.

It surprised her, too, when Delia complained to Kyle of another child. "Carla didn't come home from school, and I don't know where your brother is."

"I'll find Carla," he told her. "As for Jamie, you've gotta stop worrying. He's doing good now. He passed all his summer courses, didn't he?" Delia nodded, and Cynthia caught herself smiling along with Kyle, as though she somehow had a stake in all this. "See there? He'll be finished with school and working before you know it."

Cynthia left the store smiling. She felt as though he'd included her in some family business, and the feeling was good. She realized it was probably silly, but in a way she felt privileged. She knew his niece, Carla, from school, and now Delia, and next she would meet his brother Jamie, because Kyle had obviously taken it upon himself to include her in—

"I'll walk from here," he told her when they reached the car. It was the last thing she'd expected him to say, and he surely saw that in her face. "Got my jogging shoes on, and I haven't had my workout yet today," he explained casually.

Cynthia felt as though someone had pulled the plug on her swelling heart. "It's no trouble to drop you off. Besides, I'd like to help you look for Carla."

"Delia's laid down the law to those kids about going home after school, but that Carla..." He shook his head as he braced one hand on the hood of the car. "She probably went to a friend's house, so it'll be easier if I just make the rounds on foot."

He cut off further objections by changing the subject. "I see you're going to help chaperone my field trip next week. Did you volunteer?"

"I offered to help out," Cynthia answered, still feeling a little shell-shocked. "After all, you'll be taking the students that I would have had in class on a normal day."

He grinned, looking boyishly pleased with himself. "Then you can't quit yet. You'd leave me high and dry."

"Someone else would take my place."

"That might be hard to do. Take your place, I mean. Not too many people would give up a slack day. That was nice of you."

"I like to stay busy." Warming to his praise, she felt like a schoolgirl lingering under the porch light when it was clearly time for her to get in her car and leave. She'd made her offer. He'd turned her down.

"Are you busy Saturday night?"

It was her turn. "Actually, I do have plans."

"How about a week from Saturday? I'd like to see a play."

"A play? Which one?"

"Any one. You choose. They want me to put on a play for parents' night, and I don't know a damn thing about plays. Thought I'd go see one, if I could find myself a date."

"Actually, the Children's Playhouse would be—"

"'Actually' makes it sound like you're taking exception." He stepped closer, blanketing her with his shadow. "But I don't think you are. How well do you want to get to know me, Cynthia?" She gripped the handle on the car door, but she'd completely forgotten how the thing worked. His smile faded as his fingertips grazed her cheek. "After hours I'm not looking for any children's playhouse. If I want to play house, it's going to be on an adult level."

"I've played house before," she recalled regretfully. "With a man who neglected to mention that he didn't play for keeps. 'Getting to know you' means one thing to a man and something altogether different for a woman."

"My definition might surprise you, Cynthia." He slid his thumb beneath her chin, tilting it up. "Here's something else that might surprise you."

He lowered his head, blocking the light completely, but then he tipped his head to the side, and the light struck her eyes again. She closed them against the rude street lamp, heard the soft intake of his breath and felt the warm dewy impression of his lips on hers. The sweetness of his mouth was no surprise, but she would never have guessed how delicious his brand of sweetness was.

Chapter Four

FIRST STOP on the fifth- and sixth-grade field trip was a wildlife sanctuary in a wood north of the Twin Cities, where two canvas-draped sweat lodges of the type Kyle had described were already set up, and an old man was waiting to lead the boys in *inipi*. Lily Moore, who was officially on staff at All Nations as a classroom aide, was truly the school's on-site elder. She was prepared to lead the girls, as was traditional, in a separate sweat.

Few of the children had ever participated in such a ceremony, and they were all given the option of declining. The fire tenders, who were part of the ceremonial team, stood ready to roll in the first rocks. A dozen boys, dressed in shorts or swimming suits, went in, challenging each other as to who could stay in the longest. Without expending many words, Kyle, dressed in gym shorts, imposed one hand between two boys who were sparring while he stripped off his T-shirt with the other. "You guys might make me angry if you ruin my concentration in there," he warned before saluting Cynthia with a quick wave and disappearing inside.

Cynthia had worn shorts and a T-shirt as instructed, and she was about to heed Lily's hurry-up gesture when Carla Bear Soldier put the skids on the proceedings. "I'm not going in there."

Cynthia glanced at the men's lodge and realized that Carla had carefully calculated her timing. "That's fine. It's your choice." She smiled pleasantly. "I'll stay out here with you."

At twelve, Carla was already as tall as Cynthia. She had sturdier shoulders, more bust, and at least as much resolve. "Chicken?"

"No. I think it would be very interesting to participate." She signaled Lily to go ahead without her. Lily nodded and ducked into the cavelike door on what had been designated the women's lodge. "Well, maybe a little chicken," Cynthia confided then. "I passed out in a sauna once, and it would be awfully embarrassing if you girls had to drag me out of there."

"I can't imagine *you* passed out." Carla wandered across the clearing, away from the two young men who were busy separating rocks from the hot coals in the fire pit. "You're too neat and clean to be passed out."

Cynthia followed. "Well, it happened. I was clean, but I don't know about neat." Cynthia tossed a doubtful glance over her shoulder. "Can you be neat and naked at the same time?"

"I think *you* could." The girl took a seat on the ground, hiked her knees up and leaned back against a tree trunk. "Listen, you don't have to watch me. I can't go anywhere." She indicated the woods with a nod of her chin. "There's no place to go."

"I'm not worried that you'll skip out on us, Carla. I just thought I'd keep you company. I suppose you've done lots of sweats, huh?"

The girl shook her head. "My uncle Kyle is the one who's into it most, and he's just dying to get us kids to try it. But I'm not gonna." Glaring at the men's lodge, she snatched a twig off the ground and snapped it in half. "He was mad at me for going to Rhonda's house after school on Friday, and I told him it was no big deal."

Cynthia sat down on the ground opposite Carla. The late-summer grass crackled as she crossed her legs and settled in. "Your mother didn't know where you were. She was worried."

"They think I can't take care of myself. I'm twelve years old, you know."

"I know. I'm thirty-two years old, but people worry about me when they can't find me." Carla gave her that skeptical look again. "After a few days, anyway. If I don't talk to my mother every few days, she gets worried. But, then, I live alone, so..."

"So you don't have to explain every move you make, right?"

"It can be a comfort to know you're accountable to someone if that someone cares what happens to you. Your uncle Kyle was worried, too."

"Well, he's not my dad, and sometimes I wish he'd mind his own business." She scowled at her right knee, which bore the remnants of a week-old scrape. "But sometimes I don't. Sometimes he gets my parents to lighten up."

"You must be a very close family," Cynthia said, suddenly wishing she could say the same about hers. What little she had.

"Well, yeah, we have to be close. We're—" Carla straightened abruptly. Her eyes brightened as she cocked her head in the direction of the activity she'd stubbornly denied herself moments ago. "Listen to those boys messin' around in there. Uncle's only gonna let them go so far, and then he's gonna—"

"You guys need more steam?" they could hear Kyle say. "Add a little water, Earl."

"No more steam," a younger voice croaked. "We'll behave. We'll behave."

"I don't know. Sometimes it takes more steam to get the songs going."

"We'll sing."

"Give us a break, Kyle."

Carla and Cynthia shared secret smiles.

"Hey, I said we'll sing!"

And sing they did.

LATER, AFTER A QUICK DIP in the YMCA pool, the group was joined by the Ojibwa language teacher Marty Blue for a trip to the local science museum. The steam had sapped some of the mischief out of the boys, but the swim revived them. The stately rooms containing attractions for the curious invited active participation, which meant, as far as the kids were concerned, touching everything in sight.

Mr. Drayton, the white-haired volunteer host who introduced himself as a retired teacher, was eager to educate. "The artifacts belong to all of us," he explained, clearly proud of his part-ownership. "This is a safe place to keep them, a place where we can all see them whenever we want to, but we realize that the Native American collection is a very special..."

Cynthia hung back, herding the stragglers along. She decided her most valuable contribution to keeping order was to lend a watchful eye. It was a skill she'd learned from her mother. There was a time for touching and a time for just looking, and when a young face was pressed against a glass window, it was time to say, "Tom, don't put your mouth on that."

Tom Gorneau leaned back to admire his lip print, surrounded by the steam from his breath. "It'll wash off."

"But it's not clean," Cynthia reminded him, just as her mother, or *any* mother, might have done. "Other hands have—"

"Looks clean enough." He glanced up at her, grinning with pride. "I left my mark."

"His big flapping lips," James Red Leaf taunted. James licked his thumb and pressed it next to Tom's lip print. "Good as fingerprints. Cops can track you down now. Get you for abusing our artifacts with those big flapping smackers of yours."

"You're an *artifact,*" Tom accused, as if it were the worst insult he could come up with. Actually, Cynthia admired Tom's choice of words. "You're just lucky you're bigger than me."

"Shh. Boys, you're making people—" she glanced around, noting they were drawing a few cool adult stares "—nervous." The boys giggled. "You mustn't be so loud," she pleaded.

"This ain't no library."

"Yeah, this ain't no church, neither."

"Oh, dear." Cynthia sighed, wishing she could go back to square one and let Tom kiss the glass to his heart's content.

"C'mon over here, you guys," Kyle said, motioning to them. "Watch this demonstration."

Mr. Drayton showed the group an old Ojibwa drill, and then he took out a reproduction and demonstrated how the machine was used. He was clearly enamored of its simple efficiency and his own practiced proficiency.

"Pretty clever of us Ojibwa to come up with a thing like that," Marty observed. "Wonder how the Sioux drilled out their pipe stems." While Mr. Drayton beetled his brow and racked his brain for the answer, Marty eyed Kyle. "Bet it took them weeks to finish a pipe."

"Hey, while you guys were fooling around with that little toy, we were using the method told to us by Iktome, the trickster, which we don't reveal to too many people." He turned to Mr. Drayton, who was all ears. "But today, just for the sake of comparison..."

He picked up a piece of white ash that had been partially whittled for demonstration. "Every Lakota pipe stem was bored straight and true. We were known for this. We would build a small fire first. Then we would carve a notch in the end of the pipe stem," he explained, making the motion over the butt of the unfinished piece to demonstrate.

Cynthia watched the gathering of faces, dark-skinned and light, brown-eyed and blue. The students were curious. Marty looked skeptical, but Mr. Drayton was thoroughly absorbed.

''Then we would put a termite headfirst into the notch, tamp in some clay and suspend the whole thing over the fire. When that termite's rear end heated up, he'd *really* drill that hole in a hurry.''

Marty was the first to respond. ''Ayyy.''

James Red Leaf gave Kyle a thumbs-up.

Mr. Drayton laughed so hard Cynthia thought the man might have to be carried out on a stretcher.

The children were still full of energy when they returned to school that afternoon. Their second wind always seemed to outstrip Cynthia's first. After they were dismissed for the day, several of them dashed into the art room to check on the progress of projects still in the drying stage, or to ask what they were going to do tomorrow, or to see if a cap somebody had swiped had been stashed there. She was too tired to arbitrate the running battle between the last holdouts—James and Paula Red Leaf—so for once she went about her business organizing student portfolios and ignored the whole thing.

Kyle stuck his head in the door. ''You guys get going before you miss your bus. Paula, you left your saxophone in my room.''

''I know,'' she said on her way out the door. ''I don't want my older brother to hock it again. I almost didn't get it back.''

Cynthia motioned Kyle into the room and closed the door, scowling. ''Her brother *pawned* her saxophone?''

''The school's saxophone,'' Kyle corrected. ''And if that shocks you, I'm afraid you've led a very sheltered life, my friend. Or maybe I shouldn't say I'm

afraid. Maybe some people are supposed to lead sheltered lives." He shoved his hands into his pockets and
looked her in the eye, adding, "When they're children."

"These *are* children."

Kyle shrugged. "Money's hard to come by around
here, and the kid might have figured that hocking the
instrument was better than selling drugs. Then again,
he might have used the money to buy drugs."

"I hope not." She would not apologize for being
shocked by unfairness, nor for hoping for change, and
if that made her sound unrealistic, so be it.

"I hope not, too. I hope he used it to buy his mom
a birthday present. The good news is Paula got her
saxophone back."

"It must be quite a challenge to put a band concert
together here."

"We're all here because we just *love* the chal-
lenges," Kyle teased, which brought a reluctant smile
to Cynthia's face.

"Actually, I *did* enjoy the field trip today."

"Really? I thought you were going to lose it at the
museum. It's a hands-on museum, Cynthia."

"I know that, but hands-on has its limits."

"Does it, now?" With a twinkle in his eye, he took
a step closer and lowered his voice. "Suppose you en-
lighten me in advance, because I've always been pretty
hands-on myself."

"In advance of what?"

"In advance of further advances," he said lightly.

She folded her arms and glanced away. "Hands-on
has its limits."

"You said that." They stood in silence for a moment and then he asked, "What kind of limits do you put on your heart, Cynthia?"

She glanced up at the intercom speaker, thinking this was not the place to discuss such things. She answered quietly, "I'm cautious."

"Fair enough." He touched her arm, easing away a tension she hadn't realized was there. "When you care, you care deeply, don't you? You care about these kids."

"I care," she admitted as she released her arms slowly and let them relax at her sides. She avoided his eyes as she moved past him. "You were right. I was ready to give up before I'd really gotten started. But now..." She directed his attention to a long table. This time she had fourteen projects sitting out in various stages of completion. *Fourteen.*

"We started making papier-mâché faces yesterday, and the kids have come up with some animal masks that would scare—" she looked at his handsome face and broke into a broad smile "—the most stalwart of us."

"This ain't no mask, lady," he drawled in protest. "This is the real thing, scary or not."

"And it was inspirational, I must say. You were the model for the bear mask," she explained. He quirked one thick eyebrow, clearly amused by the idea. "I said, 'Imagine Mr. Bear Soldier's face when he's angry,' and that sparked all kinds of creativity."

"Believe it or not, I don't have to get angry much. I just keep telling them they wouldn't want to see me get angry, and they believe me." He touched the pointed nose on one of the newsprint masks. It bent beneath his finger, and she reached for his hand, gently pulling him back from doing any damage.

He turned his palm to hers. "I used to get angry a lot when I was younger. Didn't do anybody a damn bit of good. Especially not me." He smiled as he hooked his long fingers around her wrist and caressed the hollow of her palm with the heel of his hand. "I have to be cautious, too."

"Are you apt to be dangerous?"

"I'm apt to withdraw, just the way the kids do sometimes. I guess that's dangerous in a way, especially when you start gnawing at your own insides."

Flustered, she drew her hand away and began rearranging masks that needed no rearranging.

"What about you?" he asked. "Do you get angry?"

"Sometimes." To prove her point, she snatched up one of the projects. "Look what they did to this. These aren't dry yet." It was Tom Gorneau's mask, and someone had stuck a wad of pink bubble gum on the lips.

"But you stay cool, basically," Kyle observed.

"I try to, yes." She peeled the gum away. Some of the paper came with it. "I think I can fix this."

"I'd like to see you heat up a little. Maybe I'll try on that bear mask and see if it gets *your* creative juices flowing."

"Actually, it already did," she said, brightening. "I have an idea that might solve your production problems."

He offered a champion-male smile. "What am I suppposed to be producing?"

"A play."

"Oh, that." He sounded disappointed. "You've got some ideas?"

"I think we might make it a joint effort, using my masks and your knack for storytelling. You might have to write the lines yourself, but I have a feeling you're never at a loss for lines."

"You question my sincerity?" He clapped his hand over his heart. "Ms. Boyer, you wound me deeply."

"I happen to have tickets for tonight's performance at the Ordway. Will you recover from your wounds by seven o'clock?"

"I don't know," he said, eyeing her suspiciously. "Is this one of those fancy theater deals?"

"Haven't you been to the Ordway?"

"I suppose I haven't *lived* unless I've been to the Ordway."

Cynthia welcomed the excuse to link arms with him and lead him to the door. "Deliver me from my sheltered existence, and I'll deliver you to the theater."

"Such a deal," he conceded, but he needed more coaxing. "Ordinarily I'd take you up on it, but my tux is at the dry cleaner's."

"Dress comfortably." She wanted to tell him to wear his hair just as he always did, sometimes with a little queue in the back, and not to forget his boots and the Western-cut jeans that always rode nice and low at the base of his long back.

"And how will you be dressed?"

She wondered whether he could read her mind.

"Comfortably."

HER HAND-PAINTED JEANS nearly knocked his socks off. He didn't get the full effect until they'd parked the car, he'd opened the door for her and she'd stepped out onto the pavement. When she'd come to pick him up, he'd been waiting on the porch for her. Behind a pillar. Fortunately Jamie had a night class and Delia was at the store, so his nephew, Markie, was the only one who'd followed him out the door with a ten-year-old's version of a wolf whistle. Hell, his outfit had seemed like a good idea until he'd put the damn thing on.

But Cynthia's outfit... Now *there* was an outfit, and it fit her classic female shape just fine. Her hair, the color of a shiny chestnut, was done up on top of her head, and her jacket collar stood up fashionably at the back of her neck. A silky red scoop-necked blouse hinted at the presence of cleavage. He gave a low whistle, thirty-five-year-old-style, and motioned for her to do a quick turn for him. Denim made a very classy canvas, he decided as he admired the abstract artwork, punctuated with glitter and flashy fake jewels. Especially draped over a nice curvy... easel.

"You look great. That's a real work of art. One of a kind, I'd say."

"I'd say so, too. I painted both the pants and jacket myself."

"They look just—" he shook his head, clucking to himself "—great, which sounds like a puny word, but I'm a little tongue-tied. I thought you'd be wearing some real fancy dress, so I..." He looked down at his black dinner jacket, white shirt and tie, and shrugged uneasily. His shoulders felt a little cramped.

Those big blue eyes widened innocently. "Are you disappointed?"

"Hell, no," he assured her, giving her an appreciative once-over. "Are you?"

She motioned for him to give her a spin. He had tied his hair back, and he'd polished his black cowboy boots. When he completed his turn, she smiled and reported, "I'm dazzled."

"Good." He offered his arm. "I feel like the flip side of Cinderella. Tomorrow this thing has to be back in the dry cleaner's window, so I've only got a few hours to be dazzling. I plan to make the most of them."

The play was a musical, featuring some toe-tapping country-and-western tunes. Kyle had a good time holding Cynthia's hand and patting it against his thigh. He liked the way her head bobbed and her shoulders swayed just a little when she got into the swing. She'd chosen the play because she thought it would please him. And it did. He wondered if it surprised her that it pleased her, too.

She invited him to her home, explaining that she had prepared some food and that she wanted to show off a little. "Since I missed my chance to show off my fancy clothes, maybe I can impress you with my interior decorating. It's the first time I've lived in a place that's all mine."

"You haven't missed your chance with anything so far," he assured her as he took the key and unlocked the door.

Cynthia's condo was one of several that had recently been offered for sale in a converted late-nineteenth-century fire station. The architect had added wood and glass to the rich hues of old brick and had achieved dramatic high ceilings, clean lines and an airy open feeling. It was a complete departure from any place she'd lived in before, and Cynthia loved it. It was the perfect home for her Navaho rugs—the teal-and-russet Crystal pattern that graced the polished floor beneath the glass coffee table, and the highly prized Two Gray Hills she'd hung against the old brick. She had some exquisite Pueblo pottery—a white Acoma seed pot painted with fine black lines, a startlingly beautiful black Santa Clara pot, and the more colorful Jemez pieces. There were three large paintings by up-and-coming Native American artists—bold lines and bright colors exploring timeless earthy themes.

He took it all in, and she waited for his reaction. He couldn't help but like what he saw, she thought. Even the big cylindrical aquarium blended with the decor.

"So this is where you live?" Kyle's boot heels echoed against the hardwood floor. He shoved his hands into his pockets and ambled toward the huge window overlooking the lake. City lights twinkled beyond the glass like jewels in a shop window. "Pretty nice." He touched the white leather sofa and eyed the free-standing fireplace. "Kind of a lot of room for just one person and a couple of fish."

"I'm used to a house, so I've had to make some adjustments. But after the divorce, I couldn't stay in 'the house that Jack built.'"

She went to the kitchen, wondering whether the tray of cold cuts she'd carefully arranged and stashed in the refrigerator was such a good idea. She listened to the sound of his footsteps as he moved about the living room, presumably taking a closer look.

"I have an assortment of beverages here," she called out as she slipped out of her jacket and hung it on a hook. "Name your heart's desire, and I'll tell you if I've got it."

His first answer wasn't quite intelligible, but the request for "just coffee" came loud and clear. She flipped the switch on the coffeemaker, which was ready to go. She resisted the urge to peek out, see what he was inspecting and try to read his thoughts. Did "pretty nice" mean he liked the place? One of the paintings was done by a Sioux artist, and she wondered whether he recognized the name. She wondered whether he liked her color scheme, whether he was tempted to relax on her sofa, or whether he thought this was all too pretentious for relaxing.

Mostly she wondered whether surroundings like these would prevent him from kissing her again.

She turned, shutting the refrigerator door behind her, and found him standing there, leaning against the door frame, hands still in his pockets. "Who's Jack?" he wondered.

"My former husband was an architect. I decided that I didn't need a big house. I didn't need rooms full of perfectly coordinated furniture and office-suite artwork." She set the snack tray on the tiled counter and gestured toward the tall stools. "I loved this place the moment I saw it. It's something old made new again."

"Made new and neat and . . ."

"My taste in art was never to his liking. He used to criticize me for, as he put it, bringing my work home with me. For my new home I bought new things to suit my new life."

He helped himself to a block of white cheese and a black olive on a toothpick. "Sounds like the old life was a real downer."

"I married the kind of man I thought I was supposed to marry. He came from the right family, and he had all the right credentials." It was good to keep busy while she related all this. She took two mugs from the cupboard and made sure she put out the sugar. "We had no common interests, no children and no real life together. He went his way with another woman, and I—" she tried to dismiss seven years of her life with a wave of two blue paper napkins "—eventually went mine. To All Nations."

"You got left with a broken heart," he concluded for her. He rested his hip on the stool, hooking his heel on the crossbar.

"That sounds like a line from a country and western song," Cynthia said with a smile.

"It's probably in at least half of them. Deep down I'm just another cowboy poet."

"I don't know any other cowboy poets. You make me sound sweetly tragic, and I'm not." He didn't seem to notice when she served his coffee. He was watching her face, and it made her a little nervous. "It was a very civilized parting. Nothing as moving as you describe."

"You weren't hurt at all?" She pushed the sugar across the counter toward him, but he ignored that, too. "I know more about you than you think I do, Cynthia. No matter how classy the ironwork, I know a wall when I see one. And now you've got it in your head that you're gonna do your charity work with me while you keep your valuables locked up."

"What valuables?"

"Your heart, Cynthia." He captured one of her busy hands and drew her over to his side of the counter. "Your soft and tender little heart."

"Oh, Kyle," she groaned, shaking her head and smiling at him indulgently. "I wouldn't have taken you for such an incurable romantic."

"You wouldn't have taken me, period. Not the first time you saw me, anyway. You wanna talk about my heart's desire?" He slipped his arms around her waist and laid his cheek against her chest. For a moment she didn't know where her next breath was coming from. "Your heart's beating pretty fast, Cynthia. You'd better use some sophisticated trick to make it slow down."

"I don't—" her hands fluttered uselessly, then found his shoulders "—know any tricks."

"You know how to walk away. You could walk away and take this little problem with you." He raised his head slowly, coming up smiling. "It feels like it's trying to break out of this beautiful fortress, where you keep it locked up."

"I knew you'd have no trouble with lines." Tentatively she touched the silky hair that swept over his right ear. "Dreamers have all the best lines."

"Dreamers are dangerous, and this heart of yours is scared to death of me. But it's still knocking on those iron bars." She closed her eyes and he whispered, "Hear it?" And then he kissed her there. She felt the dampness of his kiss through her thin silk blouse, and her blood pounded in her ears. "You hear it now, don't you?"

"Yes, I hear it."

"I won't take it from you, Cynthia," he promised as he rose from the stool and took her in his arms. "Poor little society girl, that's all you really have to give."

"I can give my time..." He was nuzzling her neck, and she found herself rising on tiptoe to give him better access as her point, whatever it was, drifted. "My time and my—"

"Your sweet time?" he whispered close to her ear. "I'll take that, honey. I'll take your sweet, sweet..."

She put her arms around his neck, and the last words she heard were "... Indian time."

Chapter Five

DEEP INTO THE MONTH of October, rehearsals were still too loosely structured by Cynthia's standards. There were some fun times and some frustrating times. She wanted more *productive* times, and she couldn't understand where Kyle got the idea that everything was "going great."

Gopher, Badger and Bear were stirring imaginary soup in the wastepaper basket with a yardstick. Kyle had explained that the yardstick represented the sharing spoon, and they were supposed to take turns tasting the brew, which made for one antic after another. The battle over who would actually hold the yardstick had been won by Tom Gorneau, who was Bear. Gopher was in charge of salt, and Badger added the pepper.

"Fly was coming along," Kyle narrated, "and he smelled the soup."

Enter Bertram Yellow, the biggest ham in the class.

"Okay, buzz around them like a fly, Bertram," Cynthia coached. "Pester them, just like a fly."

"You know how to be a pest, Bertram."

"Yeah, just be yourself."

Bzzzz. Bzzzzzzz.

Mischief burned in Tom's brown eyes as he took a batter's stance with the yardstick. "Shall I kill it?"

"That's not in the script, Tom," Cynthia said with a sigh, but the whole crew had already cracked up. "One more time, *seriously* now."

She didn't know why she kept using that word when she was the only one who understood its meaning. Kyle was worse than the kids. He couldn't keep a straight face when Bertram stuck his foot in the trash can and Tom yelled, "There's a fly in my soup!"

It was straight downhill from there. Nobody seemed to mind when she scheduled yet another after-school rehearsal "after you've all had time to pull yourselves together." Kyle smiled innocently when she gave him a look he couldn't possibly misinterpret.

"Want to grab a bite to eat?" he asked after the children were gone.

"No, thanks, I have a prior commitment." Besides that, she was a little put out with him. She took her light wool jacket off the back of her chair and gathered up her papers, her purse and her plan book. When she finally looked up at him, it was still there. That irresistible, infuriatingly innocent look. "I'm back on the volunteer schedule for Loaves and Fishes," she told him.

"Great. That's where I was headed if you turned me down."

"For coffee?"

"Depends on what else you're serving."

She shrugged off his answer, his plans, his attitude. The program was for the have-nots, and he knew what that meant. Yet he chuckled, as if *she* was the one who didn't understand.

"It's a feed, Cynthia. I grew up on church-basement feeds, powwow feeds, marriage and funeral feeds. It's part of our..." He rubbed the back of his neck as though his efforts to get through to her produced pain there. "When there's food, everybody eats," he said simply.

"I think that's wonderful." Primly she completed the buttoning of her jacket. "But this program is meant to feed the hungry."

"Well, then, I sure can qualify." Slinging his jacket over his shoulder, he made an after-you gesture toward the door. "And I belong with the rest of the people who'll be in that line. I'm not too good to sit down and share their meal."

The gauntlet was down, and she wasn't going anywhere. "Kyle, I'm not sitting in judgment, but what if everybody in town decided to—"

"Then you take what you have and make it stretch. Isn't that the way it works with loaves and fishes?" He smiled and touched her hair. "You're a nice lady, Ms. Boyer, but you're such a stickler."

"I like to stay on track. Or nearly on track." He brushed her chin with the backs of his fingers. "I like to be within shouting distance of the track, how's that?"

"Close enough." His hand went to her shoulder, which he kneaded, loosening the muscle. "We like it that you're such good hosts. But just remember, when there's food, everybody shares it together. Where we come from, it's supposed to be that way."

"It takes a lot of work." His touch made her soften her tone. "Lots of working hands to feed so many—" at the word, he took her hand in his "—people."

"Don't get me wrong," he said quietly. He brought her fingertips to his lips, kissed them, then smiled into her astonished eyes. "These hands do good things. Fine things. Come a little closer."

"You said close enough," she reminded him.

"So close, but still so far away. Go all the way with us, Cynthia."

"You *know* how that sounds, Mr. Bear Soldier."

"Of course, I do." Still holding her hand, he led her toward the door, urging, "Fill your belly with us, Cynthia."

"This is a little heavy for cowboy poetry."

"It's Indian philosophy."

"Or humor."

"One and the same." He gave her hand a quick squeeze as they headed down the school corridor. "Suit yourself. Put the food on the table and watch us eat if that's what amuses you. What you see and what *is* are not necessarily the same thing."

LINDA KOPP PUT Cynthia to work on the serving line. Since Kyle was not one of the volunteers, they had parted company at the door, and he waited outside with the guests. She was learning to dish up the food fast and furiously, but she kept glancing up, anxious to see him in the line. *Anxious* for the man she'd come to care for to show up for a charity-sponsored meal.

Anxious to see his face, she realized, anytime, anywhere.

Finally he appeared, standing in line behind the tall man she remembered from the last time. The line moved quickly. Kyle was greeted by several of his students. He shared a laugh with the woman behind him, and Cynthia found herself wondering what *that* was about.

"Hey." The tall man gave her a deadpan stare from behind his taped glasses. "Do your gloves have holes in them?"

Cynthia glanced at Kyle, then smiled as she dished up the coleslaw. "Two great big ones."

"Good. Smart woman."

"It takes a smart woman to put on a feed like this," Kyle said. The remark surprised her, and she wasn't sure how to take it. She was a volunteer, yes, but not a benefactor.

"Hey, you're my teacher," a small voice said. One of the second graders peeked out from behind her mother and waved at Cynthia.

"Hi, Jenny."

"Is there seconds on the lasagne *without* the coleslaw?" Jenny asked.

Cynthia nodded as she watched Kyle accept a tray from the server at the end. *When there's food, everybody eats.* And there was plenty of food. Volunteers and guests were just people, and people needed to eat.

Cynthia started to fill a tray for herself, but then thought better of it. Instead, she stripped off her gloves and let the last two people behind the table fill it for her. She thanked them and took the tray from their gloved hands with her bare ones.

"May I join you?" It pleased Cynthia to see that she'd taken Kyle and his friends by surprise. "Or are we seated by gender here?"

Kyle laughed as he pushed the empty chair away from the table. "First they quit walking five paces behind us, then they want to sit on the men's side and eat their food. We're losing our traditional place, you guys."

"Earlier this evening Mr. Bear Soldier treated me to a bit of 'Indian philosophy,' which included an invitation to 'fill my belly.'" She ignored the appreciative glances and sly chuckles exchanged among the five men at the table. "I believe those were the words. He didn't tell me about any seating rules."

"You have to watch yourself around Kyle," the heftiest man warned. "He has a smooth way with words."

"This is Tony Left Hand," Kyle said. "He's from my reservation. And this is Paul and Jim—"

"This guy's such a smooth talker," Tony told Cynthia, cutting in on the introductions. "He got them to name a town after him. Kyle, South Dakota."

"*I* was named for the *town*. That's where the car broke down just before my mom went into labor." Kyle joined in the laughter, then gave Tony a nod. "You should've been there, man. We might've made it to the clinic."

"Or you could've broke down again in Porcupine," Paul chimed in. Merry men, Cynthia thought. There was surely merriment in their dark eyes.

"Or Wounded Knee. They could've called you Wounded for short," Tony said, and they all nodded, chortling.

"He did mention something about being wounded." Cynthia had come this far, and she wanted in on the fun. "Was that for sympathy or for short?"

Kyle clapped his hand over his chest and managed a pained expression. "Whoa, she got me again." His act over, he gave his old friend a nod. "Tony's a damn good mechanic. He came here looking for work."

"Looking for someplace off the reservation where they pay in U.S. dollars, instead of trying to trade me their junk cars. I've got a yard full of junk cars and no cash income."

"Anybody who can get a rez-runner back on the road is a master mechanic," Kyle told him. "You ought to be in high demand here."

"Or get yourself some training in bodywork, man," came the suggestion from Jim, sitting across the table. "These Minnesota cars rust out in a hurry."

"I feel right at home," Kyle said. "More junk cars on the road in this city than in all the yards in Pine Ridge Reservation."

"You advertise your South Dakota cars here, you can make money. No rust on a South Dakota car. Doesn't matter about the engine." Tony turned to Cynthia. "You got a car, ma'am?"

"Yes, I do. It's true about the rust here, but good mechanics are hard to find, too. I have a tough time finding a full-service gas station anymore." She let pass the arched-brow looks the men exchanged. "Either way, I'm sure you'll find work, Tony."

Tony nodded. "This is good food. Did you make it?"

"No, I—"

"Hope you were wearing your gloves," Paul said. "Wouldn't want you to be spreading germs among the guests."

With a chuckle, Kyle touched her shoulder and leaned closer. "You oughta carry those gloves in your car, for times when you have to pump your own gas."

"Rugged guy," Tony scowled. "They get inspected by the Health Department here. They gotta use gloves." He turned to Cynthia, kindly assuring her, "A lady shouldn't have to pump her own gas."

Cynthia liked Tony.

But she liked Kyle, too, impossible as he was when he got into his ribbing routine. Just to prove it, she caught up to him before he made his exit with his friends. "Can I give you a ride home this time?"

He considered the idea. "Why don't you drop me off at the co-op? Delia wants me to help her move some furniture."

Cynthia went into the store with him to say hello and ended up helping to rearrange display cases. The remodeling was taking place bit by bit, as funds allowed, but the place was shaping up nicely, as the smell of fresh paint attested. Kyle took direction from Delia, contributing his muscle to each task. Between orders he played with Ronald, Delia's little boy.

"He's good with kids, isn't he?" Delia said, noting Cynthia's interest when Kyle was out of earshot.

"I know he has a way with the older ones. It's fun to watch him with one that age."

"Kyle's looked after my husband, Jamie, off and on ever since I can remember. He's been after Jamie to go to school for a long time, got him into a program here, and now—" Delia gave a quick nod as she added more men's rings to the tray she'd been arranging "—I think Jamie might just stick it out this time. Kyle didn't have much help when he went back to school. Just the G.I. Bill. Started out at Oglala Community College back on Pine Ridge and stuck with it until he became a teacher."

"He's surely the right man for the job."

"We need a lot more like him." She set the tray in the front of the display case. "Reservation life is hard on the men. There's not much for them to do. The land is poor. There's no jobs."

"What about the women?"

Delia shrugged. "For most of us, we put the first baby to breast and there's a purpose for us, pure and simple. We know we're needed then." She slid the glass door closed.

Cynthia folded her arms across her chest almost defensively as Delia moved along to the next display case. She handed Cynthia a box of silver bracelets, along with a velvet-covered stand upon which to arrange them.

"The old way, everybody played a part in raising every child," Delia continued. "The whole village was the family. But all that was taken away back when they started the reservations and put the children in boarding schools. The mission schools, the BIA schools..." She shook her head. "I went to boarding school. So did Jamie and Kyle. Our grandparents and our parents, they had no say in it, and we were taught nothing but white culture.''

Pausing, Delia looked up at Cynthia, not for sympathy, but for understanding. ''Our generation is trying to get back some of what was lost. Even here, in a city that's about as far from Pine Ridge, South Dakota, as you can get. It's hard to leave home, but there's work here, and maybe a market for some of the things we make.''

''And there's a good school here,'' Cynthia added, hoping she might someday feel she'd contributed. ''One that's part of the community.''

''It's getting there. It's not easy, starting a new kind of school, and you can't build community pride overnight.'' Delia eyed Cynthia critically. ''You can't wait for somebody else to do it for you, either. Somebody else isn't likely to see it through.''

Cynthia studied the rows of silver rings in the case beneath her elbows. Some were excellent pieces, others less so. This was her field of expertise. In the classroom she had a lot to learn, but here she could easily take over and run the show. A few months ago, her first suggestion would have been to move the shop to another part of town. But no one had asked her, which was a good thing. She was finding easy answers harder to come by these days.

''Did Kyle tell you that I talked about quitting?''

''He said everybody's talked about quitting at one time or another.''

''Sometimes I think I'm more of a liability than an asset.''

''Are you gonna quit?'' Delia challenged.

"Not this week." Cynthia lifted her chin and smiled. "Wait till you see the play, Delia. I think it's going to be wonderful."

"LET ME DRIVE YOU HOME, Kyle," Cynthia tried again when he walked her to her car.

"Let me drive *you*," he said. He would let her get close, but he wasn't ready to let her get *that* close. Not inside his front door... "Let me get behind the wheel and drive. I miss it," he claimed as he opened the passenger door for her. "I know a real nice spot I'd like to take you to."

Indian summer had warmed the last days of October, and although the night air was crisp and sometimes frosty, there hadn't yet been a hard freeze. The harvest moon rose over the small tranquil lake that Kyle had discovered on an excursion in the country months ago. He'd returned by bus, borrowed car and on foot. Often when he'd needed time alone, he'd come here. Now he needed time with Cynthia, and he needed a place where no excuses or explanations were necessary.

"I sure like these ten thousand lakes," he told her cheerily as he parked the car at the end of a narrow, tree-lined dirt road. "Back home, we've got buttes. You take your girl up on top of a butte and show her the stars." He put his arm around her shoulders and drew her closer. "But there's something fundamentally sexy about water."

She slid easily across the leather seat, but not altogether willingly. Through her thin wool jacket he could feel the tension in her shoulders. "We could go to my place and have . . . coffee," she suggested with young-girl shyness.

He brushed her hair back from her temple and smiled. "Or we could stay right here and have...each other."

"Don't you like my place?"

"What's not to like?" He began kissing her softly, nuzzling her ear, nibbling her cheek. "I like your clothes. I like your place. I like your car." He thought "admired" would have been a better word, but he wanted her to relax while he moved deftly to the more personal. "I like your hair," he ventured as he took her face in his hands. "I *really* like your eyes."

But her lips became the object of his attention. He took several leisurely nibbles before fitting his mouth over hers, offering a gentle promise even as he hinted at the hotter demands he had in mind.

"I like your kiss," she acknowledged in a soft whisper.

"Plenty more where that came from." He slipped one button from its mooring on her jacket, and she hesitated on the verge of an objection, then slid her arms around his neck. He dispatched the second and final button. Just to make her more comfortable, he told himself as he kissed her once again.

Neither of them wanted to rush. They had found a quiet place where there was only the night sky and the moon's reflection in the lake. The time was theirs.

"I wasn't expecting anything like this when I came to All Nations," she said.

"Neither was I—" he kissed her forehead "—when I came to the city."

It was a toss-up as to who was really the visitor in whose world. He wanted her to take off her neat little jacket. She wanted him to stay longer than just a while. "I needed a change in my life," she told him honestly, "but I don't know about—"

"Shh. Nothing's going to happen. Nothing bad," he amended. "Nothing you don't want."

"I don't always want what's good for me."

The comment rankled. He fully intended to be good for her. He drew a deep breath and opened the car door. "Let's take a walk."

"Autumn chill," she said as she emerged from the car and folded her arms tightly beneath her breasts. The jacket that matched her slacks had been all she'd needed that morning. "I didn't come prepared."

"I did. I came prepared to walk home, if it comes to that." He took off his own jacket and draped it over her shoulders. "I'm prepared, Cynthia. Whenever you're ready."

They walked beneath a shadowy canopy of trees in transition. The night breeze rustled in the leaves still holding out overhead, while those that had fallen swished and crackled underfoot. Kyle had in mind a special copse of droopy willows, a particular view of the lake, an absolutely private spot. He would take the chill away, and he would do it in a natural, neutral place, a place where he owned as much of the world as she did.

He drew her by the hand, and he could feel the struggle between her hard-earned skepticism and her heartfelt willingness. "I want to be with you here in the grass." He swept the willow curtain aside and took her down with him onto a bed of leaves. "Before all the green is gone," he told her. "Before winter comes."

Wrapped in his jacket, she gave herself over to the cradle he made for her in his arms. "Oh, Kyle, this is crazy. We're out here in the middle of—"

"One lake in ten thousand. There's nothing separating us here, no..." He heard the catch in her breath when he slipped his hand inside her open jacket. "Just let me touch you, Cynthia."

His hand sneaked into her blouse. He made her shiver when he touched cold fingers to her warm breast. It took no more than that to bead her nipples. He smiled against her lips. "I'll keep the cold away from your body, but you have to warm my fingers."

"Oh, Kyle, that feels...absolutely...crazy."

He thought of her as a fragile stringed instrument, and he played upon her until she rewarded him with a soft musical moan. "Let yourself go, and I'll make it crazier."

"You'll make *me* crazy," she whispered.

"I promise."

And he kept his word. Her pleasure grew at the touch of his lips and his hand. He kept their clothing close about them even as he moved it aside for intimate touching and kissing and pressing together, flesh upon flesh. They kept their backs to the cold as they made their own heat and kept it trapped between them, cherishing it as they cherished the feel of one another. He pleasured her, and when it came time, he protected her. It was a simple gesture, performed without discussion, executed out of care and respect, and it made her heart soar. She welcomed him deep inside her, as though she were taking him home. She gave him pleasure.

LATER THEY CUDDLED together, his back braced against the trunk of the tree, hers against him. She sat between his thighs. He was wearing his jacket now, with her tucked snugly into the front of it. The lake was as smooth as glass, and Cynthia felt so light-hearted and light-headed that she was sure she could skip across to the other side without getting wet. But she would have to stir from her comfortable spot, which she was not the least bit inclined to do.

Such buoyance freed her to say whatever was on her mind, whatever popped into her head. And because he had taken such care with her, she trusted him with one of her formerly weighty thoughts, now simply a wistful wondering.

"Do you think I'm getting too old to have a baby?"

He laid his cheek against her hair. "I didn't catch the numbers."

"I'm thirty-two."

"If you're getting too old, then it's way too late for me." His lips brushed her temple. "I did right by you, honey. I said there'd be nothing separating us, but I didn't mean..."

"I know. That statement is covered under your cowboy poet's license." She turned her face toward his pleasant nuzzling. "You did right by me in more ways than one." He smiled and kissed her. "Now it's your turn to reveal numbers."

"I'm an old man. Thirty-five."

"And you don't have any children, old man?"

"No wife," he said matter-of-factly. "No kids. At least, none that anybody's told me about. I can't say I didn't sow a few wild oats, and I can't say I've always done right." His voice sounded hushed, as though in the quiet of the night their leafy bower had become a confessional. "All I can say is that I'm doing better. Almost got married once, but it didn't work out. She got a better offer."

"That's hard to believe. Like Kevin Costner saying he couldn't get a date when he was in high school."

"Whoa, that's a pretty lofty comparison. Question is, would I be a good catch for somebody like Cynthia Boyer?"

"Cynthia Boyer learned a lesson about getting caught in her own net. I don't want any more 'good catches.'"

"Damn," he said, chuckling. "You should've met me ten years ago. I was a bad catch then. Hell on wheels."

"I don't think I want a bad catch, either. I want the freedom to do something with my own life. Something that might make a difference."

It pleased her to be able to say these things to someone who actually cared to listen. That the someone was a man seemed a rarity too precious for any woman to reject. "What did you offer this woman?" she wondered aloud. "Was it hell on wheels?"

"I was in college by then, and I'd pretty much quit raisin' hell. I wanted something else, too." He moved his arms a bit higher around her shoulders, drawing her closer. "I offered her what I had. Myself in the raw-material stage and a few possibilities."

"I like what you've done with the raw material." And what he'd done with the neatly finished fabric that was Cynthia. "You're a person who makes a difference, Kyle."

"Have I made a difference to you?"

"Oh, yes. A memorable difference."

"There are a few differences I'd like to forget." She turned, and he cupped her cheek in his strong hand. "Differences between us, besides you being a woman and me being a man."

"Right now I can't think of any others that matter."

He stroked her tapered eyebrow with his thumb and smiled. "Right now neither can I."

Chapter Six

THE PLAY WAS POSTPONED twice. On parents' night, Cynthia deemed the troupe and their masks "not ready for prime time," which was just as well, since only a handful of parents showed up. On the alternate night, four key players had strep throat. A second parents' night was scheduled by a hastily formed "All Nations Alliance." Members, including parents, teachers and students, handed out flyers door-to-door, inviting people to attend the school function.

The words "Celebration and Feed" at the top of the paper helped to bring out the crowd on the Wednesday before Thanksgiving. Despite the gray clouds that filled the skies and the quarter-size snowflakes that had been falling since late afternoon, the people came. The early comers pleased Cynthia. She was glad when more came. But when they kept coming, she began to worry.

They filled all the seats in the gym. They filled the extra folding chairs that were rounded up to accommodate the overflow. She was afraid there would not be enough room, that some would be without a place to sit and would have to stand. Then they might leave. Or they might stay and keep milling around, and then what? She had to seat the older people. No, she had to seat the small children, whose pre-show antics in the middle of the gym floor threatened to ruin everything.

When showtime came and went and still neither the audience nor the players were in place, she fretted over that, too. But Kyle assured her the show would go on when the people were ready. "That's Indian time," he reminded her with a cavalier wink. "Indian time" made Cynthia all the more nervous.

She needn't have been. Kyle had assigned the narrator's role to Marvin Gates, a small boy with a big voice. When Marvin stepped up to the microphone to announce the players' names, they all appeared on cue. The colorful masks with their pointed ears, massive muzzles and brightly shining human eyes drew murmurs of approval as each was introduced.

It was all out of her hands now. Bertram, the effusive fly, was overacting to beat the band, and if Tom Gorneau decided to upstage him with an unscripted swat, there was not a thing Cynthia could do to prevent it. She didn't have to look away from the action to know it was Kyle's shoulder touching hers, his hand enveloping hers and his smile mirroring the one she wore.

"Your hand's cold." He put it between both of his and gave it a brisk rub. "Nervous?"

"I'm a wreck." She smiled brightly. "But aren't they wonderful?"

"This is definitely one of their finer moments," he agreed, returning her smile. An onlooker might have mistaken them for the proud parents of the entire fifth grade. Recalling Delia's comment about having a purpose, it occurred to her that without putting these children to breast, she had done some nurturing. And there was plenty more where that came from, she decided.

Cake and sandwiches were served in the windowless gym. The children were wound up over the success of their performance and the excitement of the season's first snowfall. As people began to leave, word drifted back that "it was really piling up out there." Kyle offered to take care of the costumes and cleanup if Cynthia wanted to get on the road, but now that they'd finally pulled off the event, she wasn't about to miss any part of the fun.

After the last of the cake had been served and the masks had been placed in the hallway display case, both Cynthia and Kyle were surprised to find at least eight inches of snow on the ground. There was a holiday atmosphere in the parking lot and the street beyond, where streetlights cast an opalescent glow over blanketed cars and stoplights and porch railings. Eight inches wasn't *that* much snow for Minnesota. The sound of spinning tires was nearly drowned out by the shrieks of children getting pelted with the season's first snowballs.

Kyle turned his collar up to his ears as they stood together on the doorstep. Somebody had shoveled a path to the street, but that was filling up fast. He shook his head. "You shouldn't try it."

"Everyone else is headed home."

"Everyone else *is* home, or close to it."

"It can't be too bad once you get going. It hasn't been snowing that long." She buttoned her long white coat and smiled up at him. "I really think we do good work together, Mr. Bear Soldier."

She was wearing low-heeled shoes, and it occurred to him that he'd never seen her without an umbrella when it rained or without sunglasses on a bright day. She always seemed to pull out the proper accessory at the proper time. "So where're your boots?"

"Where's your cap with the earflaps?" she countered with a laugh.

But Kyle wasn't laughing. "I could drive you home."

"I'm as good a driver as you are," she claimed brightly as she slipped her hand into an unlined leather glove.

"But are you as good at shoveling?"

Cynthia's smile dimmed. They stood there staring at one another while the snow sifted down around them. I'm good at many things, she thought. Just ask me. She knew if she accepted his offer, it would be a one-way trip. And he knew it, too. The thought of being snowed in with him for the holiday was delicious.

But his place was more accessible, and he had never invited her there. For some reason the idea of taking her home with him made him uncomfortable. His offer was gallant, but he had reservations about opening his own doors, reservations that might be a prelude to second thoughts. And experience had taught her that second thoughts in a man's brain had a way of cutting off the blood flow to his big feet.

"Independence becomes me, I think." She smiled bravely as she began picking her way down the shoveled path. "These days I can pump gas and shovel snow with the best of them."

"I guess you're on your own, then." He caught up to her in time to lend a hand when she started to slip. "Do you have a shovel along?"

"I'll be fine. I'm a native Minnesotan, you know. Tough as—"

"You could stay...." She slowed her steps, and he did, too. His voice trailed off, and again they searched each other's eyes. Snowflakes salted his black hair. One settled on her right eyelash.

She blinked it away. "My mother's coming for dinner tomorrow. I have those fish to feed, and I have..." Her car was only two steps away, whereas his unfinished suggestion had drifted well into the distance. "I have to get back. My car's really good on snow, so I'll be just—"

"Better get going, then."

He stood there stubbornly while she started the car, turned on the heat, the defroster, the defogger and emerged with scraper in hand.

He relieved her of the tool and brusquely ordered her back into the car. He cleared the back window, then moved around the car, reaching her side last. She rolled the window down to thank him.

"I don't think your mother's gonna make it tomorrow," he said gruffly.

"Oh, you'd be amazed. She does what she sets her mind to."

"Yeah, well, good luck following in her footsteps. Or tire tracks, or whatever." He shook the snow off her scraper and handed it back to her. "You'll need this."

He stood in the parking lot, and watched her make the turn into the street. She waved, letting him know everything was fine. He didn't wave back.

She got stuck before she reached the first intersection. The school janitor, who was on his way home, stopped to help her. One good push and she was on her way again, but the second rut she plowed into had her socked in tight. The windshield wipers were losing the battle for visibility, and she resigned herself to the fact that she would have to open the door and plant her sensible shoes in excessive snow.

Suddenly the door handle was torn from her hand. She gasped as she made a useless grab for it, but it swung out of reach. Kyle's angry face appeared in its place, his head bare, his ears red and his shoulders hunched against the wind.

"Move over."

"Kyle, you can't—"

"I won't be in the way when Mother comes for dinner," he barked as he took the seat she quickly vacated. "*If* she shows up. I'll find a way to get back."

"You don't really think that would bother me, do you? For her to—"

He ignored her anxious tone. "I don't really think I can drive this crate any better than you can, but I don't want you getting stuck by yourself."

"Thank you for the concern. I'm just wondering why—"

"About the other—" he put the car in reverse and glanced in the rearview mirror "—I don't really give a damn what bothers you."

"I see." Which was more than he could say, since, like the windshield wipers, the defogger was losing ground.

He tried a forward-reverse rocking maneuver, buried the car to the top of its wheel housings, pounded a fist on the steering wheel and muttered a colorful expletive. Still muttering, he got out and dug the front wheels out. With a couple of shouted instructions and a lot more muttering, he pushed while she manned the controls.

"We'll be doing this all night," he called finally. "You're coming home with me."

"All right."

They eyed one another for a moment. Her face was a study in artlessness, which deep down he couldn't quite buy. She knew where he lived, and damn his hide, he *would* care if it bothered her.

By white society's standards, his two-bedroom walk-up housed too many people, and he'd already had some trouble with his landlord over it. But his brother's family needed a place to stay. It was as simple as that. Jamie and Delia slept in one room with the baby. The three girls shared the other bedroom. Kyle had the sofa, and the two boys camped out on the living-room floor. The arrangements were only temporary—at least, that was the plan—but when Kyle led Cynthia in the front door he wished he'd at least moved the bed pillows out of the living room that morning.

For announcing guests, the kids were as good as having a doorman.

"Kyle brought somebody over!"

"Ms. Boyer!"

"Mom, my art teacher's here!"

"Your art teacher? Cynthia?" Delia emerged from the bedroom carrying little Ronald on her hip. "Can't get your car going?"

"She got it going, then got it stuck." Kyle handed their coats to Carla, who stared as though Cynthia had just been beamed down from the starship *Enterprise*.

"I should have left earlier, but I didn't want to miss out on anything." Cynthia took off her wet shoes and set them near the door. "Now I guess you're stuck with me until this lets up."

"According to the revised forecast—revised from 'chance of flurries' to 'no chance of travel'—nobody's going anywhere tonight," reported thirteen-year-old Arlin, whose eyes were glued to the little television set in the corner of the room.

"Did everybody make it home?" Kyle asked as he took a quick survey of all the faces. "Let's see, Tanya, Markie, Susie..."

Brother Jamie appeared behind Delia in the bedroom doorway. "We're all here, Sergeant." The resemblance between brothers was especially evident in the teasing grin that brightened Jamie's eyes. "No need to send out a search party. I got all the way across town to find my class had been canceled, so I had to hike all the way back. The buses quit running."

He turned his smile on Cynthia. "Is this the pretty blue-eyed one I've been hearing about?" Cynthia looked at Kyle, who raised a warning finger at his brother. "From the kids, I mean," Jamie clarified, palms raised in ready defense. "The new teacher, right? To hear everybody tell it, there's only one."

Cynthia introduced herself, extending her hand to Kyle's smirking brother.

"Well, I don't know about you guys, but all I got to eat tonight was one little piece of cake," Kyle said as he headed for the kitchen. "I'm making soup surprise. That means, whatever's in the cupboard added to what's left in the refrigerator."

"I've already started some," Delia said.

Since the TV was blaring and all available seating in the living room was full of kids, Cynthia followed. She remembered being snowed in at her grandmother's at Christmastime one year. She had been the only child there, besides her cousin Alex, who was always a brat. He took away anything she found to amuse herself with, be it pencil or book, claiming he'd "had it first." Grandmother's house, big as it was, had not been big enough for the two of them.

Kyle's kitchen, small as it was, accommodated all cooks. The old saying about too many cooks spoiling the broth—which was as far as Delia had gotten— didn't apply as people came and went to "see how things were coming."

Jamie peeled the potatoes, but when he was handed an onion, he relinquished the knife. "You'll have me cry, cry, cryyyyin' all night long," he crooned.

Cynthia saw the chance to make some points, and she moved in on the onion, even though Kyle assured her that she was a guest tonight and not a volunteer.

"Can't I be both?"

He'd been angry with her a little while ago. Since they'd walked into the apartment, even though his anger had dissipated, his eyes had glanced past hers more than once. Now, with her hands full of onion and his resting on the shoulders of one of the little girls, their eyes met.

She smiled, "I want to be both."

He nodded, and as he smiled the tension drained visibly from his shoulders. He gave the child a quick pat. "Can you find enough bowls for us, Tanya?"

Six-year-old Tanya deftly negotiated the jungle of adult legs, while Kyle took over in front of the simmering kettle. "Let me test it out here. Where's the spoon?"

"I can add another can of tomatoes," Delia said.

"Pepper," Kyle judged. "Come taste this, Cynthia."

Cynthia cocked her hip to one side to allow Tanya's older sister, Susie, access to the utensil drawer. A handful of spoons clanked on the counter next to Cynthia's pile of chopped onions as Susie rummaged around for more. Cynthia picked one up and took it with her to the stove, where Kyle was waiting with her taste already dipped out.

"This is the sharing spoon." He blew into the big serving spoon to cool the soup before he fed it to her. "Everybody gets a taste and everybody has a say." He didn't give her much time to consider. "Pepper, right?"

She pressed her lips together, assessing the flavor from start to finish. "I always add vinegar, too."

"Vinegar!" he called out to Delia, whose head was buried in another cupboard.

"And sugar."

"Sugar?"

"Just a little." Cynthia showed him a half inch of space between finger and thumb. "It brings out the flavor."

"I've got nothing against sugar," he said, reaching for a plastic bowl. He added a pinch and gave her a wink. "You know that."

"Now taste." It was her turn to dip, blow and hold the spoon while he sipped. He licked his lips, then smiled as he took the spoon from her hand and fed her another sample. She nodded. "It's getting there."

Custom dictated that the children be fed in the kitchen, while the adults would take their soup to the living room. While Delia and Jamie added a leaf to the table, pushing the edges close to the walls, the boys moved two chairs in from the living room. Cynthia joined Kyle in the living room for a brief moment of semi-privacy.

"Are you sure there's room for me tonight?" she asked as she stretched her shoulders and used both hands to iron the day's kinks out of her lower back.

He gave her a guarded look. "What kind of room do you need?"

"Just a chair, or a little—" she measured a square foot of air with her hands "—place to put my head down."

"Next to mine would be good," he whispered, and she feigned shock. "A guy can dream, can't he?" Smiling softly, he slipped one hand behind her and gave her a soothing back rub. "We have plenty of room for you. I just hope you're not too fussy about..."

"I thought you didn't care what bothered me."

"I do." He glanced at the rest of his family, still jockeying for space at the kitchen table. "They'll be able to get a place of their own soon, but right now they need a place to stay, and it's kinda crowded, but..."

Cynthia put her arms around his waist and gave him a hard squeeze. Then she surprised herself by kissing his cheek, right there in front of everyone. "Thanks for taking me in tonight."

He ignored the giggling and shushing that was going on in the kitchen. "Anytime."

"I won't take up much space."

"Take all you want. What's mine is yours." He was still rubbing her back, running his fingertips up and down her spine as though they'd been together a long time and he knew exactly what she needed just now. "I'll move the kids around, and you can bunk in with the girls."

As the snow piled up outside, Kyle's family regaled her with stories that had clearly been part of the entertainment on other nights, since even the young ones had an occasional punch line. Kyle was the star of many of the family tales, and everyone seemed to enjoy telling on him for Cynthia's benefit. She heard about the time the sorrel horse flopped him in the manure pile and the time the ghost his brothers had seen in the yard turned out to be Kyle draped in the bedsheets he'd just taken off the clothesline.

Following each story he gave her a secret look that said, *Don't take it too seriously.*

She returned a merry smile that said, *I believe every word.*

The laughter was part of the storytelling rhythm, and the storyteller's hands animated each incident. Meanwhile the television droned in the background, and children crawled from one lap to another. During a lull, Kyle stepped over one wrestling match and one sleeping child on his way to the kitchen, where he made popcorn in the iron skillet. It was like a big slumber party, Cynthia thought, and nobody spoiled it by announcing bedtime.

But there was a winding-down as quiet settled in over contentment. Those who had fallen asleep were either moved to another spot or just covered up with a blanket. The girls' room had twin beds, and Carla insisted that Cynthia get one all to herself. She accepted little Tanya's offer of her special pink blanket, turned off the lamp, moved close to the wall and waited. Springs creaked in the dark. She lifted the edge of the blanket, and Tanya scrambled in next to her.

Then came Carla's harsh whisper, a little-mother warning. "Tan-yaa..."

"It's okay," Cynthia said, smiling happily in the dark. "This is the sharing blanket."

SHE AWOKE the next morning to the smell of coffee. Eager for the taste of morning and for a daylight look at what the skies had delivered overnight, she slid down to the foot of the bed, slipped into her clothes and followed the aroma. Toes and cowlicks peeked out from under the blankets on the living-room floor. The two boys were still asleep, but the pillow on the sofa had been abandoned.

Cynthia put in a call to her mother, wished her a happy snow-bound Thanksgiving and promised to celebrate with her over the weekend. Then she helped herself to a cup of coffee and took it outside to the porch, where she had a hunch she would find Kyle.

He'd draped his shoulders with a striped blanket and taken his coffee to the porch, where he stood looking in amazement at the way the snow had filled up the small fenced-in box that was the front yard. Turning at the sound of her footsteps, he shook his head in mock disapproval. "Where's your coat, young lady?"

"Your niece let me share *her* blanket last night."

"And I lay awake half the night wishing you were sharing mine." He opened it now, and she stepped inside, fitting her shoulders into the shelter of his arm. "I've never seen this street so still," he said. "So quiet. It's almost like back home."

"It'll take some time to get things moving again." She sipped her coffee, savoring the rich flavor and the warmth of the rising steam. "How much did we get?"

"Almost two feet."

"How much did they get in South Dakota?"

His smile acknowledged his habit of taking note of the weather report for his home state. "The storm went around them, as usual."

"Ah, we're talking Camelot, then."

He chuckled. "When I first moved here, I met a guy—a white guy I used to know when I was in the army. Told him I'd gone back to school and become a teacher. He introduced me around as someone who'd 'come a long way.'" He glanced up at the snow-laden branches of the big sugar maple that stood in the front yard. "To him that meant I'd come up in the world. To me it meant I had traveled over a long distance. That was my first thought. It's a long way back to Pine Ridge."

"You've done both, haven't you?"

It took him a moment to answer. "We see things a little differently, your people and mine. Ordinarily I'm inclined to shrug it off, but with you . . ."

He studied the coffee that was left in his mug. Half a cup. "I know what your place is like. It's like *up* in the world," he said quietly. "And I wasn't anxious to bring you here because I didn't want you to think—" their eyes met over the coffee he'd made and the doubts he'd been unable to dismiss "—less of me, I guess."

"Less than what?"

"I don't know." There was a teasing glimmer in his eyes. "Less than you thought the first time we met?"

"I wasn't the same person then that I am now. I hadn't tasted from the sharing spoon."

"What? You mean if you were making a pot of soup in your house, you'd all taste from different spoons?" He laughed and squeezed her shoulder. "You must like to wash dishes."

"You know what I thought the first time I saw you at the church feed?" He had a ready answer, but she hugged him around the middle and cut him off.

"No, you don't, because I've never told you. The first thought that came to my mind—" she gave him a sober look "—automatically, before it occurred to me that you had some nerve putting in all those orders for coffee and sugar, what I thought might roughly translate into—" ah, she could tell by his eyes, she had him cold "—this man could probably charm an Ojibwa rabbit into a Lakota kettle."

Kyle's eyes lit up like fireflies. Then he grinned naughtily. "Easy."

Chapter Seven

"THERE'S A BUNCH of turkeys in the kitchen at the church," Kyle reported to the snowbound cardplayers as he hung up the phone. The game of hearts had gotten started over morning coffee, and now it continued through the parade of children marching back and forth between the kitchen and living room, cereal bowls in hand.

"A new street gang raiding the cupboards?" Jamie drew a few chuckles as he trumped the trick on the kitchen table. "Or are we talking real turkey here?"

"I'm talking edible turkeys, the kind we've just been talking about and wishing we had in the refrigerator."

"I was going to buy one yesterday," Delia said for the third time, "after I checked in the Phillips Village newsletter and said to myself, What? No turkey bingo here?"

"That can be your next project," her husband told her, then grimaced when she played a card. "Eee, this one. We're supposed to be partners, and she's thumping her trump over *my* trump."

"Sometimes your trump needs thumping." Kyle tapped his brother's shoulder with a playful fist while he took a peek at Cynthia's hand. He'd turned his seat over to Carla, whom he'd trained as a hearts partner. He didn't know how Delia and Jamie had managed to make so many babies when they couldn't get it together on a game of cards.

"It's not snowing in New York," Susie announced as she passed by in search of more cereal. "But the wind is picking up, and it looked like the gigantic Miss Piggy balloon *almost* took off."

"You'll thump my trump when pigs fly, brother," Jamie said with a laugh as he swept the cards off the table. "And 'almosts' don't count."

"We have a turkey crisis to consider," Kyle reminded the foursome. "It's Thanksgiving, and we've got no turkey, and the church has a whole flock of birds, all thawed out and waiting to be cooked. But they've got no cooks." Cynthia looked up at him, then Delia. "The cooks can't get over here. The teams that were scheduled are from way out in the suburbs."

"Will there be people showing up for dinner in this weather?" Cynthia asked.

"Will the people show up for dinner?" Kyle repeated slowly as he moved behind her, resting his hands on her shoulders. "We have here a woman who has seen but does not yet believe."

"If you cook it, they will come," Delia said solemnly. Carla giggled.

Cynthia shrugged. "Then we'll cook it."

As he spoke, Kyle massaged. "I like your spirit, Pilgrim. Trouble is, the padre says we'll have to round up the mashed potatoes and corn and pumpkin pie." Cynthia was getting into the massage, and Jamie was getting a peek at her hand. "The volunteers were bringing that stuff, so all there is now is turkey."

"We'll go to the store." She tipped her head back against his stomach and smiled up at him.

Carla groaned and threw in her hand in utter adolescent disgust as Kyle returned the smile, along with a question. "You got a team of sled dogs handy?"

"Mary White Eagle has a four-wheel drive," Delia said as she added her cards to Carla's. "We'll do it the way we do at home. We'll round up donations."

"How far away is the church?" Cynthia asked.

"About six blocks," Kyle told her. "We'll have to hoof it."

Cynthia shifted in her chair, stuck her legs out to her side and looked at her feet. She was wearing a thick pair of Kyle's socks.

"I've got boots you can wear, Ms. Boyer. I can wear my high-tops," Carla said.

It pleased Cynthia to realize that the children had gotten the hang of calling her "Ms.," even though it probably sounded funny to them. It was beginning to sound funny to her, too. "Call me Cynthia."

Carla gave her uncle a knowing look. "Probably be callin' you 'Auntie' pretty soon."

THE FIRST CHALLENGE came in breaking a trail through the city snow. In the course of six blocks much of the sidewalk was still covered with snow, although many people were working their shovels in that direction. Lola Johnson, one of the neighborhood's black elders, agreed to watch baby Ronald in return for some help with the chore. Arlin and Markie stayed behind in trade.

At the church, an anxious young curate, Father Preston, greeted them gratefully. He said that while the word of the need for local effort was getting out, only a few helping hands had made their way to the massive old brick landmark that was St. Jude's.

"No one expected all this snow." Father Preston gestured dramatically as he bustled ahead of the small group on the way to the kitchen. "So, of course, the turkeys were thawed out. It would be a *sin* to waste all that food." He chuckled. "So to speak."

An elderly nun and three of the church's closest neighbors were visibly relieved when they saw that help had arrived. "We're tired after just unloading the coolers," one woman said. "But if we don't get them started, these things won't be done before Sunday."

"Cynthia is on the official volunteer schedule," Kyle announced. "She knows just what to do."

Cynthia failed to take the bait. She was too busy taking account of the birds, still in their packages. "I've never seen such big turkeys." She took a slow turn around a steam table that was piled high. "I've also never seen this *many* turkeys—" a plastic-covered breast yielded beneath the pressure of her forefinger "—thawed out, all at once."

"Next she's gonna tell us she's never *cooked* a turkey," Delia predicted with a smile.

Kyle laid a hand on Cynthia's shoulder and recited with mock solemnity, "But when the guests arrive, she'll be happy to pour."

"In your ear, Mr. B.S." Cynthia's comeback gained her several appreciative snickers, along with Jamie's unrestrained hoot. "I certainly know how to cook *a* turkey."

"All you have to do is cook *a* turkey." Kyle gave her a conciliatory pat on the back. "Times twenty."

But there were plenty of hands to help with the preparations, and they were hands of all races. They were the face of all nations, too. They came by twos and threes, bringing sacks of potatoes and flour, cans of fruits and vegetables. Up to her elbows in giblets, Cynthia was awed by the increasing stockpile. She decided not to worry about what kind of a mixture all these foods would make. It would be a neighborly blend.

Carla and two of her pals took charge of the ever-present little ones in the dining hall. In the kitchen, few of the helpers needed directions, other than where to find the right pot or spoon. Since it would have taken too long to cook stuffed turkeys, the bread stuffing—which was a recipe never to be duplicated, since no one was measuring—was prepared on the side. And since pumpkin pie was out of the question, a team of women set about making traditional Indian frybread, while another group improvised a fruit compote.

Mary White Eagle was a large woman with an imposing voice, and when she appeared at the top of the steps and announced that she had rounded up several four-wheel drive vehicles, all heads turned. Mary was dressed like a cossack. She was used to giving orders.

"I've got three four-by-fours outside and two more stuck somewhere between here and Franklin Avenue. This was your idea, Kyle Bear Soldier." She tossed him a ring of keys. "Blue Suburban. Start hauling the old folks in."

And so the feast was prepared, and the people came. As always, they came in all age groups, all shapes, sizes and colors. The elders and the children were fed first. Some of the people came to be served. Others took their meal, then spelled those who had been working in the kitchen.

Cynthia was happily exhausted by the time Kyle made her sit down with her own tray. He said it was time she met some people, and he introduced her to the editor of the neighborhood newsletter, the chairman of the neighborhood safety committee and the head of the neighborhood-renewal task force.

These were people Cynthia had read about or had seen in television interviews. But she never would have met them, really met them, had she not come to work at All Nations. These were the community leaders who had led the fight to close down a liquor store near the school, who had objected to the plan for locating a city garbage-transfer station in their neighborhood and who organized property cleanups and street patrols. They were the people who were making a difference. They welcomed her to their table simply because she was willing to come. She was willing to share. She wanted to be part of it all.

And from people she had once presumed to be stoic, she was learning a lot about the nature of humor and the benefits of laughter.

"Did you hear the one about the boy whose mother was Chippewa and his dad was Sioux?" Anna Martinez, the newsletter editor, asked. "Went out hunting, took along a dog. Out on the flat he saw a rabbit." She pointed toward the far wall. "Dog took after it. Boy didn't know which one to shoot."

Everyone laughed—except Cynthia. Wide-eyed and perfectly innocent, she said, "What did he decide?" Kyle groaned as she lifted a hand for truce. "No, wait, I can figure this out. Just tell me, was his mother cooking that night, or his dad?"

Now *everyone* laughed.

"Okay, time out," Cynthia pleaded. "Now, explain to me why you guys give each other such a hard time over rabbits and dogs."

"The Chippewa like to take credit for chasing the Sioux out of the woods and pushing them onto the prairie," Anna explained. Cynthia wondered which side Anna might be on, then decided it didn't matter.

"But the way the Sioux remember it," Kyle said, "it was a much more powerful tribe that had us on the run." He paused for effect. "It was the north-woods mosquito people," he said, garnering a round of chuckles. "Anyway, they were rabbit-chokers, according to us, and we were dog-eaters, according to them."

"So you're traditional enemies," Cynthia concluded. "And you're able to laugh about it. Meanwhile, you can probably find ancient enemies still killing each other at any given time somewhere in the world for reasons that probably don't matter anymore."

"Maybe it started out when somebody served up the wrong kind of meat to his guests." Kyle pushed his empty tray back a little. "And while they were fighting over it, maybe somebody else came along and pulled the rug out from under them both."

"Maybe," Cynthia allowed.

"Sooner or later, you have to pull together," Kyle said. "Can't say we don't get into it sometimes, even now. You oughta go to an intertribal basketball tournament sometime if you wanna see traditional enemies battle it out." Murmurs of agreement drifted around the table. With a nod, Kyle raised an admonishing finger. "You Pilgrims were lucky you met up with our relations on the East Coast, instead of any of us. Otherwise the traditional Thanksgiving spread would have looked a lot different."

"When the Pilgrim shall come to dinner, the rabbit shall lie down with the dog." Cynthia smiled, making a mental note to submit her new saying to a greeting-card company. She speared a piece of dark meat, studied it, then giggled. "And the turkey shall wish he had long ears and a wagging tail."

"Ow-owww," came the response from one of the men, and the laughter flowed freely.

IT WAS WELL PAST nightfall by the time everything was cleaned up and put away. The rest of the family had gone home, but Kyle and Cynthia waited to stroll back at their leisure—alone. The streets were snow-bright, and the traffic, both automotive and pedestrian, was sparse. The dominant sound was that of a backup beeper on a snowplow that was probably a block away.

"That was the best Thanksgiving meal I've ever had," Cynthia declared. "I've never worked or laughed so hard."

"That reminds me—" Kyle put his arm around her shoulders and gave several playful squeezes as they shambled along the narrowly shoveled path "—where do you get off, calling me Mr. B.S.?"

"I couldn't help it." She glanced up, offering her sweetest smile. "It just came to me. Sprang to my lips and I couldn't hold it back."

"I like to hear you laugh," he said.

"I like your crazy sense of humor." She slid her arm around his waist. "And I enjoyed meeting people tonight. Some very well-known local people, people I've read about."

"Whether they're famous or notorious depends upon your point of view."

"I was glad to meet them. It was a good time, and a good place. And I thought about something Delia said." Their eyes met, and his were expectant. "Something I'm only beginning to understand. That it takes a whole community to raise a child."

"It used to work that way." He shrugged as they came to a stop at a quiet street corner. "I don't know. The community's getting to be a pretty big place."

"And you've let a lot of pilgrims in."

"They just sorta showed up, and you know how it is." He took both her hands in his, and she looked into his eyes, waiting to be told how it was. "When there's food, everybody eats."

"From the sharing spoon."

"You guys have a sharing cup, don't you?" The light turned red as she nodded. "That works, too," he said.

There was no traffic. There was no reason not to cross the street, except that they were mutually stunned by each other's eyes.

"The main arteries are open now."

"I really need to get home," she said softly.

"After all, you've got those tropical fish," he reminded her. "I wouldn't mind digging your car out and driving you home. 'Course, then you'd have to drive me back, and then I'd be worried about you going in the ditch, so I'd have to drive you back again..." He tipped his head from side to side, suggesting a perpetual motion.

"Let's just do it once."

He grinned slowly. "Just once?"

"One trip." The light turned green and she hopped off the curb, towing him along. "Then I'll make us a cup of coffee—"

"Just *one?*"

"—and we'll share." She tossed her hair as she turned, smiling, feeling light-hearted as a child. "We'll keep the cup brim-full. Bottomless. Runneth-ing over. And we'll keep on sharing."

A Note from Kathleen Eagle

I know I wasn't the first pilgrim to be treated to Native American hospitality on Thanksgiving, but I'm one who gives credit where it's due. More than 370 years ago, a group of Pilgrims got off the boat in Massachusetts, got themselves invited to dinner and made themselves at home. More than 20 years ago, one very proper pilgrim left Massachusetts, got off the plane on the Dakota prairie and did pretty much the same thing. But this pilgrim's experience leads her to question those cutouts that appear on every classroom bulletin board during the month of November. You've seen the pilgrim ladies laying out a big spread, the pilgrim men hauling in the turkeys and the one or two Indian guys standing off in a corner waiting to be called to dinner. I suspect we've always had the picture backward. I know for a fact that in Indian country, when there's food, everyone eats. Even the stiff-necked pilgrim, yours truly. I have a feeling that, like me, those first Pilgrims learned a lot about sharing from the *real* hosts of the Thanksgiving feast.

As I write this, times are tough in our cities, but tough times can bring out the best in people. "Loaves and Fishes Too," an interdenominational program sponsored by Minneapolis churches, is a good example. Serving as an occasional volunteer, I'm reminded of the day I actually experienced the miracle of the loaves and fishes. It was during my first summer at Standing Rock Reservation, when my friend Karen and I were volunteer Bible school teachers. On our first day at a little church in one of the more isolated, very traditional Indian districts, a woman came down to the church basement with two loaves of bread, four little cans of meat spread and a packet of Kool-Aid. "When the children get hungry, feed them," she said.

I looked at Karen; Karen looked at me. "What are we supposed to do with this?" I muttered. "We've got fifty kids here." Karen's faith overrode my doubts. No one complained that the meat was spread too thin or the Kool-

Aid was watery. And everyone ate, even the haughty pilgrim.

I believe life is a journey, and there are signs and signals for us all along the way. So many of the milestones in my life have occurred in the autumn. Thanksgiving has often been a meaningful time. It was a time for parades and football, for family and guests, for a fire in the hearth. It was the time of my brother's wedding, and, later in the circle of years, it was the day of my mother's death.

Thanksgiving is a wonderful tradition. It reminds Americans that our native people shared their bounty with our immigrant people, and that they all thanked God for life and sustenance. I'm sure the feast went over big on both sides. But my husband assures me that the conversation was flat because those stiff-necked pilgrims failed to appreciate good Indian humor.

LOVE IS THANKS ENOUGH
Sandra Kitt

Chapter One

EVAN HOLDEN SMILED good-naturedly, even though his neck was wrapped in a fierce stranglehold and his cheek was being pressed to that of someone considerably shorter than his six feet.

"Evan, we don't know how to thank you. You were heaven-sent."

"Yes, yes. He knows you're grateful, Gladys. Now let the poor man go before you kill him," came a raspy voice next to Gladys.

Gentle laughter erupted around the crowded table as Harry Jackson attempted to restrain his overexcited wife. Mrs. Jackson clasped her hands together, looked lovingly at Evan Holden and promptly burst into tears. For the fourth time.

Down the length of the three tables that had been pushed together to accommodate the celebrating group, Evan caught the steady gaze of Vanessa Moran. Her large dark eyes sparkled, and her brown face hinted at an ironic but affectionate smile meant only for him. Her expression was sympathetic as Evan, once again, shrugged in resignation. He had hoped for some time to relax with Vanessa. He had hoped that dinner and wine would have been just the two of them and not a cast of thousands. Still, Evan gave his full and undivided attention to Gladys Jackson, who was sincerely trying to express her admiration for him—the lawyer who'd just won their civil court case.

Conversation began again. The eleven people present, all colleagues and friends of Evan's who were interested in the case and its outcome, were talking mostly shop. Law. Cases. Fees. Juries. Justice. A waiter brought another carafe of wine, and Vanessa, patiently listening but not fully participating in the discussion, found some of their anecdotes both funny and sad. If these people were typical, then the only thing that seemed to matter to lawyers was winning. Today Evan had done that; he'd won a victory that was both legal *and* just. But Vanessa was nonetheless appalled at the casual recounting of the many ways people tried to hurt and destroy one another.

Vanessa Moran wanted Evan to enjoy himself at this celebration party. He was not one to gloat and crow after a victory, and his ego would not have been damaged if the case hadn't gone well. But as Vanessa glanced around the table with its eclectic grouping of people and professions, she hoped that all of them fully realized and appreciated the significance of the day. Evan Holden, civil attorney, had successfully won a racially motivated bias case for an elderly black couple.

Vanessa pursed her lips as she saw the way Gladys Jackson regarded Evan as a new kind of hero—someone who cared, someone she trusted. A far cry from the first time the Jacksons had met Evan and openly expressed their mistrust of him and his motives. Understandably the elderly couple's fight against being terrorized in their own apartment had left them weary, frightened and angry, anxious only for peace. Evan had convinced them on a third visit that he would fight *with* them in their suit against the new owner of their apartment complex—and that he could win. Vanessa could tell, from the quietly exchanged words at their end of the table, that Evan had the Jacksons' lifelong regard.

Evan didn't see it that way, of course. Yes, the jury's verdict on the bias case he'd been working on for eight months was just, but he hardly deserved praise. As far as Evan was concerned, the system had proved it could right a wrong and provide for just compensation. He glanced at Gladys. She had changed considerably since their first meeting. Her face, the rich deep color of oak, had become more expressive, no longer grim and wary but smiling and animated. That had come with trust. The older woman's lipstick was slightly smeared and faded from all the kissing and hugging, though her iron gray hair was still precisely fixed in place. Gladys said she'd had it done that morning just for her court appearance. Her cheeks wet with tears of joy, she pressed an already shredded tissue to her eyes, then reached for her husband's hand.

Evan was charmed by the Jacksons. There was a solid connection between them that reminded him of his grandmother Clair and granddad Bill. The Jacksons had more than forty years of marriage together, a love that adversity and tragedy had not diminished. The callousness of a big city and too many people who looked the other way, even bigotry, had not defeated them. Evan admired their strength and wondered about the lives that had forged it.

The Jacksons were the victors, not him, Evan believed. He had been merely an instrument in helping them even the odds. Their kindness to each other, their dignity throughout months of uncertainty and trying times, their eventual trust and faith in him, was a wonderful testimony to what love was really all about—trust, faith and grace under fire, no matter what. Love that would always win out. Evan glanced at Vanessa again, seated too far away for him to even touch. He wondered if she was thinking the same thing he was. Was it possible for *their* love to survive, despite the odds against them?

"How much did you say the jury awarded them?"

Evan turned to Brian Wesley, a lawyer in the DA's office, and a friend. "Just over a million."

Brian grimaced. "That doesn't seem like an awful lot when you consider what they went through. They could have been badly burned or even killed in that apartment fire. It was vicious and hateful."

"You're right. But the Jacksons weren't after revenge, just fairness," Evan explained. "The building owner has to pay the judgment and replace all their lost possessions. Another building owner has offered them a new apartment. And the Jacksons were relieved that the building manager was willing to testify on their behalf against his boss."

"But wasn't the manager the one placing the threatening letters in their mailbox?"

Evan's smile was sardonic. "If the threats had worked and Gladys and Harry had left the building peacefully, he figured no real harm would have been done. But they decided they weren't going to be intimidated or forced out of their home, so it's just as well that the manager's conscience drew the line at possible homicide. Actually, the manager was one of the people who helped get Gladys and Harry out of the building. When the fire started he got scared and came to his senses."

"So what happens to him?"

"Well, he's not going to jail for two years like his boss, who's in for arson and attempted murder. He received a suspended sentence and probation. The financial judgment may seem small, but Gladys and Harry were more concerned about being able to live safely and with some dignity. There's no price tag on that."

Brian nodded and took a gulp from his mug of beer. "You're right. It's fair. So how much was your fee?"

Evan played at the loosened knot of his tie and shifted in his chair. "Nothing."

"Nothing?" Brian asked blankly.

"It was pro bono."

Brian groaned. "Another big win and no pay. You're going to single-handedly give lawyers a bad name."

"We already have a bad name. I didn't need the money that badly—"

"Oh, really? Your car's going to die any day now."

"—and the case was a good one. I learned a lot from it."

Brian shook his head in bewilderment. "I thought you were looking forward to a quickie vacation with

Vanessa when this was all over. What did she say when you told her you weren't taking a fee?"

Evan's smile was warm and his gaze on Vanessa held a lot more than admiration. "It was her idea."

Evan didn't go into the details of how the Jacksons' case had come to him. That had been Vanessa's doing, too. Even though at the time she'd suggested he take on the case, Evan knew it was a challenge thrown in his face. That challenge had been made early in their relationship when Vanessa still believed that Evan's intentions were suspect. Would a preppie white civil attorney, who'd proved he was smart enough to make big bucks, take the case of an elderly black couple who were without resources but had an awful lot of pride?

Evan was still angry when he recalled the reign of terror perpetrated to force the Jacksons out of their six-room rent-controlled apartment. The building's new owner wanted to convert the space into two apartments and increase the rent. For Evan there had been no hesitation in taking the case. His first reaction was a genuine rage at what the Jacksons had endured for more than four years prior to his meeting them. At the time Vanessa had introduced him to the desperate and angry couple, they were barely surviving in a shelter sponsored by a community church.

Evan watched as Harry Jackson leaned on his cane and tried to stretch out his left leg. It had been injured when he'd fallen during the rescue from the burning building, and he'd been left with a painful limp. He was once again dumbfounded as to why people willfully treated other people so badly and with such cruel disregard. He'd had no personal experience with anyone whose life hung in the balance because of the color of his skin. Evan would always remember the look of pleasure on Vanessa's face when he'd told her he would take the case. He would also remember the Jacksons' defensiveness, which had taken weeks to overcome. But it had taken months for Vanessa to trust him, too...

Except for Pastor Hitchcock, who ran the temporary shelter where the Jacksons had lived ever since the fire, Vanessa Moran was only casually acquainted with everyone else at the table. But they were a friendly bunch. Outgoing, smart and aware. They had all rallied around her and Evan when it seemed inevitable that the two of them had deeper feelings for each other than just friendship. But Vanessa's instinct was still to be alert to signs of rejection and malice, the kind she and Evan had been encountering for the eight months during which they'd fallen in love.

Vanessa looked at Evan now, with his disordered wavy hair, and thought of his inclination toward being laid-back, his fondness for old movies and penchant for racquetball. She was still confused by how it had all happened. She and Evan, together. Yet there were two things Vanessa had learned quickly about this man. First, he had steamrollered his way into her life with absolutely no preconceived ideas about her. And second, he was always fair. That was how Vanessa had come to trust Evan. That was why she'd finally fallen in love with him. But, admittedly, this emotional awareness had been wrenched out of her against her will, whereas Evan had looked at Vanessa and accepted her as she was: whole, complete and distinctly, uniquely, herself. That was the meaning of love.

Vanessa saw Evan glance at the door of the restaurant again as he'd done frequently all evening. Only now did she wonder if he'd invited his parents to come and see him perform in court and then attend the celebration afterward. She knew they'd come to similar affairs in the past. Irrationally, Vanessa hoped they wouldn't show up. Not now. She was unprepared for an audience with Marsha and Stuart Holden, whom she'd never met.

"You know, I just realized this is probably an anniversary celebration, as well."

Vanessa raised an eyebrow at the young woman seated next to her who was reaching for a slice of pizza from the three varieties growing cold on trays in the center of the table. "Whose anniversary?"

Carol James licked an oily finger and pulled napkins from the dispenser. "Yours and Evan's. Wasn't it about a year ago that you two first met? Before he got into this case with the Jacksons?"

Vanessa shrugged. "Well, more or less—Evan was handling a contract dispute between a small company and the city. But it was a few months before we started dating." She stared at Carol. "Why would you call that an anniversary?"

"Well, it's at least a landmark moment. When you're starting a career in law there's no such thing as a relationship. There's work, and then there's more work. I'd love to know how you two managed it, let alone how it's lasted so long."

Vanessa's smile was ironic. "Especially since no one would have taken bets on our chances from the beginning. Right?"

"Oops," Carol murmured, shaking her head in embarrassment. "Just hang on while I take my foot out of my mouth."

Vanessa sighed inwardly. "Don't worry about it." Carol was a law student clerking in Brian's office, and her comment was not mean-spirited, just...annoying. "I didn't realize Evan and I were a hot topic of conversation among his friends."

Carol rushed to reassure her. "You're not. But I guess *I* want to know. Isn't it hard? My family would kill me."

Vanessa frowned, thinking about the changes she'd gone through, the revelations—and the stand she and Evan had taken for themselves. For each other. "I hope you never have to put that to a test," Vanessa murmured.

"I mean, relationships are hard enough."

Vanessa grew uneasy. She didn't want to have this conversation. Again. She was tired of explaining, tired of people's voyeuristic questions. There had been difficult moments, but nothing impossible, either. She and Evan together, a black woman and a white man, did make some people angry. It stirred up too much history, fed too many fantasies and made for too many questions. Vanessa turned and looked squarely at Carol.

"Not if there's trust and love. Anyway, my relationship with Evan isn't public property," Vanessa said softly. But her mother's stony silence when she'd first told her about Evan sat uneasily in her memory. Her mother's prediction that no good would come from their affair had struck a chord of suspicion in Vanessa. Was her relationship with Evan and his pursuit of her nothing more than an affair? Temporary, and an illusion? What more could it possibly be?

Carol nodded and munched thoughtfully on a piece of crust. She studied Vanessa. "Evan said the first time he met you, you threw him out of your office."

"That's not true, but I *did* lock him out. He wanted some records in the archives, but the office was closing."

"What happened?" Vanessa smiled and felt the memory pull her back in time. What *did* happen exactly? It was one of those events that seems surreal and dreamlike when you recall it. The course of their lives, hers and Evan's, had been completely changed.

It had happened at five-ten on a Wednesday afternoon almost a year ago. All the research patrons and her two assistants had gone home for the day. Vanessa had just locked the door to the archives when, down the hallway from the bank of elevators, a deep male voice thundered, the sound echoing off the walls, "Wait! Wait! I need to get in there."

Vanessa had stopped in her tracks, paralyzed by the demand and staring as an apparent madman charged down the hallway toward her. He wore a black leather overcoat, open and flapping as he ran. A thick folder was tucked under one arm like a football, and he was sprinting as if for a touchdown. He'd slowed as he neared Vanessa. She couldn't begin to guess at her expression, but even as the man gasped for breath, he started to laugh.

"I...I'm sorry. I didn't...mean to scare you. I promise you I'm not a murderer, just desperate."

"For what?" Vanessa had asked, suspicion clipping her words.

"I need to get into your archives."

She chortled. "Not today you won't. We're closed. You'll have to come back tomorrow." She began to walk around him, but he grabbed her arm.

"Look, it's only a few minutes after five. I tried to get here as fast as I could, but I was in court and—"

Vanessa eased her arm free. "I'm sorry. The office is closed." Again she started to walk away, wondering if this stranger was prone to violence if he didn't get his way.

"All I need is a few photocopies. It'll only take a minute. Maybe two," he called out after her.

"Good ni...ight," Vanessa sang out, almost to the safety of the elevators.

"Please," she heard quietly from behind. She stopped. She turned around and saw his silhouetted shape. She slowly walked back and looked more carefully at him.

He was tall and dressed in charcoal gray, like many of the lawyers who came in and out of her building. His eyes were hazel, and Vanessa noticed a very small scar near his chin. He played sports, she guessed. He was used to attention, to winning. But he didn't seem dangerous or demented. He gave her a tentative smile.

"It will *not* take two minutes just to photocopy," Vanessa said firmly. "It'll probably take fifteen minutes to identify what you're looking for. Then it'll take fifteen minutes to retrieve the records. They might be in storage. They might be on microfilm—which means another fifteen minutes to set up the reader. The records you want might be missing. We're talking an hour minimum, and you know it." She shook her head. "You'll have to come back."

The man sighed. "You're right, you're right. But I have a brief due tomorrow morning. The data I need is in your archives. I *have* to get it and work on this thing tonight."

Vanessa looked at her watch. She was suddenly glad she had a legitimate excuse to resist his plea. "And if I don't leave right now, I'm going to be late for class."

"School?"

"Yes. Graduate."

The man's eyes sparkled mischievously and he arched a brow. "Let's make a deal. You get me my records, and I'll help you do all your term papers. I'm very good at research and writing."

"Let's *not* make a deal. I'll do my own papers, and you come back tomorrow."

He sighed again. "You mean I'm going to be left with nothing to do tonight but watch videos?"

Vanessa began walking backward away from him. "That's not such a bad idea. I wish I could. I don't think you'll be drawn and quartered if your brief is late. See you tomorrow." She'd turned and continued to the elevators, half expecting to hear him plead some more. But he didn't, and she let the doors close without once looking back.

Thinking about the incident now, Vanessa wondered if she'd been unkind. It might have taken only ten minutes to find the records and make copies. But at the time she'd resented Evan's manner, his certainty that he could get his own way. Of course, she didn't learn his name until the next day when he'd returned to apologize. It hadn't taken long to forgive him.

"I recall that those records were a really important part of his case. When did you finally give them to him?" Carol asked.

"The next day."

Vanessa had found Evan waiting outside her department the following morning before the doors had even opened. He carried an umbrella with a white handkerchief tied to the end. The word "truce" had been written on it in red marker. Evan Holden was a surprise. He had a sense of humor. He could be humble, admit a mistake. He could also be persuasive.

"I guess you weren't so desperate, after all," Vanessa couldn't help teasing him the next day, charmed despite herself.

"I was," he said smoothly as she'd unlocked the door and he'd followed her into the archives. "But I got a delay."

"Good." Vanessa had smiled wickedly at him. "That's what a lawyer's supposed to do. Stall." Evan Holden had burst out laughing, and their professional association had begun.

That had been the easy part, as Vanessa was to reflect later. Evan became a regular at the municipal archives. He was always friendly and frequently amusing, with his observations of life as a lawyer. Vanessa also noticed the determined way Evan attacked his cases. And the thoughtfulness with which he sometimes brought her doughnuts and coffee.

But even then Vanessa knew. Already her imagination had come out of nowhere, without prelude, to let her know that Evan Holden was different from any man she'd ever known. It was during his fourth or fifth visit to the archives that Vanessa found she was anticipating his coming, looking for his quick smile and the way he combed his hair with his fingers. She found herself looking forward to his incessant questions about his research—and eventually about her. So she began to fight Evan Holden's appeal. She didn't want to like him too much.

But before long she was using spare moments to dig out additional information for him, saving him time when he used his entire lunch hour to pore through old city documents. She began to set aside special resources for him, secretly enjoying his sincere thanks. Once, when he didn't come by for materials he'd reserved, Vanessa had gone to his office and found him with stocking feet propped on a desk spread with legal forms and texts. He's shown real surprise and pleasure at her sudden appearance, and he'd introduced her around his office as a "national treasure." Their odd working arrangement lasted about four months. Then one afternoon Evan stopped by Vanessa's office wanting to take her to dinner. That had been late February, eight months ago.

"You know, you could probably bill me for all the hours of your time I've used," Evan had teased.

"I don't mind." Vanessa had shrugged. "That's what I'm here for."

Evan had arched a brow at her, and there had been something titillating and seductive about the look. And he'd been seated next to Vanessa, at her desk, instead of a safe distance away on the other side. "I was hoping it was a little more than just dedication to duty."

Evan had made her uneasy. She felt awkward and thrown off balance. How could he be so bold? What was he thinking, anyway? "Then consider it my way of making up for being such a shrew the first time you came here."

Evan looked momentarily embarrassed. "You had a right to be angry. I was pretty arrogant."

Vanessa responded softly, "Yes, you were."

Evan laughed. "I knew I could count on you to be honest." He became sober and direct. "Thanks, Vanessa. The Case from Hell was a lot easier with you working on my side."

She'd laughed nervously. "Too bad I can't use that as an endorsement to get a raise. Thanks, anyway." She hadn't meant to sound flippant, but she was also feeling curiously shy.

"You're welcome. Now, can we go to dinner?"

"Excuse me?" Vanessa had asked. Warning bells began to clang in her head.

"How about dinner? There's a great Mexican place I've been meaning—"

"No."

Evan had been totally unprepared for her refusal. "No?" he'd repeated blankly.

"Right."

"Why?"

"Just because," she'd said patiently, keeping the anxiety in check.

"I can't accept that. That's not a reason."

"It's my reason. Look, it's very nice of you to want to take me to dinner to thank me, but—"

"No, no, no..." Evan shook his head. He sat forward, leaning closer, so that Vanessa was suddenly aware of him, not as a client, but as a man.

"What?"

"I want to take you to dinner because—" Evan gestured helplessly with his large hands "—because I want to take you to dinner."

"Haven't we spent enough time together in the past few months?"

He'd stared earnestly at her. "Not the kind of time I'd prefer. Come on, Vanessa. We're practically related, we see each other so often. I like you. I want you to have dinner with me. Just the two of us. No documents, no clients, no colleagues, no 'it's five o'clock and I have to close the office.' A *date*."

At that point, Vanessa wasn't entirely sure of Evan's motives. She should have paid more attention to the word "date," but she'd been too busy realizing that her excuses for saying no to Evan's invitation seemed so mean-spirited and groundless. She rather liked him because he was so open and friendly, so confident. She liked the fact that he asked her questions, never doubting that she'd have an answer he could rely on. She liked the fact that Evan confided in her, often voicing personal opinions, often opening up avenues of serious conversation better left between friends. But that was Evan. Apparently he wasn't afraid to ask for what he wanted. And it was only dinner. It didn't mean anything. Vanessa finally said yes.

But dinner *had* meant something. To both of them. Of course, there had been uncertainties, fears. Did Evan think she was an easy target? Did he think that because she'd agreed to dinner, it gave him special privileges? Was it really okay for them to be together?

Vanessa had expected that dinner would have been just that one time. That both Evan's curiosity and hers would have been satisfied. Instead, it had only opened the door to more questions—and the desire to explore them further. That took time. When Evan had driven her home that first evening, Vanessa had belatedly panicked, wondering if a simple "thank you and good night" would serve as a way to close the evening. But it hadn't been an issue. Before leaving for his own apartment, Evan had only said that the evening together had been the most enjoyable and relaxing he'd spent in months. And wondered if she wanted to do it again. She did. . . .

Down the length of the table, Vanessa stared at Evan, but it was no longer possible to see the Evan Holden she'd first met. There was only the Evan she loved, and *that* no longer seemed so strange. Would it have been easier if he didn't have dark blond hair, hazel eyes—and white skin? Or if she had not already experienced bias and indifference? Perhaps not. The first time Evan had kissed her, taking her off guard, he'd sighed and said, "that was nice." The world as

Vanessa had known it tilted several degrees on its axis, and all bets had gone out the window....

Someone at the table got up to leave. Everyone else took it as a signal and followed suit. Pastor Hitchcock went to get his car so he could take the Jacksons back to their temporary home. In three minutes the babble had died to a hum. Vanessa changed seats, coming to sit next to Mr. Jackson. He bowed gallantly over her hand and gave it an enthusiastic kiss.

"Vanessa, I want to thank you, too." Harry beamed at her, continuing to hold her hand.

"I haven't done anything."

"Sure you did. You brought Evan to the shelter." Harry laughed wickedly and shook his head at Evan. "Lord knows Gladys and I gave him a hard-enough time, and all he wanted to do was help. It's a good thing we listened to you, after all. You were a lifesaver."

"I don't think making gallons of black coffee counts," Vanessa said dryly. She was acutely aware that Evan, so far, wasn't saying anything. He was merely smiling complacently, listening to the exchange.

"I'm so glad this is over," Gladys sighed. "I'm looking forward to having my own place again. But I'll miss the shelter in a way. Especially the young people and the children. I'm going to miss Terry. That poor child—how's she doing?"

"Pretty good," Evan answered. "She's taking classes to get her high-school diploma, and there are plenty of people to baby-sit Kevin for her so she can study."

Gladys nodded. "I'm glad to hear that. She sure could use a few breaks after all she's been through. And so young!"

Vanessa leaned forward. "You can always come back to visit. I'll tell you what. When you and Harry get settled, maybe Terry and the baby can come to see you."

Gladys nodded, patting her husband's hand. "Oh, yes. We'd both enjoy that."

Harry looked pensively at Vanessa. "Gladys and I sure do wish we could have had children—we'd have wanted a daughter just like you."

"Or a son like Evan," Gladys added softly.

"Your families must be very proud of you both. And if they don't watch out, we're going to start adoption proceedings. Any more like you two at home?" Harry asked.

"One older brother, married with kids," Evan responded with a grin.

Vanessa's smile was regretful. She shook her head. "One older brother, deceased."

Gladys Jackson drew in a soft breath. "Oh, my..."

Harry remained momentarily silent and thoughtful, and Evan's expression was knowing. He'd heard the story of Richard, Mrs. Moran's pride and joy.

"Well, thank goodness your folks still have you," Gladys said to Vanessa.

Vanessa chose not to inform Gladys that her father was also deceased. And it was questionable whether or not her mother was as proud of her as she'd been of Richard. Richard had never disappointed Katherine Moran.

"As soon as we get settled in our new apartment, we hope you'll both come for dinner. Gladys here makes a great ham with honey glaze."

"Thank you," Evan answered for both of them. "We'd love to."

"You two make a very good team," Gladys observed. "You work so well together."

"I agree," Evan said smoothly.

Harry squinted at him. "Is there something going on between you two?"

"Harry!" Gladys said, shocked. She poked Harry sharply in the arm. "What kind of question is that? Why, it's none of your business!"

"I'm an old man, but my eyesight is still good enough to see the truth," Harry defended himself, causing Evan to laugh in amusement. "Are you a couple, or what?"

Vanessa opened her mouth to speak, but nothing came out. She felt trapped. She felt terribly vulnerable, but she wasn't inclined to lie. What would have been the point? For some reason, Vanessa thought that the way she and Evan felt about each other was still largely a secret. She thought it was private and that somehow she could protect it from the world, from the opposition that was sure to come. Harry was proving her wrong; people *did* know.

"Well? Are we?" Evan asked her softly.

Vanessa couldn't ignore him. She couldn't pretend that this was a new idea or that Harry Jackson was being sentimental. Vanessa nodded slightly, her eyes large and round as she gazed at Evan. Doubt might sometimes cloud her eyes, but her heart knew better.

"Yes," she confirmed. "Yes, we are."

EVAN HAD BEEN SILENT and thoughtful for the entire drive to his apartment. There had been no time for just the two of them before the three-day trial, and now Vanessa realized that what she and Evan both needed was time to be alone with each other. When they were, things always became easier. There were few barriers left between them. Still, as they entered Evan's place, Vanessa thought carefully about what she should say, or even if she should say anything at all. The excitement and tension of the day had drained away, replaced by a certain disappointment she sensed in Evan.

He hung up their coats and, distracted, crossed to the living room window to gaze out over the nighttime city. Vanessa followed quietly. She looked at Evan's profile, at the pursing of his full mouth and the furrowing of his forehead. She reached out and took his hand. He threaded his fingers with hers, glanced briefly at her and made the little kissing sound Vanessa always found funny, but reassuring.

"I'm sorry, Evan."

"What for?" He frowned.

"You invited your parents to be in court to see you today, didn't you? And they didn't come."

He shrugged. "It wasn't that important. They've seen me try cases before."

"Maybe something came up at the last minute and they couldn't make it."

Evan was silent for a moment. "You took the day off from work. You had a graduate class this evening. You came."

"Well . . . it's a long trip for them to make. Almost two hours." Vanessa hugged his arm and rested her chin against it. "Anyway, they knew you were going to win. They had complete confidence in—"

"Van," Evan said patiently. "You don't have to make excuses for them."

Nonetheless Vanessa felt the old uneasiness slip over her. The tension rose in her body until she thought she needed to scream to release it. She again examined Evan's strong profile, expecting to see anger and bitterness. But there was only the disappointment.

"Maybe you should have listened to me," she said softly, her own sense of guilt and anxiety, her own confusion, making her feel defensive.

"What about?"

"About us. Don't you think our relationship is affecting your parents?"

"No," Evan said shortly.

"What do you mean, no?"

"I mean they haven't even met you."

"What have you told them about me?"

"That I'd fallen in love with Vanessa Moran. That was the most important thing they needed to know."

Vanessa saw no reason to doubt him. "To you I'm the woman you love. To your parents I'm something else."

"I don't understand what."

"But it bothers you. You know it does," she said urgently.

Evan tilted his head to look down at her. "I think it bothers you more. I can handle my parents. I don't need their approval."

"Evan, your parents are only thinking about what's best for you."

"I know, but that doesn't mean they're right."

"I don't think this is about who's right. It's about family and tradition and what parents expect of their children. You and I are more different than your parents can deal with. I don't think they imagined you would fall in love with someone like me."

"Someone like you?" Evan repeated. "Van, we're not types—we're people. I haven't tried to hide anything from my parents. I've told them all about you. I've shown them your picture."

"And what did they say?" Vanessa asked in a quiet voice.

"My father said you're very attractive."

Vanessa leaned her head against his arm. "You can't divorce your family, you know."

Evan put an arm around her and drew her to his side. "Well, maybe we should redefine family. The Jacksons are ready to take us in, no questions asked. What do you think?"

She only smiled vaguely. Evan might make light of his parents' silence, but it made her nervous. She recalled the conversation with Carol and the ones she'd tried to have with her mother. Family *was* important, and she didn't want Evan to forget that. Family was about togetherness and belonging and strength and love, and Vanessa ached that she had lost most of that when Richard and her father had died and her mother had continued to grieve, taking the child left behind for granted.

It had been some time since she and Evan had come together, perhaps out of curiosity at first, but then purely out of love. Was their relationship really about just the two of them? Could they survive even if Evan's parents and her mother didn't give their blessing?

"Thanksgiving's coming up in a few weeks," Vanessa murmured. "I've always loved Thanksgiving. I remember the songs we used to sing at school assembly. 'We gather together to ask the Lord's blessings...the wicked oppressing, ccases from distressing...'"

"'Thy name be ever praised, oh Lord make us free." Evan grinned. "Yeah, we sang that one, too. I remember I had to dress up as a pilgrim and wear white stockings for the school play."

"I got to play a native American," Vanessa said wryly.

"Better than being the turkey."

Vanessa laughed. "Know what I always liked best about Thanksgiving?" Evan asked.

"Yeah. All that food."

"Okay, that, too. But I liked everyone sitting around the dining table, laughing and eating and being happy. I liked the turkey drumstick."

"I liked slices of breast meat with lots of gravy."

"Messy. I could get away with eating the drumstick with my hands. And I loved stuffing."

"Yeah. And we had buttered squash and macaroni with three kinds of cheese."

"After dinner, my dad would take Jason and me and a bunch of cousins out for a game of touch foot-

ball. There would be hot apple cider and dessert when
we got home. Blueberry pie.''

''My mother made sweet-potato pie.''

Evan sighed. ''Thanksgiving always made me
feel—''

''Safe and warm,'' she supplied. She nodded. ''Me,
too.''

Evan turned to put both arms around Vanessa,
sighing as he smiled down at her. Her eyes were so
dark they appeared almost black. And she had a way
of smiling, lifting one corner of her mouth, that suggested irony. Evan slid a hand along her jaw, his fingers caressing the side of her neck. ''The funny thing
is my parents would really like you. You're independent and smart and professional—''

''Evan, I really don't think—''

''—and patient and pretty and clever.''

''That depends.'' Vanessa shook her head.

''My father would love that you're a baseball fan
and that you make great French toast.'' Evan closed
his eyes briefly. ''But the fact is, it only comes down
to how *I* feel.''

Vanessa sighed. That was Evan the man talking, not
the well-brought-up son. Evan's family, and to the
same extent her own mother, had not exactly drawn
battle lines, but there was an unmarked boundary, and
neither family expected to cross it. Vanessa actually
felt more sadness than anything, as well as a sense of
bewilderment. All she wanted was to be able to love
Evan Holden. Was that so wrong?

''What about Thanksgiving?''

Evan's expression was cryptic, his answer indirect. "Don't worry. We'll have a Thanksgiving."

Vanessa stared at Evan, always amazed at his strength. "You're so sure of yourself," she murmured.

He brushed a hand over her hair. The short curls and waves were soft and springy to the touch. Evan flicked the small gold loop earring she wore. Sometimes he felt totally unable to explain to Vanessa just how important she'd become in his life. It had just happened. It just *was*. The feelings they shared were of care and comfort and trust. Evan was sure those feelings had always been there, right from the time they'd first met. He realized he'd never thought even for a moment that loving Vanessa Moran was a mistake.

"I get a little confused by a lot of things, by a lot of people, Vanessa. You just don't happen to be one of them. I'm in love with you. Period."

The reassurance warmed her, and she smiled. "I believe you."

"Then that's all that matters. Right?"

Vanessa conceded with a chuckle. "Right." She pulled away from Evan and gasped. "I almost forgot! I have a present for you."

"I hope this isn't an attempt to make up for my parents' absence," Evan said a bit caustically as she walked to her leather bag left by the closet. He settled on the living room sofa, kicking off his shoes, pulling off his tie. His eyes were half-closed as he watched Vanessa, his body already sinking into comfortable lethargy in the cushions. Vanessa returned and curled herself next to him. She held out a couple of brightly wrapped gifts.

"You didn't have to do this," Evan murmured.

"You're supposed to be gracious and say thank you. The party was fun and you'll go on record for having done a brilliant job today, but this is just between the two of us."

He gave her a quick kiss before opening the first package. It was a sleek Mont Blanc pen, just perfect for Evan, who favored fountain pens and had sprawling handwriting. He whistled as he examined it. He knew it was expensive.

"I always promised myself one of these," he said.

"I know computers are quicker, but this is more personal. You can sign all your contracts with it."

"And a love letter or two," Evan said softly, kissing her again. He slipped the pen into his shirt pocket.

The second gift was two video films—*Twelve Angry Men* and *To Kill a Mockingbird*.

"These are great," Evan said enthusiastically. He held up *Twelve Angry Men*. "This is a classic, but I don't think I've ever seen *To Kill a Mockingbird*."

"Well, that's a classic, too. I think all lawyers should see both of these films at least once a year so they don't forget the true meaning of what they do."

Evan examined the films once more, an ironic grin on his face. "My father always loved *Twelve Angry Men*."

Vanessa drew up her feet and grinned. "My dad always liked *To Kill a Mockingbird*."

They looked at each other. "They'd have had a lot in common, wouldn't they?" he said quietly.

Vanessa nodded. "Maybe more than they'd be willing to admit."

Evan took her hand. "Then there's no problem. We both come from good stock. Thanks for the pen and the films." He reached out to curve his hand around the back of Vanessa's neck, pulling her closer. Her dark eyes sparkled brightly in anticipation. Evan kissed her, sighing as their lips met, smelling the sweetness of her skin that was scented with nothing more than baby powder. Her mouth was soft and full, and Evan enjoyed the slow sensuous buildup, the promise of passion.

"There is one more thing," Vanessa whispered, pulling away.

"Not another present!" he said.

"No... I won't be able to see you Saturday."

Evan frowned. "Why not? I thought we were going to try and find that winery on the other side of the river."

"I know, but I promised the pastor some time at the shelter. I also need to study, and restock my kitchen." As Evan started to speak, Vanessa touched her fingertips to his mouth to silence him. "And as for you, you're going to take the weekend to go visit your parents."

Evan pulled her hand away from his mouth. "You don't need to play peacemaker between me and my folks."

"Evan, believe me, my reasons are selfish ones. I don't want your parents to think I'm keeping you from them."

"My *parents* are the ones keeping me from them. Yes, I probably should go see them, but for other reasons," he said clearly.

"For whatever reasons, then."

Evan toyed with one of her curls. "I have another idea." He saw the light in her eyes, the slow secret smile that curved her mouth. "Why don't we microwave some popcorn, get into bed, turn out all the lights and watch a video. Preferably something romantic." He pulled Vanessa onto his lap, and she giggled as she looped her arms around his neck.

"Anything else, Counselor?" she asked suggestively.

He grinned. "Someone told me I was brilliant today. So, yes, I'm pretty sure I can think of something else."

Chapter Two

WHEN EVAN LEFT his bedroom in the house he'd been raised in, the smell of cinnamon and cloves filled the hallway and stairwell. As he made his way downstairs carrying his weekend leather duffel and dressed in jeans and blue chambray shirt, he felt thrown back into childhood, back to the thousands of times he'd raced, jumped or rolled down these same stairs, drawn by his mother's wonderful cooking. At the time he'd simply accepted that he lived in a happy home, had everything he needed and most things he wanted. Now that poignant memory was mixed with the sense of how much he'd taken for granted.

Evan left the duffel by the main door, since his car was parked out front on the road. When he entered the kitchen he found his mother surrounded by bowls of peeled fruit, flour, sugar and other ingredients for baking. The air was warm and fragrant, and he inhaled deeply.

"Mmm-mmm. Love that smell." He peered into the oven and was met with a blast of hot air aromatic with the spices of two baking apple pies. "I don't suppose I can talk you into letting me take one home with me," Evan said to his mother, who was seated on a stool at the counter assembling yet another pie.

"No, you cannot," Marsha Holden said calmly. But she tempered the response with a warm smile at her youngest son.

"It's a great smell. I wish I could bottle it."

"It's called the smell of home. It would be a lot easier if you'd just stay for dinner. Then you can enjoy the smell *and* sample the pie."

Evan went to the refrigerator and got out a bottle of beer. He leaned back against the counter next to his mother and watched the familiar routine of all the early preparations that went into Thanksgiving. "I can't," Evan said.

Marsha Holden didn't answer right away, nor did she stop what she was doing. Over the top of her half-glasses her hazel eyes, so like Evan's, examined him. She shifted her gaze back to meticulously lattice-working the crust on top of a blueberry pie. "I guess that means you have a date tonight."

Evan looked at his mother. Her once blond hair was now mostly gray, and she wore it in a short naturally curling bob. Retired from an administrative position at a local college, she now favored jeans, sneakers and sweatshirts. She cultivated a garden all spring and summer, and quilted her way through the fall and winter. Evan had always thought of his mother as funny, understanding, firm but caring. He also knew his mother well enough to recognize that her reference to his "date" was a thinly veiled attempt to grant Vanessa Moran only temporary status in his life. "Yes, I have a date," he finally answered, taking a deep gulp of the beer.

"Too bad. You're going to miss Jason and Eleanor and the kids. And a *very* good pot roast," Mrs. Holden teased in a quick harnessing of her disapproval.

Evan finished the beer and put the empty bottle in the proper recycling bin. "I have to be back tomorrow morning, anyway." He peered into a pot simmering on the stove and found boiling potatoes. "Vanessa and I are helping a couple we know move into their new apartment."

"Is it someone in your office or someone you went to law school with?"

Evan arched a brow and took up his position next to the counter again. He folded his arms over his chest. "Not exactly. This is the couple I defended recently in a lawsuit. I told you and Dad about it. Harry and Gladys Jackson."

Marsha Holden glanced briefly away from her son, but not before he noticed the flush on her cheeks and neck. "Oh, yes. Well, that's very nice of you, but how can these people be more important than your family?"

"They're not," Evan said, picking a slice of apple from a bowl and popping it into his mouth. "But they're in need of my help."

Marsha Holden looked puzzled. "I thought that case was over. Aren't you finished representing them?"

Evan met her gaze and slowly smiled. "Yes. But I'm also their friend." His mother sighed. Evan wasn't angry at his mother's apparent lapse of memory, but he was surprised and disillusioned. "I wanted you and Dad to meet them. They're wonderful people."

"I'm sure they are. Especially if you represented them." She smiled kindly and pushing the assembled pie aside, began vigorously slicing carrots.

Evan reached out and touched her arm. The slicing stopped and she glanced up into his serious expression. "Mom, I wanted you to meet Vanessa, too."

Marsha Holden's eyes looked helpless and confused, and Evan waited for her to say something, anything, to explain her and his father's absence that evening more than a week ago. It had remained unspoken when he'd visited, at Vanessa's insistence, the weekend after the trial. There had been another celebration because he'd won, and no time to really talk to his parents about the Jacksons. Or Vanessa. But Evan quickly realized that his parents had deftly avoided the issue this weekend, as well.

"I'm sorry," Mrs. Holden finally whispered. Evan did not doubt that his mother was sincere. But "sorry" didn't help, and it didn't explain the reluctance to meet Vanessa.

Evan slowly took the paring knife from his mother and put it on the counter. Then he held her hand as he gazed into her eyes so that he wouldn't miss her reaction. "I love her, Mom. I love Vanessa. You and Dad can't continue to ignore that."

"But why *her,* Evan? Why not someone like... like..." She gnawed her lip.

"Like?" he prompted.

She squeezed his hand and her eyes pleaded with him. "Evan," she said, her voice quavering, "you know what I mean."

Evan smiled sadly, shaking his head. "I guess you've forgotten how you always told me and Jason that *what* a person is wasn't nearly as important as *who* that person is."

She took a deep breath and pulled her hand free. Retrieving the knife, she got up and moved to the stove. With renewed purpose she dumped the sliced carrots into the pot with the potatoes and began to work on an onion. "I haven't forgotten for a minute, and it's still true. But you're my son and I have the right to be concerned about you. I . . . your Dad and me, we just don't want to see you make a terrible mistake." She abandoned the onion and turned to her son. "I hope you realize that I don't *dislike* this...this young woman."

"Vanessa," Evan quietly supplied.

"I just don't think she's right for you."

"How do you know that? You haven't even met her."

"Have you thought about how it would look to other people?"

Evan frowned. "Is that relevant? Isn't your life *your* business? Isn't my life *my* business?"

"It isn't that simple."

"Sure, it is," he said a bit too impatiently.

"No." She shook her head and her eyes shimmered with tears.

Evan saw that she was becoming upset. "Mom..." he began, cursing himself for his heavy-handed approach.

A car could be heard turning into the driveway at the back of the house. Tires crackled and crunched over the pebbled surface.

"That must be your father," Mrs. Holden said, clearing her throat and wiping her eyes.

Evan put his hands on his mother's shoulders and kissed her forehead. "I'm sorry, Mom. I didn't mean to upset you. I just wish that... Never mind. I'll go give Dad a hand." She nodded silently.

Evan opened the kitchen door that opened into the garage. The gate was up and his father's Jeep Cherokee was parked in the opening. Stuart Holden was already unloading bags from the back seat. The early afternoon was overcast and cold, and Evan wondered if snow had been predicted for the evening. He hoped not. He wanted to be on the road before it started to fall and the temperature dropped, but he couldn't leave before coming to some understanding with his parents about Vanessa. He'd allowed the avoidance to go on too long in the hopes that his parents would come around; but it had already been the greater part of a year. He needed the reassurance that they were willing to give Vanessa a fair chance. He stuffed his hands into the front pockets of his jeans and ambled over toward his father.

Stuart Holden lifted out a twenty-five-pound bag of Ice-Melt which he placed on the ground, then took out a bright orange outdoor extension cord, a sixty-gallon garbage can and a twenty-pound turkey. He playfully heaved the heavy bird in his son's direction, and Evan was agile in catching it even as he stumbled backward with the weight.

"Mom's expecting half the state to Thanksgiving dinner, I see."

Mr. Holden shook his head wryly. "Your mother loves nothing better than feeding and taking care of people. She's on her annual preholiday cooking marathon. That's how she landed me. I overdosed on her lemon tarts." Evan laughed as he hoisted the plastic-wrapped turkey onto his shoulder, the cold seeping through his shirt.

When his father had put away the other purchases in the garage, he said, "Did you change your mind about staying until Sunday?"

"No. I was just telling Mom that Vanessa and I are helping the Jacksons move tomorrow afternoon."

Mr. Holden pursed his lips and frowned. "The Jacksons? Oh, yeah. The bias case—*Jackson v. Lowell and Cranbrook Realty.*" He glanced up at his son, who was nearly three inches taller, and continued to frown. "I'm sorry your mother and I didn't make it to court. Something came up."

Evan laughed shortly. "Vanessa defended your absence with the same comment. Was it true or just an excuse?"

Stuart shook his head. "I can tell you've already talked to your mother about that."

"I'm not sure it helped much. Mom hasn't changed her mind about Vanessa, and neither have I."

His father sighed. He looked furtively toward the house and, assured he and his son wouldn't be overheard, took a step closer to Evan and spoke in a low voice. "Look, I want you to know I understand what you're going through."

"Do you? Then how come you and Mom won't meet Vanessa?"

"Your mother is much more emotional than I am..." Mr. Holden hedged.

Evan smiled. "That's sexist."

Mr. Holden ignored the remark. "She feels very strongly that a relationship—an intimate relationship across races—is...wrong."

"Wrong? Do you know why she feels that way? Do you agree?" Evan asked, discouraged.

"I believe it's...difficult." Mr. Holden said thoughtfully. "A wrong decision in your personal life right now can affect your professional life now *and* later."

"My personal life is just that, personal."

His father grimaced. "Don't be foolish. Of course it's not. How would you feel if you lost an important job opportunity because you were involved with the wrong sort of person?"

Evan felt his jaw muscles tense. "Vanessa happens to be a person who happens to be black. What's 'wrong' about that?"

"No, no..." Stuart Holden shook his head and struggled to justify his comment. He couldn't. He looked long and hard at his son. "Evan, one of the ironies of being a lawyer is that you have to understand both sides of the argument. I know what your mother's position is, and it's to see you not get hurt or your future destroyed. I know all about your position. *I've* listened, remember? You think you love her—"

"I know I do."

"But things change. Quickly."

"And what about Vanessa's position?"

"What?" Mr. Holden asked blankly.

"What about how *she* feels? Doesn't she count?"

"How she feels is not the issue," Stuart snapped, jabbing a finger at Evan's chest.

"Sorry, Dad. It is exactly the issue," Evan said. He balanced the turkey on his shoulder and turned back to the house.

"Evan! Evan, for God's sake. How much do you really know about her?"

Evan stopped and turned to his father. His breath came sharply, painfully, in the cold air. "Vanessa. Her name is Vanessa Moran. I know all I need to know. She makes me happy and I love her. You know what's pathetically funny about this? Vanessa's mother doesn't approve of me, either. She doesn't think I'm good enough."

Stuart Holden's face stiffened with indignation. "That's ridiculous!"

"Her mother's probably right." Once again Evan started to walk away, trying to contain his rising anger.

"Evan, wait. Please!"

Evan responded to the urgency in his father's tone. He turned around and saw him standing against the desolate winter backdrop of naked trees. Mr. Holden looked bewildered just then and hesitant. Evan frowned in concern. "Dad?"

"I love your mother very much. I consider myself extremely fortunate to have met and married her." He stood waiting for a reaction from Evan, who slowly retraced his steps until he stood directly in front of his father. "She was beautiful and smart. She was talented, and she thought I was the handsomest, most clever man in the world. Somewhere around our third date, at a movie I think it was, I knew I was going to marry her. I've never once regretted it."

Evan stared at his father silently, surprised by this speech and wondering where it was going. There was memory and pain in his father's eyes.

"Just after the Korean war, before I ever met your mother, there was another woman. Her name was Kimiko. She was Japanese-American, the daughter of a surgeon. She was a research assistant at my law-school library and..." Stuart stopped and took a deep breath.

"Did you love her?" None of Evan's astonishment showed in his voice.

"I...I thought I did. I...yes, I think I did." He looked at Evan. "But she was afraid of her family's finding out about me. With good reason, as it turned out. When her father did find out we'd met several times for lunch or just to talk, he threatened to have me expelled from law school. He threatened to send Kimiko to relatives on the West Coast."

"So you stopped seeing her," Evan said flatly. "And your parents? What did they think?" He watched his father flush, in much the same way as his mother had in the kitchen.

"My sister knew. But it happened so quickly—was over so quickly. It was probably nothing more than infatuation. She was very sweet, very exotic."

"On the other hand, maybe it wasn't just infatuation. Haven't there been times when you've wondered?"

Stuart lost the thoughtful distance in his gaze. He stared at Evan. "I love your mother."

Evan sighed. "I know, Dad. I've never doubted it and I guess Mom hasn't, either. That only leaves Kimiko to wonder. But you have to understand, I'm not in any doubt about how I feel about Vanessa."

Evan turned then and walked into the house, leaving his father to follow. He ignored his mother's questioning look as he entered the kitchen and continued on to the door leading to the basement. He went downstairs to put the turkey into the freezer, but didn't return upstairs right away. Instead, giving himself time to swallow the bitter taste of defeat, he wandered around the playroom where he and Jason had hung out as kids. Now it was used mostly as a woodworking shop by his father.

Evan lifted the lid from the box housing Jason's Lionel train set and the table hockey game. He absently twirled one of the game levers, remembering the noisy and rambunctious Saturday afternoons when as many as eight boys had crammed the lower level of the house with imaginative play and high spirits. The group had included Dennis Kwok, a Korean, and Miguel Piñeo, who was half Filipino. When Jason was a sophomore in college he'd gone off to summer school in Mexico and had sent back photos of himself with a beautiful girl named Elena Maria, whom he'd dated for a while. The next year the family had been host to an exchange student from Ghana.

What had all that been about? Had so much openness and generosity of spirit been a fraud? Was all the talk about equality and fairness nothing more than talk? When had his parents stopped practicing what they'd always preached? When did they start to qualify their humanity?

"Evan?"

He vaguely heard his name being called from the kitchen above, but his mother had to call twice before Evan emerged from his reverie.

"Evan, Jason and Eleanor are here with the kids."

"I'm coming," Evan responded, but still made no move to leave the basement.

He thought suddenly of all the times Vanessa had tried to tell him that a relationship between the two of them was different than that of a couple of the same race. They would be watched. They would be questioned. They would be challenged and forced to be stronger and more committed than anyone else was asked to be. They would be measured by a different standard. It meant they had to be absolutely sure their love was strong enough to survive all the difficulties. It now came to Evan that Vanessa knew exactly what she was talking about. She'd had twenty-eight years to adjust to a world, an environment, a society that expected less from her—but that would ultimately always demand more. If Vanessa faulted either way, she couldn't win.

She had taken a risk by loving him, trusting him.
Evan bounded up the basement stairs, two at a time.
He was not going to let Vanessa or himself down.

When he reached the kitchen there was a crowd of
people and a cacophony of voices. Four adults were
exchanging affectionate greetings while two young
children—Christy, almost three, and Michael, seven—
created enough chaos for a legion.

"Glad we caught you." Jason grinned through his
ginger beard, shaking his brother's hand.

"Why? Do you have a rich new client to recommend, or are you going to share the winnings from
your lottery ticket?"

"Don't hold your breath." Eleanor chuckled as she
stood on tiptoe to kiss her brother-in-law's cheek.

Evan's mother was helping Christy out of her
snowsuit, which was an interesting exercise since the
curly-haired toddler refused to give up a bottle filled
with apple juice. As Evan squatted next to his niece to
get a sticky wet kiss, thirty-five pounds of pure energy climbed onto his back.

"Michael, behave," Jason ordered his son, but was
ignored as Evan stood up with Michael hanging from
his neck.

What Michael was doing obviously looked like more
fun than being coddled by Grandma, so Christy put
down the bottle and reached chubby arms up to her
uncle.

"Me, too! Me, too!"

Stuart Holden shook his head indulgently. "There
was more peace when they were too small to get
around."

Evan helped Michael somersault clear over his head, then put him gently down onto the floor. "Who's next?" he asked.

Eleanor shook her head wryly as her daughter was lifted, squealing in joy as she was tossed into the air, safely caught, and then dangled upside down from her knees. Marsha Holden gasped.

"Evan, for goodness' sake, be careful with that child!"

"She loves it." Evan laughed, but already he was setting Christy down and trying to pull himself to rights.

"Where's Vanessa?" Michael asked. The innocent question immediately silenced the room.

Jason and his wife glanced at one another, but it was Evan's mother and father who were clearly taken aback.

"Where's Vanessa?" Michael asked again, yanking on his uncle's sweater.

Marsha Holden stared round-eyed at her oldest grandchild. "How...how does Michael know about her?"

Jason took a deep breath and ruffled his son's blond hair. "Michael and Christy know Vanessa quite well."

"They've met her? When?" Stuart asked.

"When Vanessa comes with Evan to visit, of course," Eleanor responded smoothly.

Evan gave her a warm smile. He looked down at Michael. "Vanessa couldn't make it today, sport."

"How come?" Michael asked.

The four other adults exchanged awkward looks; Evan simply stood there and waited for someone else to come up with a good reason.

"Because she needed a rest from you," Eleanor teased, lifting the fretting Christy into her arms. She looked at her in-laws. "The children like Vanessa."

"'Nessa." Christy bobbed her head.

"Yeah, she knows this neat story about pickles and peppers, right, Uncle Evan?"

Evan smiled. "Right."

"Well, is she coming to Thanksgiving with us?"

Now the silence was like a great bottomless pit that threatened to pull them all in. Everyone stared at Michael's expectant young face. Evan crossed his arms and winked at the boy.

"We'll see," was his quiet response.

"WELL? WHAT DO YOU THINK?" Katherine Moran asked. She was slowly pivoting and turning before a full-length mirror as she modeled a black knit jumpsuit. It had long dolman sleeves, and the neckline was rounded and plain. It was a flattering outfit, one that took at least ten pounds off her still-shapely figure.

Vanessa smiled. It wasn't as if her mother really needed the reassurance. She had excellent taste, a good sense of style. "It's very becoming," Vanessa nonetheless answered.

Her smile continued with a certain pride and bemusement. Vanessa knew her mother was basically unconscious of her attractiveness. She wore simply tailored clothing and always managed to project the image of a woman who was independent and in charge. She still worked as Manager of Library Services for a local hospital.

"You don't think it looks too young, do you?"

"Mother, it looks fine."

"I just don't want to look foolish," Katherine Moran sighed in resignation, clearly having made up her mind to purchase the jumpsuit. She began to remove the outfit and to change into her street clothes—a pair of olive twill slacks and a thick off-white sweater that offset the smooth flawlessness of her toffee-colored skin. Except for her short salt-and-pepper hair, she could easily have been mistaken for Vanessa's older sister. She combed her hair, gazing at her daughter's reflection in the mirror as she did so.

"How's school?"

"Just one more semester. I'll be finished by next May."

"I know it's been difficult working and going to school for your master's, but I'm glad you stuck with it. Are you still volunteering at that church shelter?"

"Yes, that too."

Her mother sighed. "All those people. It's so sad."

"They don't think they're sad. Some of the residents have lots of problems, true, but they're trying to get on with their lives."

"And are you still seeing that . . . man?"

"Yes, I'm still seeing Evan Holden."

"Is that why you sent me that newspaper article? To remind me?"

"No. I sent you that clipping because I wanted you to read about the great job Evan did with the Jacksons' court case. And I wanted you to see who he was, since you've been avoiding every chance to meet him.''

''I don't see the point of meeting him.''

''Are you hoping he'll just go away?''

''I disapprove.''

''Because Evan is white? I've already used that argument on myself, and I already know all the reasons you're going to give me. It took me months to realize that none of them were going to hold up. Evan showed me they wouldn't.''

''Is he worth the heartache?''

Vanessa smiled. ''There hasn't been any.''

Katherine Moran looked doubtful. ''You mean, not yet.''

''Evan is one man. He's not *every* white man. He's himself. You and Daddy always told me to judge people individually, on their own merits.''

Mrs. Moran scoffed. ''*Please* don't throw that back at me. You haven't lived long enough to know how cruel and blind people can be.''

''I've lived long enough to know that not all people are the same. Evan loves me,'' Vanessa said firmly, but her stomach roiled with the tension of knowing she fought a lonely battle. Worse was the thought that she was opposing her own mother. She stood up suddenly and began gathering their packages. ''I don't want to fight with you about Evan, Mother.''

''I'm glad to hear that,'' she said dryly. ''I didn't raise you to be disrespectful.''

The comment was so outrageous Vanessa laughed. It was a deliberate attempt by her mother to say,

"Don't mind me if I still treat you like a child. I have the right."

"You haven't bought a thing," the older woman observed, looking at all the bags. "This shopping trip was your idea."

"I know, but it was more just to spend some time together. And I did buy something. A catnip toy for Ming, and some candy for Evan. He has a sweet tooth."

Mrs. Moran looked sharply at her daughter. "Is he as thoughtful to you?"

Vanessa smiled privately to herself. Evan was more than just thoughtful. He was romantic. Should she tell her mother that it was not unlike Evan to call her in the middle of the afternoon and when she answered the phone say simply, "I love you"? Should she mention that both she and Evan left silly little gifts for each other, to be found and laughed over together? Vanessa wasn't sure it would make a difference to her mother.

Mrs. Moran sighed as she put on her coat and they headed to the cashier to pay for the jumpsuit. "Your daddy was thoughtful. He used to do the most unexpected things," she reminisced. "And not a week went by that he didn't bring me flowers or a small houseplant."

"Evan and I have rituals, too. We rent videos on Wednesday nights and cook dinner together." Vanessa paused. "I'm sorry, Mother, but nothing you say is going to make me feel less for Evan."

"Oh, Vanessa." Katherine Moran sighed impatiently. "Love is overrated! What's really important is

familiarity and common background and traditions.
Family. All I can say is your daddy would have a fit if
he was alive. Lord, I can hear him now. 'Is that girl
out of her mind? Did I raise her to be a fool?' "

Vanessa let the hurtful words creep over her. Her
mother made it sound as though she'd given no
thought to the consequences of loving Evan Holden,
as though she'd turned a deaf ear to warnings and had
blanked out all of history. Love was *not* overrated. It
was more powerful, more compelling, than Vanessa
had ever found hate or bitterness to be. And if people
couldn't believe in the power of love, then how would
things ever change?

"Daddy's been dead for almost ten years. Maybe he
wouldn't feel like you do. Daddy always tried to be
fair."

"But the world *isn't* fair. What I think, Vanessa, is
that the world hasn't changed so much from when I
was a girl that you should get involved with someone
of another race. You're going to get hurt. There are
plenty of good black men out there like your father.
Like your brother."

"I'd hoped you would meet Evan and judge him for
himself."

"I've been busy," Mrs. Moran prevaricated.

"Doing what?"

"I've been asked to set up a literacy program at the
local library. And you've been after me forever to send
you Nana's trunk with all her old linen. You used to
love those damask table cloths and the big napkins she
used for family gatherings. Well, they all have to be
washed and ironed. These things take time."

They left the store and found themselves standing in a cold drizzle. For dinner Vanessa and her mother decided on a trendy café that served pasta dishes. As they took a booth and arranged themselves and their bounty, Vanessa tried to remember the last time her mother had actually cooked dinner at home and they'd eaten together as a family. Last Thanksgiving her mother had gone on a cruise with a couple of colleagues; Vanessa had gone to a friend's place. Her mother had summarily decided ten years ago, when her husband had died, that there was no reason to continue the tradition of Thanksgiving for just the two of them. But that wasn't how Vanessa wanted it.

As if reading her daughter's mind or sensing her longing, Katherine peered at her over the top of her menu.

"I got a call from your uncle Walter. He and Lee invited me to spend Thanksgiving with them."

Vanessa fixed her mother with a stare. "Why don't we have our own Thanksgiving this year?"

"What do you mean, our own Thanksgiving?"

"I mean, we stay here, instead of you flying all over the country to relatives, like you've been doing, and we make dinner. We haven't done that in a long time."

"That was a million years ago. There won't ever be Thanksgivings like those again."

"Why not? We can use Nana's beautiful table-cloths like we did when I was little and Uncle Walter and Aunt Lee only lived an hour away, and Nana would do the cooking, and all the cousins—"

Mrs. Moran laughed softly. "Oh, yes. Your father would carry on and make such a production out of carving the turkey. And Aunt Lee would set the table and tell everyone where they were sitting. You kids would be making all kinds of noise.''

Vanessa chuckled, hoping she'd captured her mother's imagination, her memories of the joyous times of the past. ''I liked when we closed our eyes and held hands around the table and Daddy said grace.'' She paused. ''We can do that. The three of us.''

''Three?''

Vanessa stared at her mother. ''I thought I'd invite Evan.''

''No.''

''This is important to me—''

''I can't, Vanessa. I just can't. What kind of Thanksgiving are you talking about? What would it be without your father and Richard? Without Nana?''

''Have you forgotten that I'm still here? You and I are still a family.''

Vanessa detected a sudden flash of pain in her mother's eyes, and she blinked in surprise. Only then did she wonder if perhaps her mother was afraid of losing her, too. Not to death, but to another force she couldn't control—love.

''Did he invite you to his family's?'' Mrs. Moran asked. Her tone of voice held a kind of knowing smugness. ''Or did he come up with some excuse?''

The question caused the muscles in Vanessa's stomach to tighten suddenly, because the question of how they might spend this Thanksgiving hadn't been discussed. It was hard to say if they were avoiding it, or if they hoped that by not making it an issue, it would somehow work itself out.

"No. I haven't been invited yet," Vanessa answered truthfully. She bent over her menu but knew her mother was looking closely at her with maternal concern and exasperation.

"You've been seeing him most of the year. If you haven't met his family, Vanessa, then there is no serious relationship between you."

"Have you forgotten that Evan hasn't met you either?"

"That's different."

"How?"

"You have more to lose. I hope you're not indulging in fantasies that you'll live happily ever after with him."

Vanessa felt the stab precariously close to her heart. "Don't you think that someone could love me enough to ask?"

Her mother quickly reached out a hand to pat her cheek. "Oh, honey, yes. I do. I want to see you married. *I* want to have grandkids. But why stack the odds so heavily against it happening?"

"Because I know I love Evan. And if there isn't a future for us, then I want to love him for as long as I can."

Katherine Moran slowly shook her head, and her eyes filled with sadness and helplessness. "Then what else can I say?"

"That I can invite Evan to have Thanksgiving with us."

Her mother chuckled. "You are so stubborn. Daddy always said you never did things the easy way.

You always wanted to do what you wanted to do when you wanted to do it.''

"I'm only talking about Thanksgiving," Vanessa coaxed. "Will you think about it?"

"All right, all right. I'll think about it."

Vanessa couldn't speak for a moment. It had never occurred to her that she'd have to barter with her mother over the simple desire to be loved. "Thank you," she finally whispered, suddenly realizing just how much she had to lose.

Chapter Three

ALREADY THE CITY seemed infused with the spirit of
the season. Thanksgiving was just two weeks away, but
Christmas was more prominently anticipated in the
sounds, colors and window displays of the shops and
stores. The weather was cold, but clear and very
sunny. The streets were filled with people who were
thickly dressed for warmth, and the atmosphere was
almost cheerful.

Vanessa, however, apparently didn't quite feel part
of it. "You know, it doesn't seem like the holidays to
me yet," she said as she and Evan turned away from
gazing at the window of a toy store. A giant red rib-
bon with a bow had been attached to the front door to
make it look like an oversize present.

Evan squeezed Vanessa's gloved hand and smiled at
her. "That's because you haven't started your Christmas shopping, I'll bet."

Vanessa chortled. "I haven't even made up my list.
It's too soon," she said. Besides, there was still
Thanksgiving to deal with. Vanessa threw a parting
glance at the store window. "I'd love to be able to get
some of the things in that store for the kids at the
shelter."

Evan pulled Vanessa closer to him and they side-
stepped a delivery man piling boxes and packages on
a dolly from the back of his truck. "First things first.

I thought you were setting up the food drive for Thanksgiving," Evan said.

"I am, and it's going well. I think there'll be plenty of food."

They waited at the corner for the light to change. Evan looked at Vanessa's face. The sunlight caught the earth tones in her skin, and he was momentarily transfixed by her subtle beauty and by the way her smile completely animated her features. A fringe of curly dark hair sprouted from beneath a bright orange beret, pulled at an attractive angle on her head. The collar of her black wool coat was pulled up around her neck and ears, and a scarf of a softer, lighter orange was tied loosely around her throat. It was on the tip of his tongue to say to her, "What about us? How are we going to spend Thanksgiving?" They hadn't talked about it yet, but Evan was sure that their not talking about it had more to do with their respective families than it did with the two of them. His expression was concerned. "Aren't you taking on too much?"

"No, I don't think so. I mean, I realize I can't solve all the problems of the shelter, but there's a lot I *can* do."

Evan thought for a moment. "Tell you what. I'll set up a collection box in my office for toys and clothing for the kids."

They began to cross the street. Vanessa gave Evan a sidelong glance. His eyes squinted against the sunlight, which heightened the blond in his hair. "You don't have to do that. You've done more than enough for the church. First there was Gladys and Harry

Jackson's case, and now you're trying to help the pastor find a suitable building to convert to a church-owned temporary residence. And there's Terry..."

Evan looked quizzical. "When is it enough?" he asked. "It needs to be done. I don't mind taking a few hours to make sure a handful of kids have a decent Christmas. I think I've contributed to enough Girl Scout cookie drives in my office and school candy sales to be able to call in a few markers. What's the big deal?"

Vanessa could only smile. It was so typical of Evan to want to dive right in to a problem and try to solve it. But it still sometimes surprised Vanessa. She felt that strange sensation come over her again. The one that split and divided over the way their lives connected that made her feel sometimes breathless with joy—and terrified with uncertainty. She had not yet gotten beyond treating their relationship, their love, as something that existed one day at a time. She was still afraid to count on it. Somehow, to do so seemed presumptuous. And risky.

Vanessa took a deep breath. "The big deal is, you're going to be busy enough with your own family."

Evan glanced off for a moment down the street. He was aware that the shelter wasn't the only problem on their minds. And he was again reminded of the unsettled situation between him and his parents. It wasn't about his feelings, but theirs. Yet he didn't believe that his love for them and his love for Vanessa needed to be mutually exclusive. He squeezed her hand and gave her a quiet smile. "Let me worry about my family."

Vanessa nodded, but she felt uncomfortable with Evan's comment. It suggested there might be a conflict in his family; she didn't want to be responsible for that.

They continued together down the street, the lunchtime crowds swarming around them. "I'm sorry we can't have lunch," Evan said. He held up a manila envelope in his free hand. "I want to get this registered for the pastor."

"What is it?"

"An application to bid on the purchase of a building. The need for shelters isn't going away anytime soon, and I think it's a good idea to have a more permanent and better-equipped shelter than the basement of the church. When you go to the church this afternoon, tell the pastor he'll get a hearing date in the mail."

"I will."

"Are you and I going to see each other tonight?" Evan asked casually, but there was a sensual note in his tone that sent a little thrill through Vanessa. He had never been shy about the time he wanted to spend with her.

"I'd planned to work on my project paper. The outline's due before the holiday."

"Work on it at my place."

"Why not at my place?"

"Because your cat is jealous of me."

Vanessa laughed. "Don't tell me you're afraid of a small furry animal. Ming's just being protective."

"She plays dirty. She claws."

"That's because you lock her out of the bedroom."

Evan's gaze was suddenly wicked and suggestive. "Only when I think she'll see something she shouldn't."

Vanessa laughed again. "So... I can't expect to get any work done on my paper either way, is that it?" Their steps slowed and they stood in front of the courthouse, a Greek-revival structure fronted by enormous columns.

"I'll help you with it on the weekend," Evan coaxed. He turned to face Vanessa, releasing her hand and cupping his under the collar of her coat. Her chin was framed and tilted up to him.

Vanessa loved it when they did this. When they teased and flirted and bantered. It was one of the routines that had sprung up easily and naturally between them. It was one of the ways in which their love flourished.

"That's what you said last weekend," she reminded him.

He shrugged, grinning at her. "So I lied. Sue me."

"I'll have to find a good lawyer first."

"I can recommend one."

"How self-serving."

"Absolutely."

They stood gazing at one another, oblivious to the cold, the curious glances, the noise of traffic. For just a moment Evan and Vanessa locked themselves away in a world that was utterly private, utterly peaceful. It was solid and safe. The laughter in their eyes grew warm. Evan tugged playfully on the ends of Vanessa's scarf.

"I know you've been busy with classes and the shelter. I just want to make sure there's time for *us*."

Vanessa nodded and smiled. "I'll see you tonight."

"And tell Terry Williams I've set up a meeting with Family Services to talk about keeping her baby while she tries to finish school."

Vanessa nodded again. "But it'd be a lot better if she had a more stable home, right?"

"Well—" Evan sighed and glanced into the distance "—the laws and the courts are still entrenched in a definition of family that's changed drastically over the years. They haven't caught up with real life yet."

When Vanessa frowned Evan smoothed her brow with an index finger. "Don't worry. I'm working on another angle that might help. I've got to go..." As he stepped back, Vanessa caught his hand.

"Evan..."

He waited, a puzzled half smile on his face.

"I'm sorry," Vanessa said fervently.

His expression was blank. "What for?"

Vanessa gnawed on the inside of her mouth and stared at the stitching of his black leather trench coat. "Because I once accused you of being arrogant, of promoting your own career and your own interests, rather than helping people who really needed it. I was so wrong."

Evan was silent for a moment. He clearly remembered Vanessa throwing those accusations at him. But there had been much more at work than a mere character attack. It had been her defense against an attraction that had taken them both by surprise. He'd understood Vanessa's motives even then; if she could prove he wasn't a person she could like or respect, then she could be safe from loving him.

Evan stepped closer now and leaned toward her. "I seem to remember telling you that you were a self-righteous snob. I was wrong, too. We got past all that a long time ago, Van."

She took a deep breath. "I know, but... I just want to tell you that..."

"I'm glad I was wrong." Evan said it first. His gaze swept across her face.

"I love you," Vanessa said softly, her heart pumping with the strength of her convictions.

"I loved you first," he responded with a lopsided grin.

"I didn't believe you."

"You were scared. I wasn't. I'm just glad you got over it."

Vanessa blinked and cast a glance around them. "Should we be talking like this in the middle of the street? What will people think?"

Evan grinned and kissed her. Her lips were cool and soft. "Ask me if I care."

"Sorry about lunch," she said once again.

"We'll make up for it tonight."

With a brief wave Evan started up the entrance and into the courthouse.

THE LOWER LEVEL of the United Presbyterian Church usually doubled as an auditorium or dining room. It was easily converted from one to the other, depending on the placement of chairs. At the moment there weren't many. The space was partitioned so that it could serve as a temporary home to about two dozen men, women and children. There was also a low platform at one end of the room that was a nursery-cum-day-care, filled with cribs, toddler cots and playpens, all occupied.

The room was lined almost in military fashion with an assortment of cots and folding beds, tables and chairs and milk crates stacked and arranged for storage space.

Couples—there were only two now that the Jacksons had won their case and moved into a new apartment—were given the use of an empty office and a supply room for privacy.

Vanessa had first heard of the shelter when she read a bulletin-board notice at the school where she was working on her master's degree in public administration. She'd decided to make homelessness the topic of her degree paper, but ever since she'd begun devoting time and concern to the people at the church, had found herself becoming emotionally and personally involved in the issue. The residents' lives meant far more than material for a research paper.

There were no luxuries at the shelter, and certainly no one was here because he or she wanted to be; for the time being, there was little choice. Yet Vanessa was impressed by the amount of cooperation and sharing among the residents. Perhaps because all any of them had was each other—and their individual pride. Life had dealt them a hard blow, but there was no self-pity here. The problems the residents had were not insur-

mountable, and Pastor Hitchcock had done a good
job of demonstrating that even they, with their mea-
ger possessions and difficult lives, had much to be
thankful for.

Vanessa was glad to help with getting donations of
clothing and dry goods, with tutoring the children or
finding agencies for the adults that were specific to
their individual problems. But it was Evan who'd discovered that the church was eligible for private funding because they housed children and because they
were nonsectarian. It was Evan who'd persuaded the
Jacksons to pursue a case against the owner of their
former residence. And Evan who had succeeded in
getting Terry Williams to return to school.

In a way not understood by others who weren't in
their circumstances, the people who lived at the church
were one big family. There was a level of acceptance
among them that Vanessa envied. It was pure. Not
defined by class or wealth or race or accomplish-
ments, but by the simple human need for dignity and
respect. Those needs made them all equal.

Vanessa glanced quickly through the notes in her
hand to make sure she'd done all the things at the
shelter she needed to do before leaving for the evening. She was on her way to the pastor's office when
she heard the plaintive cry of a baby over the general
hum of activity. She slowed her steps and looked over
at the nursery. Seeing no one on duty in the area, she
detoured to attend to the distressed infant, reaching
the crib at the same time as a girl of about seventeen.
It was Terry, the baby's mother.

"I'll get him," the girl said defensively, lifting Kevin out of the crib. The baby's fist closed around a beaded extension braid from his mother's exotic hairdo and pulled. The young mother awkwardly tried to free her hair.

"I'll hold him for a while, Terry. You need to finish your schoolwork," Vanessa quickly offered.

"I thought he'd stay asleep for a while," Terry mumbled, trying unsuccessfully to quiet the screaming child.

Vanessa smiled at the girl, then gently reached to take the baby from Terry's arms. "I don't think babies follow any timetable but their own. I promise to be careful with him." Vanessa could see Terry's ambivalence about her child; she wanted to take care of him, but was sometimes overwhelmed by the responsibility. "I think he just needs a change of diaper. Why don't I do that while you finish your homework? Then you can feed him, okay?"

Terry nodded, and Vanessa walked away with Kevin in her arms to a space where she could change him.

"Yes, yes, yes..." Vanessa cooed. The baby was already settling down to hiccups and sucking on his fist. When she was done, Vanessa picked him up and held him against her shoulder. She loved the way his warm little body felt so helpless and soft. Patting and gently rocking the baby, she began to hum a tune under her breath and realized with a wry chuckle that it was a song from *The Little Mermaid*—a clear indication of how often she'd seen the video with the children on the VCR in the pastor's office.

Vanessa, who had no nieces or nephews of her own, had come to love those moments in the office with half-a-dozen children all wanting to sit in her lap. She recalled the second or third time she and Evan had visited his brother Jason's family. Christy had taken her hand and said she wanted 'Nessa to put her to bed. Michael had asked if she knew any good bedtime stories. Vanessa had tried to teach him the tongue twister "How much wood would a woodchuck chuck..." that her own brother Richard had once taught her, sending the little boy into peels of delighted laughter. Vanessa also loved the open and totally unself-conscious way the children accepted her.

The baby in Vanessa's arms now was a bright-eyed boy with a full head of soft curls. He stared at Vanessa from the crook of her arm where he nestled, lulled by her humming. Kevin suddenly offered her a wide gummy smile and a gurgle. She wondered if, as he grew older, someone would play word games with him and tuck him carefully into bed, then kiss him good-night and always have a hug and time to listen to him. Would Terry be able to do for her son what was never done for her and break the cycle?

A hand touched her shoulder, and Vanessa turned to face the young mother. In the three months she'd known Terry, the girl had never done anything spontaneously, had never laughed out loud, had never asked questions. When Vanessa looked into Terry's eyes, she saw only resignation. Certainly no joy. No happy memories of childhood. The irony of the situation wasn't lost on Vanessa. While she herself was agonizing over loving Evan Holden and where they might spend Thanksgiving, the concepts of love and family were probably completely foreign to Terry.

"I can feed him now," Terry said. Vanessa handed her son over and watched as Terry settled into a chair to give him his bottle.

"Mr. Holden told me to remind you about your meeting with Family Services," Vanessa said to the girl. Terry silently nodded. "Are you ready for the interview?"

Terry nodded again. She might seem indifferent, but Vanessa knew she was not. Vanessa wondered how someone so young got to be old so fast.

"They say I gotta finish high school. They say I have to show I can take care of Kevin." Terry looked up at Vanessa suddenly, her dark face briefly flashing fear and defiance. "I want to keep my baby. He's all I got."

Vanessa touched Terry's arm. "No one is going to take Kevin away from you. Don't forget that Pastor Hitchcock said he'd write letters, and Mr. Holden said he'd come to court with you. And Mrs. Jackson said she would baby-sit and help you with your schoolwork. There are lots of people who believe in you, Terry. But you have to believe in yourself, too. The most important thing right now is to keep you in school, find you and Kevin a home and figure out how you can work part-time. You concentrate on school, and I'll try to work on everything else."

"Miss Moran?" Terry said as Vanessa began to walk away. "Do you like Mr. Holden?"

Vanessa blinked. "Excuse me?"

"Do you like Mr. Holden?"

The question had come out of left field. "Yeah, I do."

"I know, but do you like him a lot?"

"Why are you asking?"

"Because you talk about him all the time, like he knows everything."

Vanessa laughed lightly. "Well, yes, I do like him 'a lot.'" Vanessa frowned at Terry. "Don't you? Or is it that you don't trust him?"

"I don't understand why Mr. Holden cares what happens to me."

Vanessa sighed deeply. "He cares about people. Wouldn't you rather know someone like that than someone who walked away when you needed help?"

"I guess so."

"I think the next time Mr. Holden is here you should ask him."

Terry stared at her. "What if he gets mad at me?"

"I bet he doesn't. Mr. Holden doesn't have to be here—neither do I. So maybe that means we really do care what happens to you." Vanessa smiled. "I have to go talk to the pastor. If you need some help with your schoolwork, I'll be here for another hour. Or if you just want to talk."

"Okay." Terry nodded.

When Vanessa reached the pastor's office, he was finishing a phone conversation and beckoning her to a seat.

"Yes, Mr. Castelli. That's very generous of you. We'd be happy to accept your gift. I'm sure I can arrange for a pickup from your store... Sometime this week? No problem. I'll call as soon as I can arrange it.

Good-bye.'' The pastor hung up and sighed. He made a check mark next to a name on the list before him and looked up at Vanessa. "Well, we're going to have lots of pasta for Thanksgiving. Not exactly traditional, but I don't think the residents will mind."

"Did we get a turkey?"

"I'm working on it. We also need more tables and chairs, dishes and cutlery, dessert . . . There're always so many things. But—" he sat back in his chair and smiled at Vanessa "—I'm sure everything will work out."

"You're an optimist, Pastor."

"That's what faith and love is. And don't think I'm fooled by that cool tone, young lady. You're an optimist, too, otherwise you wouldn't come here as often as you do. Long before there were city agencies to help people, there were just folks like you and Evan. You give something our government can't. Genuine concern. Love. The kind of thing there's no substitute for."

Vanessa felt embarrased by the pastor's praise. She was not without selfish motives for what she did—it was nice to be wanted and accepted—although she was glad she had something to offer. "So, will there be a place for me in heaven?"

"For all God's children. He smiles on those who are generous in sharing their love. I'm not sure anything else is as important."

"Sounds like a good topic for your Sunday sermons."

The pastor sighed deeply and peered at his list of names again. He reached for the telephone to continue his soliciting. "I have. Often. Unfortunately actions still speak louder than words."

WHEN EVAN LET HIMSELF into his apartment, the silence made him feel tired. And lonely. The day had been hectic and too long. Not that he minded the work. Though it was sometimes mechanical and cold, it was often challenging and exciting; he liked arguing, liked the debates of facts and logic and coming to irrefutable conclusions. It used to be that after a day of court briefs, depositions and filings, the arguments would continue over dinner with four or five colleagues; or over a round of drinks with a couple of the senior partners. Evan had never appreciated before the peace of not talking law for twelve hours a day—until he'd met Vanessa.

Vanessa brought him back down to earth. She stabilized him. She was his reality check, both to what else was going on in the world—such as the lives of the residents at the shelter—and to his own feelings. But even more than that, Vanessa had cared about him, the way only a woman could. She made Evan comfortable; she was empathetic and always willing to listen; she knew how to distract him, how to love him. Which was why the silence seemed so much worse after a day like the one he had. It made Evan feel isolated.

A certain relief and rejuvenation began to take place, however, when he opened the closet door to hang up his coat. Vanessa's black wool coat was there between a rain poncho and his aviation jacket. And taped to the inside of the door was a piece of white bond paper—with a lipstick print smack in the center.

A grin quickly transformed Evan's face, and a sense of peaceful pleasure made him sigh. He walked into the small kitchen. There was another piece of paper on the counter, this one a note. "You're getting warmer," it read. A third piece of paper with the word "Bingo" outlined by a heart in the middle of it, Evan found taped on the back of a chair in the living room. The chair was stacked with Vanessa's books and papers, and Vanessa herself was stretched out on the sofa, asleep. Evan stood watching her for a long moment, and then she began to stir and stretch into wakefulness. Evan sat on the edge of the coffee table facing her as she blinked her eyes open. She covered her yawn with the back of her hand and arched her back. It was a graceful, almost feline movement that made Evan want to hold her. Instead, he leaned forward and kissed her mouth.

"Was I sleeping?" Vanessa asked, her voice raspy and surprised. "What time is it?"

"Almost ten," Evan said. "I'm sorry I'm so late."

Her smile was sleepy and had a seductive warmth. "I'm sorry I didn't stay awake. I was in the middle of not-for-profit funding sources..."

Evan laughed and, taking Vanessa's hand, pulled her into a sitting position. He sat next to her and put his arm around her. As she snuggled closer, he said, "No wonder you fell asleep."

"Why *are* you so late?"

Evan sighed. He kicked off his shoes and lifted his long legs to the coffee table. "A late-afternoon deposition; a court date pushed up from next month to next week; a flat tire; a misplaced legal document..."

Vanessa chuckled. "All of the above, I take it?"

"Mmm." He closed his eyes briefly. "I'm glad you're here, Van. I found all your clues. What's the prize?"

"What would you like?"

"For you to stay with me."

Vanessa sighed. "I hadn't planned on that. I thought we'd have dinner."

"We can still do that."

She shook her head and laughed. "Not unless you shopped on the way home. There's a tomato, half a loaf of bread and some milk in the refrigerator."

"We'll order a pizza."

Vanessa sat away from Evan and grimaced. "I hope I never have to face you in court. You have an answer for everything, don't you?"

"Almost."

She sighed. "Ming will never forgive me."

Evan watched her mouth. Her top lip was clearly sculpted, lifting and flaring so that she always seemed on the verge of smiling. Her bottom lip was fuller. Evan reached out to touch her face, still surprised sometimes by the paleness of his skin against hers, though it was no longer the first thing he saw. "There's a solution to that," he said quietly.

Vanessa knew exactly what he meant. "No," she whispered.

"Why? Are you afraid that living with me will turn you into a pumpkin? Or that I'll turn out to be a toad?"

It was more than just a teasing question. She watched the way his jaw muscles worked and flexed. It was such a small thing, but it fascinated her. A masculine trait that showed intensity, strength. Her gaze swept over his face, a strong face with a prominent nose, though not unattractively so, gray-geen eyes that always looked directly at her and that had learned to read her with surprising accuracy.

She tried to jest her way out of the conversation. "Your bathroom isn't big enough and I don't have a real living room. Besides, this way we won't get bored."

"I'm not talking about the size of a room and whether we're going to bump into each other in a tight space. I'm talking about having a life together that's together, and not in two places across the city. I'm talking about waking up with you and going to bed with you and making long-range plans."

"Yes," Vanessa answered as she uncurled herself and got to her feet. "I'm still afraid." She held out her hand to Evan. He took it and silently stood up, too, recognizing the end of the conversation. They moved to the kitchen where Evan phoned in an order for a pizza and Vanessa made coffee.

There was a part of Evan that didn't want to admit Vanessa's concerns were valid. And hc had not come to know and love her without seeing firsthand the parts of her identity, her *self*, that could not connect with his. It was the nature of their being different that neither had any control over and that the world wouldn't let them forget. Nonetheless, Evan believed completely that their love was enough.

After the pizza arrived they found they weren't all that hungry, and in the end most of the pizza was wrapped and refrigerated. Vanessa washed plates and cups, while Evan dried. But he abandoned the duty as unnecessary and, instead, stood behind Vanessa with his arms around her middle, nibbling on her earlobe until she, too, figured out the immediate priority.

Evan eased her sweater over her head, and Vanessa slowly pulled his shirt free of his slacks and started on the row of buttons. They made it to the bedroom with much of their clothing already removed. Everything else came off in leisurely fits and starts. They continued the gentle sensual foreplay on top of the quilt Evan's grandmother had made. And then he just lay back watching her.

Vanessa always wondered what Evan was thinking as he gazed at her brown body, the even darker aureoles of her pert breasts. He sometimes just smiled as though he had a secret he didn't want to share. Only his sure touch and dizzying kisses hinted at his pleasure. They curled languidly against each other, their limbs interlocked like an abstract mosaic.

Their lovemaking built slowly, no need to rush for fulfillment. The stroking and sighs and whispers, the rhythmic dance of their bodies, were familiar and warm. Both knew the tempo would soon rise to a frenzy—but it didn't get that far. The telephone rang.

Both Evan and Vanessa were startled and the soft sexual mood cracked at the intrusive, persistent ringing. Evan swore under his breath. He dropped his weight completely and lay still on top of Vanessa.

She sighed and stroked his back. "Maybe you'd better answer," she said regretfully.

Evan shook his head. "No," he mumbled, his breath hot against her neck. After the third ring the answering machine switched on.

"Hi, Ev. It's Mom calling. Sweetie, I know it's late, but I kept missing you at your office today. I guess you've been very busy, but...well, I just thought I'd better call. It's...about Thanksgiving...."

Evan slowly raised his head and looked into Vanessa's dark eyes. He saw the pain gathering, the apprehension. He felt the way her body stiffened and her guard went up.

"Let me go," Vanessa whispered urgently.

"No." Evan responded. Vanessa tried to draw away, pushing against his chest, but Evan squeezed his arms and legs around her to hold her still.

"...Evan, you know how Dad and I feel. We just think you're confused right now and that you just need some time to...work things out. Thanksgiving is a family affair, and of course we're expecting to see you. But it would really be better for everyone if you didn't bring...your friend. Besides, I'm sure she'll want to be with *her* family...."

"Evan, please let me go."

Evan braced himself on his elbows. He cupped his hands around Vanessa's face. She was crying silently, her chest rising and falling deeply with every breath.

"...We're expecting a lot of people. Oh, and I've invited Christina de Haviland and her family. We all used to be so close. It should be a wonderful dinner. Give us a call. 'Bye."

The phone clicked off. The silence was smothering. Suddenly Vanessa couldn't seem to breathe. She tried to get up, but Evan hugged her closer, instead.

"Shh..." he whispered against her lips. He kissed the tears from her face, then gently kissed her mouth. Vanessa's body shuddered, but she sighed deeply and relaxed.

They had to start over again, but the buildup was quick, spurred on by frustration and surprise, disappointment... and love. Their need for each other was greater now. When the need wrapped tightly around them, demanding fulfillment, Evan reached to turn out the bedside lamp and settled down in Vanessa's open arms.

In the dark, love didn't have a color.

Chapter Four

FOUR HOURS LATER when Ming padded into the quiet of the living room and meowed in her lazy half-hearted way, Vanessa knew that Evan was awake. She glanced up from the letter she was writing, drank the last of her tea and put the mug on the coffee table. Vanessa herself had been up since six-thirty, uncomfortable dreams and emotional anxiety forcing her out of bed.

Ming planted her hind legs stiffly, walked the front ones out and arched her body in a full feline stretch. Then she leapt gracefully onto the sofa and into Vanessa's lap. The purring of the contented animal vibrated against Vanessa's thighs and stomach.

"Traitor," she whispered affectionately, stroking her pet's sleek back.

When Vanessa and Evan had first become serious about each other, when their relationship demanded physical intimacy and the desire to be together meant time at his place or hers, Ming and Evan had been wary of one another. Evan was not used to cats, and Ming was not used to sharing the affections of her mistress. Ming would hiss whenever Evan came into the apartment, and hide under the bed. Now, Vanessa mused as she heard Evan stirring sleepily in the bedroom, Ming either slept on Evan's chest or shared his pillow. The cat had checked him out, shown disdain and indifference initially, then finally come to the same conclusion Vanessa had: Evan Holden was worthy of attention and love.

But love had not been enough to insulate her from the phone call four nights ago. She'd been an unwilling eavesdropper on a conversation that had been filled with opinions, attitudes and coaxing, and one that she'd not been meant to hear. But she had, and the resentment and pain had sent her into a tailspin of emotional confusion. And sleepless nights. It had been a jolting reminder that she and Evan were considered, even by his own parents, an aberration, instead of a man and a woman who loved each other.

Evan had expressed remorse about the phone call and explained that it had nothing to do with her. Vanessa hadn't asked him what *he* thought of it, because he hadn't given her a chance. Instead, he had made love to her with a tenderness and concern meant to replace the layer of hurt. But the succeeding nights in Evan's arms had left Vanessa awake, pensive . . . and torn.

"Van?" Evan croaked from the depths of the bedroom.

She closed her eyes briefly against the appeal in his tone. Sleep made his voice an octave deeper, the sound forging up from his chest. She loved his voice in the morning. Grating and sexy. Intimate. She hesitated only a moment longer before uncurling herself from the sofa and responding.

"I'm coming," she called out as Ming protested against being summarily roused from her comfortable warm spot.

Vanessa tightened the sash of her short kimono. Her bare feet were silent on the floor, and when she appeared suddenly in the bedroom door, Evan smiled.

He'd been disappointed not to find Vanessa next to him in bed when he awoke. He sensed that Vanessa's restless wakefulness had to do with more than just being ready to get up or having things to do. She had developed a habit of reaching out in the night to rest a hand on his chest. And it was not unusual for the two of them to thread their fingers together while asleep. But since the phone call Evan had sensed a withdrawal in Vanessa.

"Couldn't sleep again?" he asked.

Vanessa only shrugged. She played with the knot of her robe, but came to join Evan on the bed when he held out a hand to her. Instead of sliding under the sheet and letting him warm and comfort her as she knew he would, Vanessa sat atop the spread. Evan's face was still flushed with sleep, his facial muscles still slack, his hair tousled. He took her hand and scrutinized her carefully.

"What have you been up to?"

Vanessa looked at their hands. "Reading. Writing some letters. Making lists." She gave him a brief smile. "Checking them twice."

"Brooding?" Evan asked quietly.

She forced a smile. "No."

"You haven't been sleeping well."

Vanessa hesitated. "No."

Evan stroked her thigh. "Want to tell me about it?"

Vanessa looked at him and knew his concern was genuine. For a second she considered asking him what he'd been thinking since that night. But she didn't, because she was afraid to know the answer. She shook her head.

"No." She reached out and rubbed Evan's chest. The hair there was pale ginger, and soft. "I thought you had a racquetball game with Brian this morning," she said, hoping to deflect Evan's probing questions.

He yawned. "I do. But I've got time."

"Not if you want breakfast. The kitchen closes in thirty minutes," Vanessa said playfully, then quickly got up, because she knew that otherwise Evan would coax her back into bed and any resolve she'd formulated would melt under the magic insistence of his caress.

"Van..." Evan tried to grab her wrist but she easily evaded his grasp.

"Twenty-nine minutes," she said over her shoulder as she left the room.

"What's for breakfast?" Evan called out, but got no answer. He collapsed back against the pillows, frowning, wondering how wide the gap between them was going to get.

Vanessa was whisking eggs, milk and nutmeg together when Evan came into the kitchen. He'd shaved, but hadn't combed his hair. He was dressed in navy blue sweats and slouchy gray athletic socks. Ming trailed behind him, meowing and brushing her long body against his leg. But Evan ignored the cat in favor of Vanessa, moving up behind her and sliding his arms around her waist.

"French toast," Vanessa said.

Evan maintained his position. "Uh-oh," he groaned dramatically.

"What does that mean?" Vanessa asked. Evan bent forward to rest his cheek against hers and peer over her shoulder.

"That means I know this is some kind of setup. My mother does the same thing. She'll use my favorite foods as a means of persuasion." As soon as the words were out Evan regretted them. He could feel Vanessa's body stiffen.

"What would I be trying to persuade you to do?" Her voice sounded low and cool.

Evan didn't move. "I don't know. You tell me." Then a thought occurred to him. He stood straight and turned Vanessa around to face him. Her gaze was uncertain and searching. "Or are you trying to soften an imminent blow?"

Vanessa shrugged, and her easy grin was not convincing. "I just thought I'd make something you really like. You have to keep your energy up if you expect to beat Brian."

Evan absently shook his head, but his gaze rolled over her face. "He'll probably win, anyway." Her features were smooth and still. Only her eyes gave her away. He smiled tenderly. "You don't have to convince me that you love me, Van. And I don't care if my stomach is satisfied as long as my heart is."

Vanessa studied Evan with equal care and thoroughness. She wanted to be absorbed into the look in his eyes that said he loved her, too. *No matter what.* But her concern stretched way beyond herself and Evan. To his family, and hers. Vanessa blinked and took a deep breath. She glanced at the wall clock. "Fifteen minutes," she murmured. Her voice shook.

Evan frowned and released her. "I'll set the table."

When they finally sat down, the distance between them was greater than the width of the table. The silence didn't hold the comfortable familiarity of the present, but the murky unknown of the future. It had nothing to do with breakfast or the ritual Saturday games of racquetball or errands done together. It had to do with Thanksgiving and the longer-standing traditions, and love of family.

Vanessa felt tortured. Behind their easy banter was a kind of no-man's land, strewn with hopes and dreams they weren't sure could ever be fulfilled. It had been established and perpetrated by history and, through that phone call from Evan's mother, had reared its ugly head. Finally Evan, sensing the tension in her and guessing its cause, reached across the table for Vanessa's hand and held it tightly.

"Talk to me," he urged in a low voice. "Tell me what's bothering you."

She stared at him. "I don't think we can have it both ways, you and I. I don't think we can love each other and not lose ourselves." She paused for a breath. "We can't pretend we don't care about the rest of the world. We *are* part of the same world."

He sighed. "This is about my family."

She sighed, too. "And mine."

"Vanessa, I've told my folks I won't be coming to their house for Thanksgiving." She didn't respond and Evan squeezed her hand. "Did you hear what I said?"

"Why?" Vanessa asked.

"Because I want to bring you with me. If I can't do that, I'm not going."

Her reaction surprised Evan. She pulled her hand free and glared at him. "No."

"My parents have the right to say who will and will not be welcome at their house. I have a right to decide who I will or will not love. I'm disappointed, but I can't help the way they feel," Evan insisted urgently.

Vanessa looked anguished, closing her eyes, her hands clenching into fists. "You can't do this, Evan."

"I already have."

"But you should have told me what you were going to do first," she said, her voice quivering.

"It was my decision, Van."

"It was *my* decision, too."

Evan shook his head, incredulous. "The idea was that we should be together. That's what *I* want. What about you?"

"It doesn't matter what I want. What you're suggesting isn't right. We're talking about your family, not total strangers. What they feel matters."

"Is your mother extending an invitation to Thanksgiving at her house?"

Vanessa made an impatient grimace. "My mother has plans to go away for Thanksgiving." She didn't bother to add that she'd asked her mother to stay and have Thanksgiving with her and Evan.

"Because of me?" Evan shot back. "Did that make it easier for her to deal with the possibility that you might want me to be there?"

"I don't know," Vanessa answered quietly.

"Yes, you do," he countered softly. "Your mother is doing the same thing as my mother. And it has nothing to do with either of us."

Vanessa shook her head, bewildered. "I never expected you to ask me to come with you, especially since I haven't met your parents."

"And I never expected this to be an issue."

Vanessa fidgeted nervously in her chair. "Evan, please. It's not worth it."

He stood up to pour himself more coffee. Still standing, he took a sip, scalding his tongue on the too-hot liquid. "If this isn't worth it, Van, then what is? I know what I want. I've made up my mind. What about you?"

Vanessa tilted her face up to him. For a moment she felt overwhelming love, but then it was swept aside by another more immediate emotion. "Are you sure enough to risk a split from your family? Can your love for me really survive that?"

"I think *our* love can." Evan nodded. "I'm willing to risk it."

"I'm not," she said, her voice barely audible. Then her tone became pleading. "I don't mind staying by myself. I've done it before. I want you to tell your mother you'll come for Thanksgiving."

Evan sighed and abruptly put his coffee cup down. The sudden sound—or was it the build-up of tension in the room?—frightened Ming. With an uncertain meow, the cat scurried out of the room.

"No." he said, glaring down at her. "If it wasn't Thanksgiving, it'd be some other gathering. Christmas. The next family wedding. A birthday. When is it supposed to end?''

"Your parents have already made up their minds. If you push them, Evan, it'll only create bad feelings." Vanessa got up and began to clear the table. She brought the plates to the counter but Evan took them from her and placed them, clattering, into the sink. He took a firm hold of her upper arms, forcing her to face him, see his troubled eyes.

"Van, my parents aren't bigots."

"Neither is my mother. My parents raised me to be fair, to see people as individuals. I wasn't raised to think of people in terms of their race. But it hurts when I'm not seen as a person who can be hurt. So what do you think the problem is?"

"Fear," Evan answered promptly.

"Of what? What do they think I'm going to do to you?"

Evan sighed. "This is crazy. Why are *we* fighting?"

"I'm going to stay here, and you're going to your parents."

"I've already made my decision. Listen, let's not even get a turkey. What would we do with the leftovers, anyway?"

"Evan, don't joke," Vanessa said tightly.

"We'll have spaghetti and meatballs. Pot roast. Hot dogs. Maybe we won't eat at all. What difference does it make as long as we can do it together?"

"Evan, I . . . I can't."

"I don't understand why not," Evan insisted.

Vanessa couldn't say she was scared exactly. But she felt bewildered, caught between a rock and a hard place. Could Evan not see that his decision to disappoint his parents made her vulnerable? Did he not see that what was happening had everything to do with her, and that Thanksgiving was beside the point? If their love was allowed to tear them from their families, it would eventually tear them from each other, as well.

The problem was not that the Holdens had said no to her, but that Evan had so firmly said yes to her. In doing so he had set in motion a new course for their relationship, one she was unprepared for. Evan had always said to her that their love was not an affair. For months he'd been trying to persuade Vanessa that they should live together. The idea had been appealing, exciting—and frightening. Vanessa felt catapulted forward without any time to catch her breath, take stock of the possibilities or regain her balance.

She placed her hands on Evan's chest. She was afraid to trust the power of their love. "Your family will be disappointed."

"That's not our problem. My parents, unfortunately, aren't paying any attention to what I want. Just like your mother. So what does that tell you? Not that it's our duty to make them happy, but that we should make each other happy."

Something in Vanessa snapped. She began to cry silently, and two large tears spilled from her eyes and rolled down her cheeks. Immediately Evan gathered her to him, murmuring her name, rubbing her back. With her face pressed to his chest Vanessa could smell

Evan's body. It was a scent that was intoxicating and familiar; masculine and strong. It normally made her feel safe.

"You're going to be late," she mumbled. "Brian's waiting."

"He'll wait. I'm not leaving until we settle this."

Vanessa took a deep breath and pushed back from Evan's embrace. She sniffled and wiped her wet face with the back of her hand. She was caught between wanting to stay where she was, believing Evan, and an unwillingness to test him. "It's settled. You might as well go."

Evan stared at Vanessa, trying desperately to understand what was happening. He thought his decision was the right one. He thought he'd made himself clear. Was Vanessa really trying to tell him something different?

"Vanessa?" Evan said uneasily. His hands circled her jaw so that her quivering chin rested in his palms and her face was turned up to him. "Don't you realize by now that I love you? *I love you!*"

"And I love you. I really do. But if we hurt each other, if our families turn away from us, I don't think love is going to be enough."

For once Evan didn't have a response, because he didn't want to consider that Vanessa might be right. He continued to try to gauge her, to read past the noble words. He probed deeply into her wet sable eyes, feeling as if his chest were being crushed.

His relationship with her had come as a surprise to Evan. He'd had no idea what he'd been looking for in

love until he'd met Vanessa, and now it was difficult
to remember before that.

Once, back in July when she'd gone away with girl-
friends for a weekend, Evan had realized in the emp-
tiness that he wanted only her. He remembered
fearing, however groundlessly, that he'd lost her. Perhaps to another man. Or to the reasoning of her
mother. Their racial differences had only lent a certain irony, because their sensibilities were so similar,
and their coming together had been so instinctive and
easy. Natural. Whatever doubts Evan might have had,
and he admittedly had one or two the instant he was
aware of his attraction to Vanessa, they had vapor-
ized as the relationship—and trust—had grown. With
their love any doubts had become meaningless.

"Van, love is enough if you believe in it. I do."

"I want to."

They stared at one another.

Ming made a tentative appearance in the doorway
again and looked up at both of them. She meowed
softly, as if sensing the thick painful emotion that
hung in the air. Then she turned around and, meowing plaintively, slunk back to the bedroom.

The phone rang, making Vanessa jump. Almost
grateful for the interruption she picked up the cellular
phone from the counter.

"Hello?" She kept her gaze on Evan, wondering if
he understood at all what she'd been saying, how she
was feeling. "Hi, Brian. Yes, he's here. Hold on a
second..."

Vanessa held out the telephone to Evan. He ignored it, continuing to stare at her. For a moment Va-

nessa was tempted to shout, "I'm sorry. I didn't know what I was saying. Yes, I love you. Let's not worry about your parents or mine." But she didn't. Instead, she asked quietly, pointedly, "Are you going?"

They both understood what she meant. Anger and disappointment made Evan's eyes darken, his jaw muscles flex, his mouth turn grim.

"Tell Brian I'm on my way," he said flatly, and turned to walk out of the kitchen.

WITH ONE HAND Vanessa slid the fiberglass fabric along the wooden rod. With the other she maintained a firm grip on the upper ledge of the window frame and tried to keep her balance. From atop the six-foot metal ladder, she glanced down at Gladys Jackson. The older woman stood hands on hips, head tilted and eyes squinting at Vanessa's work.

"I don't think the opening is quite centered. Maybe you could pull the material in a little bit more from the left side . . . that's it. Now you come down from there and rest. You're supposed to be visiting, not working."

"I don't mind," Vanessa said, but she slowly descended the ladder.

"I appreciate your hanging those curtains for me, but you're not to do another thing."

Gladys walked around her living room as she spoke, gathering up extra panels of drapery yet to be hung and folding them. She placed the fabric on the stool pulled up in front of a secondhand sewing machine someone had given to her.

Vanessa retucked her blouse in the waistband of her jeans and smiled at Gladys. "You did a lovely job with these curtains."

"Thank you, dear. I've always loved to sew. It's nice to be able to again. I also love to cook. I've been trying out the new oven. I baked some muffins, and we'll have some as soon as they cool." With a heavy sigh, Gladys sat on the sofa, also secondhand, and patted the space next to her. "Come and sit. We haven't really talked since you walked in the door."

Vanessa sat, but she would have preferred to keep working. Do something constructive with her hands rather than let her mind spin with turmoil. "The apartment is coming along nicely."

Gladys smiled gently. "Yes, yes. I suppose so." She shook her head, her expression regretful but calm. "Harry and I will never be able to replace everything we lost, but we did save quite a bit, and we're so lucky to have this place."

"And each other," Vanessa nodded. "How's he doing?"

Gladys grimaced. "His leg still hurts him sometimes. Right now he's taking a nap, which he'll never admit is a nap, you understand. He's just resting his eyes." She rolled hers heavenward, but her laugh was loving and indulgent. Then she looked more closely at Vanessa, noting the abstract air, the pensive drifting. "You know, when I saw you at the door I expected to see Evan, as well. Couldn't he make it?"

Vanessa averted her gaze, giving herself time to compose her features. She shrugged and played with the turned-up collar of her blouse. "I think he had something else planned,'' she improvised. ''I know he'd be sorry he didn't make it today.''

Gladys tisked. ''So am I, but that doesn't mean I'm not glad to see you. How's everyone at the shelter? How's Terry and the baby?''

''Terry wanted me to tell you hello.''

''Did she?'' Gladys brightened. ''You tell her to keep at school. And anytime she wants to, she can come and visit Harry and me.''

Vanessa smiled. ''I think she'd like that. She refers to you as Grandmother Jackson.''

Gladys whooped with delight.

Vanessa glanced briefly around the living room. It was quite spacious and bright but there were only a half dozen or so cartons of personal belongings to be unpacked. Again, she felt the tragedy of the Jacksons' having lost so much. She turned a sympathetic gaze back to Gladys.

''I guess you lost a lifetime worth of memories, didn't you?''

Mrs. Jackson's smile was sad but wise. ''No, dear. The things that are gone are just that. Things. Yes, some of them were gorgeous and expensive. Some were family heirlooms. There were mementos and gifts and lots of junk with sentimental value. But I don't mind losing any of it all that much. I just didn't want to lose Harry.''

Gladys's priority touched a sudden awareness in Vanessa. She felt foolish for not having considered that. ''You're right, of course. Nothing else really matters.''

Gladys sighed and looked off into the distance. "We've always regretted not having children. It just never happened. We regret it even more now that we're getting on."

Vanessa smiled. "I know. No grandchildren."

"How did you guess?"

"My mother. All of her friends are grandparents, or soon to be. She feels left out. And I think being alone makes her feel older than she wants to."

"But she has you. Someday you'll marry and have children of your own."

Vanessa didn't answer right away. She stared down at the floral pattern of the sofa. "Yes..." she felt obliged to say, just so the silence wouldn't continue.

"You do want children, don't you? You do expect to get married?"

Vanessa smiled weakly. She made a movement with her head, neither yes or no. "I... guess. It's possible. There's time, after all, and—"

"What happened," Gladys asked quietly.

Vanessa glanced sharply at the older woman and saw reflected the clear recognition that something was wrong. She gnawed on her bottom lip. "What do you mean?"

"I mean, what happened with you and Evan? If you were hoping I wouldn't notice, then you were wrong. I've seen you excited, annoyed and surprised. I've seen you laugh and cry for the same reasons, but I've *never* seen you so unhappy. Not since I've known you." Gladys tilted her head, her eyes filled with compassion. "Is it Evan?"

"I don't know." Vanessa whispered. Maybe it was only herself and not Evan...

Gladys sighed and reached out a hand to stroke Vanessa's arm. "You two had a fight, I bet."

Had they? wondered Vanessa. Three days ago she and Evan had both been upset and angry. Three days ago they'd both tried to talk about his mother's phone call, but had really only talked *around* it. Being careful not to offend, they talked in vague intellectual terms about something that had cut an emotional trench between them. Three days ago they'd turned away from each other. Had that been a fight? Or a sudden confrontation with the truth? In all honesty Vanessa wasn't sure whom she was angry with, or at what. And maybe what happened with her and Evan had not been necessary. Had she sacrificed her own happiness out of a misplaced sense of loyalty?

Vanessa tried to tell Gladys what had happened. And she tried to be fair. It was actually a relief to unburden herself to someone who might understand. But when she finished the telling Vanessa still had no answers. There seemed something ironic in the devotion to celebrating Thanksgiving, a tradition that embodied togetherness and family while selectively deciding what made up a family. It wasn't just the Holdens. It was her mother, as well. True, Mrs. Moran had skirted any involvement by her apparent decision to be somewhere else on that day. But her intentions were clear, nonetheless.

"Well," Gladys said briskly, "what about what *you* want? And Evan? It seems to me that if you two love each other, the solution is simpler than you think."

"If you mean simply ignoring our families, you're probably right. But that won't change how they feel."

"That's probably true, too. But honey—" Gladys looked into Vanessa's eyes with sage and simple insights "—there's *nothing* you can do about the way other people feel. You can only be responsible for yourself. You know what I think the real problem is? You wonder if your love for Evan—or his for you—is strong enough to hold out against what other people think."

"But this isn't just other people," Vanessa said patiently. "We're talking about our families."

"I repeat," Gladys said firmly, "what is it *you* want?"

Suddenly Vanessa felt emotion well up in her. Suddenly she was afraid to say what she wanted, as though she was asking for too much and had no right to the kind of happiness she'd found with Evan. She recalled the moment she'd known she was in love with him. Actually it was not a single moment. The revelation had not come like a flash of light, but had evolved slowly over a number of small moments, the sum total of which had made her sure.

There'd been the bouquet of flowers and balloons when she'd been promoted to department head. When his firm had won a major case there'd been a victory dinner at his office to which Vanessa had been invited. Evan had changed the place cards so they were seated together; then he'd sat holding her hand under the table during most of the meal. There'd been the Saturday she'd gotten sick and Evan had given up tickets to a basketball game to spend the evening feeding her soup and hot tea. . . .

Vanessa blinked from her deep reverie and stared at Gladys. She felt only a momentary tug of ambivalence, but one truth remained the same. "I love Evan," she whispered.

"Honey, I know that. Now let's go sample those muffins and fix some tea." Gladys got up from the sofa and headed into the kitchen, directing Vanessa to sit at the small dining table. Gladys put a plate with a fragrant warm muffin in front of Vanessa then put out jam and cream cheese and tea with milk. At last Gladys joined her at the table.

"I met Harry at a church social," the woman suddenly began. "I thought he was handsome—and full of himself." She laughed. "Harry was raised an orphan, but he didn't let that stop him. He could quote from poetry and books. He bowed over my hand and never tried to kiss me when he shouldn't. And I loved him because he never pretended to be anything but what he was. A man with lots of dreams and the energy to make them come true.

"I married Harry against my family's wishes. We've been married more than forty years, and no one believed it would last four months. Harry and I began teaching school. And he began to write. My family gradually came around. When Harry published his one and only book of poetry, they thought he was the greatest thing since sliced bread. But I already knew he was a wonderful man, a good man. They didn't think he was good enough for me, and they were all wrong."

"You were lucky," Vanessa said softly. The analogy was not lost on her.

"No, I don't think it was luck. I think it was believing in each other, and believing in our love. Like you and Evan can do."

Vanessa stared at her muffin. It smelled heavenly, but her stomach was too tied in knots for her to eat. "Not if our families have anything to do with it."

Gladys tisked again. "Don't you know that love is a gift? It can't be taken, only given. It's what life is all about."

"But what if I lose everything else?"

Gladys sighed and reached over to firmly clasp Vanessa's hand. "Lord, child, I don't have all the answers. But there is such a thing as faith. Take it from there. True love is hard enough to find. Some people never experience it at all. Why would you doubt what's in your heart?"

Vanessa sighed. "It's not what's in *my* heart that I'm afraid of."

Chapter Five

THE BALL SLAMMED off the far wall, ricocheting with lethal speed. Brian made a valiant attempt to return it, but wasn't even close. The ball shot past his awkward off-balance stance and popped off the back wall with almost as much force.

Brian grunted as he landed in a sweaty heap on the court floor. He rolled onto his back and his chest heaved as he gasped for air. In exhaustion he put up his hands and racquet, and conceded defeat.

"That's . . . it. I've . . . had it. You . . . win."

Evan, panting just as hard and sweating just as profusely, walked calmly over to his prone partner and glared down on him. "You can't . . . give up now. I'm just hitting . . . my stride. Let's finish the game."

Brian coughed and groaned his way into an upright position. His hair was dark with moisture and plastered to his scalp. His T-shirt was drenched and sweat dripped from his nose. Brian shook his head as he leaned back, bracing his hands behind himself on the floor.

"No way. You're out for blood. I don't want it to be mine."

Evan looked down on Brian for a moment longer. Then his tightly wound body relaxed. The sinews and muscles of his legs and arms unknotted, and he dropped to the floor next to his friend. "I thought we were here to work out. We still have forty minutes before we have to get back to our office."

"Uh-uh," Brian said. "*I'm* here to work out. *You're* here to kill—the ball, the court or anything else in your way." There was no response and Brian shot a probing look at Evan. His gaze took in the tautness around the mouth, the flushed face. The furrowed brow. Evan looked defeated, too, except that he had just played like someone trying to exorcise a demon. "Okay." Brian exhaled slowly. "You have my undivided attention. What gives?"

Evan wiped his brow with his forearm and shook his head. "I don't know what you mean," he muttered.

Brian groaned. "Give me a break. Monday you nearly ripped my head off over lunch about some case I had nothing to do with. Yesterday when I saw you in court you were drawing more doodles than taking notes, and you grunted whenever you were asked a question. Today you're determined to annihilate me. Thank God we have a long weekend coming up."

Evan listened carefully, a wry grin finally crossing his features as Brian listed the ill treatment. "I'm sorry. I'm not angry at you, Brian. I'm not angry at anyone."

"So you're telling me that this need to destroy anything in your path is...what? You're having a bad week?"

"I'm frustrated, that's all. I didn't mean to take it out on you. It'll work out."

"Ahhh," Brian breathed in exaggeration. "Vanessa."

"No, it's *not* Vanessa." Evan said firmly.

"I know. I think it's pretty obvious to everyone you love the woman. But this is *about* her, right?"

Evan frowned. "I'm not sure. I thought it was about my parents, but I'm not sure it's that, either. I only know I can't seem to make my parents *or* Vanessa happy at the moment."

"Then don't even try. You can't succeed. What you have to do, good buddy, is whatever will make *you* happy. You can share that with whomever you please."

"Right," Evan responded skeptically.

"Look, I don't know what's going on and I don't want to know. But you're a good lawyer and you know as well as I do that sometimes you don't have all the answers. You just have to trust your gut."

Evan looked steadily at Brian, as if trying to decide whether to confide in him. Then he shrugged. "Van and I don't know what to do about Thanksgiving. Her mother...and my folks..."

"Okay, I get the picture. Easy answer. Forget Thanksgiving."

"That's your best advice?"

"You obviously haven't been able to come up with anything else that works."

"Actually I suggested something like that to Vanessa. But she has this idea that if I don't spend it with my family..."

"...that it's going to be her fault."

Evan frowned. "I hadn't thought of it that way. I don't want to see Vanessa hurt."

"And she doesn't want to see your parents hurt. You two are protecting each other. Sounds like love to me."

Evan sighed in relief and sudden insight. He shook his head. "We were doing just fine until we let everyone else's feelings get in the way."

Brian lay flat on the floor again and casually crossed his ankles, his hands behind his head. He took on the veneer of a sage adviser and surveyed Evan through half-closed lids. "That's probably true, but short of running away to an island in the south seas, the reality is there's always going to be someone who goes ballistic at the thought of you two together. Who are these guys, and do they matter? The thing you have to ask yourself and Vanessa is—what are you most afraid of losing?"

"Vanessa," Evan said simply.

Brian raised one hand in the air in a gesture of triumph. "I rest my case."

Evan began to chuckle. "Thanks."

"Don't thank me. Wait till you get my bill."

Evan jumped to his feet. "I'll give you a fair chance to try and beat me next week."

"Oh, don't worry. I plan on getting even. Where are you going?" he called after Evan, but never got an answer as Evan headed into the locker room. Brian laughed softly to himself. "Dumb question," he murmured wryly.

VANESSA TILTED her umbrella against the wind and rain and hurried blindly toward the building on the corner. Her mind had already run through a half-dozen worst-case scenarios as to why Gladys Jackson "urgently needs to see you," which was the message Vanessa's secretary had taken. However, two attempts to reach Gladys by phone had resulted in busy signals, making Vanessa's imagination kick into fifth gear.

Thinking perhaps there was a problem with the Jacksons' new building management or some legality from the courts, Vanessa had tried to reach Evan. She had done so with indecent eagerness, glad for a neutral reason to call him. She wanted a roundabout way to bridge the distance between them. But on this Wednesday before Thanksgiving, Vanessa had been informed that Evan Holden had been called away to a midafternoon meeting and would probably not be returning to his office.

It had been only four days since their disagreement over Thanksgiving, but Vanessa was ready to admit they were the longest four days of her life. When she cut through all the arguments and rhetoric, she knew she didn't want to lose Evan. If they could just agree on what their priorities were—what they both wanted, and what they were willing to sacrifice.

At the entrance to the corner building, someone graciously held open the door while Vanessa shook out her umbrella and folded it. She hurried into the lobby, hoping that Gladys hadn't been foolish enough to try to climb that ladder to hang more curtains. Hoping that Harry's leg had not suddenly collapsed beneath him or that either of them had taken ill, Vanessa waited for the elevator, her anxiety mounting with each passing moment.

She hadn't heard from her mother. Resignedly she reasoned that her mother was probably already on her way to the airport. Vanessa looked down at the soggy brown bag tucked under her arm. Another idea gone awry. The package was a peace offering intended for Evan. It had been her plan to go to his office earlier in the day with an apology. But that had been before she'd gotten up the courage, and before she'd learned he'd already left.

When she exited the elevator and turned down the corridor, there was a fresh trail of water on the floor leading all the way to the Jacksons' apartment. Vanessa picked up her pace. Someone had arrived before her. The police? An ambulance? She frantically pushed the buzzer.

But when the door opened Vanessa's rampant imagination stopped dead in its tracks. "Mr. Jackson?" she said, looking Harry up and down as if surprised to even see him standing. He looked fine. As a matter of fact he had a broad smile on his face, and the look of the devil in his eye. "Are you okay?"

"I'm fine. Fine. Come on in. Here, let me take your umbrella."

"But I got this call. It said that—"

"I know. I told Gladys not to leave a message like that. It probably scared you silly."

Vanessa allowed Harry to relieve her of her umbrella, package, purse and coat. Everything was dripping wet. "That's an accurate guess," she said dryly. "So there's no emergency? Nothing wrong?"

"Now, I didn't say that," Harry hedged.

Vanessa could hear voices and she turned her head in their direction—down the hall and toward the living room. She could hear Gladys's animated voice and merry laugh.

"Go on." Harry encouraged. "See for yourself."

Curiosity propelled Vanessa forward. That, and the dawning suspicion that the urgency didn't involve the Jacksons at all. Vanessa could now clearly make out the second voice, but just in case this, too, turned out to be a mistake, she said nothing until she was in the room. Not only was there no emergency, there was no sense of anxiety. Only Gladys and Evan, laughing together as they shared some amusing story. Evan saw her first. He stood up and stared at her.

Vanessa tried to ignore the sudden pulsing of her blood, the swish of emotional tension and surprise in her stomach. She tried to ignore the surge of breathlessness that made speech impossible.

"Oh, good. You're here." Gladys beamed at her.

"Are you okay?" Vanessa heard herself ask even though she was looking at Evan. Still, when both Evan and Gladys answered that they were fine, it was Evan's answer that gave her the greatest relief. She quickly assessed him, trying to determine the amount of damage their last encounter might have inflicted. But all she could see in his eyes, thank goodness, was the same kind of yearning she was feeling.

Gladys and Harry erupted in a babble of explanations and excuses and apologies for having sent out a false alarm. But as Vanessa stared at Evan all she felt was gratitude.

"We just thought we'd get things moving again," Harry said, reaching for his wife's arm.

"That's right. We hope you're not mad at us for what we did. But you two can't waste your lives on things you can't change. What you have to do is stay true to each other and love each other..." Gladys lectured even as Harry was gently pulling her from the room.

"Now don't mind us," Harry said. "You two take as long as you like."

"Oh, and one more thing," Gladys said, sticking her head back through the door opening, "why don't you two have Thanksgiving dinner with us?"

"Come on," Harry patiently urged, and the Jacksons disappeared.

Which only left Evan and Vanessa, the air thick with anticipation, about six feet of space between them. Now that they were alone, instinct and familiarity took over. The space magically vanished as they drifted into each other's arms.

"Van..." Evan whispered. He closed his eyes and, cupping Vanessa's face, kissed her with a languid intensity that suggested a great longing, but also all the time in the world to satisfy it. The soft pliancy of her mouth and the feel of her body pressed to his made Evan feel normal again for the first time in days. Nothing had changed. They still loved and needed each other. *No matter what...*

Vanessa sighed when Evan released her mouth. She put her arms around him and kissed the side of his neck. As she rested her head on his shoulder she'd never felt more sure of where she belonged.

"It's not us, is it?" Vanessa murmured.

"No," Evan said, the sound rumbling deep in his chest.

Vanessa began to smile, feeling Evan's large hand on the back of her neck. "Was this your idea?"

He chuckled. "I decided to take the legal approach. Bring the principals together in a neutral zone to talk it out. Try to reconcile the differences."

"You had Gladys and Harry lie to me?" she asked incredulously.

"No, that was purely their idea. They just wanted to be part of the plan."

Vanessa smiled nonetheless. "You can't trust anyone these days. Very good idea, Counselor. Wish I'd thought of it—although I did have something else in mind."

"What?"

"I was going to go to your office with a white flag of truce tied to my umbrella—" Evan laughed out loud "—and if you weren't there I was going to leave a milk-chocolate turkey on your desk."

"Bribing a lawyer?" he asked in mock scandal.

"Absolutely."

Evan's eyes were filled with warmth and suppressed amusement. He kissed Vanessa briefly and hugged her. "I love you."

"It's a good thing," she whispered, her voice suddenly husky and thick with relief. "Otherwise I would have looked pretty silly with that turkey."

For a long moment, just for the sheer pleasure of it, they gazed into each other's eyes.

"What do we do now?" she asked.

"We thank Gladys and Harry. We go back to my place—"

"I know. And we microwave popcorn and watch a video."

Evan grinned wickedly as he gathered Vanessa into a close embrace once more. "Eventually. There's something else we need to do first."

She sighed in anticipation. "I agree. But I was talking about tomorrow."

"We're going to have Thanksgiving."

"Shall we tell Gladys and Harry we'll accept their invitation?"

Evan began to smile somewhat cryptically. He framed Vanessa's face and kissed her several times. He trailed kisses across her cheek and the edge of her jaw. "I have another idea." he whispered into her ear.

VANESSA GLANCED around the kitchen.

The turkey, stuffed with sausage-and-chestnut dressing, was in the oven. Waiting to be cooked or prepared were rice pilaf with pine nuts and raisins, glazed carrots and brussels sprouts. There were also turnips, kasha and couscous; macaroni-and-cheese, collard greens and at least a half-dozen other ethnic dishes that reflected the input of the residents. The day was going to be a multicultural celebration and feast offered up for the purpose of saying thanks.

When Evan had told Vanessa of his idea to help with Thanksgiving dinner at the church shelter, she'd been moved almost to tears. Because in Evan's suggestion was the very essence of what she thought Thanksgiving was about. Not the self-gratification of eating from a table of plenty, surrounded by people you were assured loved you. The significance was about giving to others, sharing the good times and the bad. The food, after all, was just a symbol for generosity and love.

Vanessa had stopped worrying about her mother, had stopped being stung by the Holdens' rejection. She and Evan would love each other and take their chances like everyone else. Certain of *his* love and respect, Vanessa believed that together they could do anything.

Feeling a hand slide across her shoulders, she turned to smile into Evan's eyes. "Hi," she said softly. "How's it going?"

"Fine. Pastor Hitchcock and I have somehow jerry-rigged five tables. Each one'll seat ten people." He took a deep whiff of the kitchen air. "Smells like Thanksgiving to me. Are there any samples yet?"

Vanessa laughed and gave Evan one of the freshly made deviled eggs she was arranging on a platter.

"Mmm-mmm," he said in exaggerated fashion.

"Gladys Jackson made them. She also made a casserole of candied yams."

"I think I could fall in love with her," Evan said as he tried to pull Vanessa into his arms. "But my heart has already been staked out."

Vanessa evaded the amorous embrace with a gentle push on his chest and a light laugh. "I'm very pleased to hear that. But no more samples."

"Vanessa?"

Both Vanessa and Evan turned guiltily at the sound of the pastor's voice. The man was struggling through the kitchen door with two hugh plastic containers, one in each arm.

"Morgenstern's Deli just dropped off five pounds each of coleslaw and potato salad. Thank you," Pastor Hitchcock said as Evan quickly relieved him of the load. "Will all this fit into the refrigerator? You know, I was thinking perhaps we shouldn't try to serve dinner buffet fashion, after all. It might take too long. On the other hand I don't see how we can easily carry almost fifty plates of food to the tables..." He glanced around in distraction. "Is everything okay here?"

Evan laughed. "*We're* doing great. *You're* a nervous wreck, Pastor. Calm down. Everything's under control. What do you want me to do next?"

"Well, I'm sure we're going to need more chairs. If you'll come with me I think there're some in the storage shed out back..." The pastor was already headed for the rear exit. "Oh! And Vanessa. Forgive me for almost forgetting. Your mother's here."

Evan stopped in his movements and looked sharply at Vanessa. Her reaction would have been hard for anyone else to decipher. Her eyes stared blankly at the pastor. And although the pastor might have taken her momentary silence as acknowledgment and acceptance, Evan knew that Vanessa was feeling surprise—and trepidation.

Vanessa gave Pastor Hitchcock a quick nod of thanks. "Where is she?"

"She was right behind me. Perhaps all the activity caught her attention. Now, Evan, if you'll follow me..."

The pastor went through the rear exit, but Evan hesitated and walked back to Vanessa. Her initial shock was gone, however, and when Evan touched her arm she looked at him and smiled. "It's okay," she said to his silent question before she walked out of the kitchen and into the open resident hall.

Katherine Moran, dressed in the black knit jump-suit she'd purchased with her daughter and carrying a shopping bag, was slowly walking around the shelter, taking in its occupants and the temporary state of their existence. Occasionally she'd stop to say something to someone. An older man, a young girl, a teenager. She paused to watch a game three little boys were playing and said something to them that made them laugh. Vanessa silently watched her mother's progress, wondering what impressions she was forming of what she saw.

"Mother?"

Mrs. Moran turned, saw Vanessa watching her and made her way across the room to her side.

"I thought you might be here at the shelter," Mrs. Moran said smoothly. "I tried to get here sooner, but I couldn't recall the name of the church. I had to look for that article you sent me about Evan. Now I'm glad I never throw anything away."

"What are you doing here? I assumed you left yesterday for Sacramento and Uncle Walter's."

Her mother sighed. "No...no. I decided not to go, after all. I thought about it, and quite frankly, I decided Walter didn't need me in California. The house will be filled with Lee's family and their friends, and I won't know anyone."

"Is that the only reason?" Vanessa asked. She took the shopping bag from her mother and began helping her out of her coat.

"Well...I also don't need to be running all over the country to spend the holidays with other people's family when *my* family is here." She turned to look at her daughter, and her expression was guileless. "Am I too late?"

Vanessa smiled. "No, you're not too late." With a short shake of her head she took her mother's arm and kissed her on the cheek. The softly pliant and sweet-smelling skin recalled for Vanessa how, when she was a little girl, she'd climb into her mother's lap for hugs and kisses and the reassurance that she'd always be loved, always be safe. Now, as then, Vanessa found herself seeking her mother's acceptance. Did her sudden appearance mean she had it?

"Actually, once I figured out you were here, I thought I could help." Katherine Moran glanced over at the still-bare tables set up for Thanksgiving dinner. "Hand me that bag." She reached for the shopping bag.

"What is all this?" Vanessa asked, giving the bag to her mother.

Mrs. Moran began pulling something from the top of the bag. "Nana's old table cloths. The damask white-on-white ones you wanted. Don't you think they'd work on the tables?"

Vanessa grinned. "I think they'd be perfect."

"Van?"

Mrs. Moran stared over her daughter's shoulder and into the face of a man standing several feet behind her.

Vanessa turned and held out her hand. He came forward to place his hand around Vanessa's waist, instead.

"Mother, this is Evan."

There was a brief moment during which Evan and Vanessa's mother looked sharply at one another. The moment was not hostile, only uncertain. Vanessa found herself leaning back into Evan's chest as if to both give and get support. Finally he held out his hand to Mrs. Moran and smiled at her. She returned the gesture with the kind of formality that Evan took as poise and self-confidence—a quality Vanessa shared.

Vanessa realized her mother was trying to probe the intentions of this man she'd thought of as alien. She knew her mother would see nothing but sincerity there. And she would also see that her daughter was allied with him, not with herself. As Vanessa continued to watch her mother, she saw no sign of resentment, only acquiescence, and she breathed a silent sigh of relief.

"I'm glad we're finally able to meet," Evan said smoothly.

"Well, it hasn't been for want of trying on Vanessa's part," Mrs. Moran said honestly.

"I know. I understand." Evan nodded. "We're both glad you're here now."

"Me, too," the older woman said, and her expression showed she meant it. "I'm sorry it's taken so long."

Katherine Moran took on the chore of setting the tables, using her late-mother's table linens to bring a bright and pristine magic to the room. There was no time for Vanessa and Evan, separately or together, to react to Mrs. Moran's unexpected appearance and apparent change of heart. But they both felt as if they'd been relieved of one formidable barrier and had gained a valuable supporter.

Prepared dishes of food began to accumulate in the kitchen, and Vanessa wondered if perhaps there was too much, then decided better that than not enough. She sat Harry Jackson down at a table and assigned him the task of folding napkins. Gladys played with and tended to baby Kevin, while Terry made herself Vanessa's assistant. Mrs. Moran came to the rescue when no one knew how to enlarge the recipe to make enough gravy to serve fifty people.

Once, as Vanessa and Evan passed each other, both on their way to other tasks, he caught her arm and pulled her into the small alcove beneath the stairs. And he kissed her. It was a kiss that was thoroughly intimate, but more warm and reassuring than passionate. It was a kiss to express love, not desire, although it also served as a prelude to much later, when they would be alone to fulfill this promise.

A little after two in the afternoon Vanessa took off her apron and surveyed the foil-covered platters of steaming food. She and Terry and the rest of the kitchen squad went to join everyone else now getting settled and ready for Pastor Hitchcock's nonsectarian service, to be followed by Thanksgiving dinner. Vanessa glanced around the now-crowded room. She spotted her mother and Gladys in conversation. Harry and the pastor stood by the podium at the front of the room. Evan was nowhere to be seen. Deciding there must have been something else that had required Evan's attention, Vanessa moved to join her mother and Gladys. Then she heard Evan call her name.

With a smile already curving her lips Vanessa turned around, prepared to ask him what he'd been up to. But he wasn't alone. She stood still as he approached. His expression was cautious as he tried to gauge Vanessa's reaction to the couple with him. For she could see a striking family resemblance. The two other people were obviously Evan's parents.

She crossed to meet the trio halfway. Evan took her hand and his smile was supportive. Vanessa wondered if any of them could hear the way her heart was galloping, or if they could detect the protective cloak that had dropped over her features. But in the older Holdens' faces Vanessa did not see animosity or contention. She saw hesitancy and almost shyness.

"Vanessa, these are my parents," Evan said unnecessarily.

She shook hands blindly with each in turn, and they introduced themselves by their first names. But because she'd never met the Holdens before and could not yet emotionally connect them to the person she knew Evan to be, Vanessa only saw in that instant a white couple in their sixties. It was an eerie sensation, and Vanessa realized his parents must have been experiencing something similar. They would just be seeing a slender young woman, certainly very pretty, with the erect bearing of a dancer. One with cinnamon-colored skin and large dark eyes.

For Vanessa the moment began to change when she noticed that Evan had his mother's eyes and the shape of her mouth and chin. From his father he'd inherited certain physical mannerisms. She saw the moment change for the Holdens, too. Their smiles grew warmer, and Vanessa sensed they were now seeing the woman their son loved. Not just a concept, but a real flesh-and-blood woman.

"We didn't tell Evan we were coming," Mr. Holden explained to Vanessa as if to absolve Evan. "We wanted to surprise him."

"It worked," Evan commented dryly.

"Maybe you want a little time alone with Evan," Vanessa said, already taking a step away and trying to free her hand.

"No!" the Holdens exclaimed in one voice.

"Actually we wanted to see you both," Mr. Holden said somewhat awkwardly. He looked at Vanessa. "To apologize."

Vanessa felt Evan squeeze her hand tightly, but they stood still and let Mr. Holden struggle through.

"I guess we forgot for a moment that we raised Evan, both of our sons, to use more than their eyes to see and to treat people as individuals." He paused and exchanged an uncertain glance with his wife. She smiled even more warmly at Vanessa.

"Unfortunately we let our fear get the better of our judgment, and we were very unfair to you."

Vanessa felt no resentment, just sadness for the unnecessary hurt Evan's parents had inflicted not just on her, but on themselves. "Please don't apologize. I think it's been difficult for all of us." She glanced meaningfully at Evan. "But I know and trust . . . and love Evan enough to believe his parents couldn't be cruel people.''

''No. Just victims of ignorance.'' Mrs. Holden's voice shook.

Evan leaned over to kiss his mother's forehead. ''It's okay, Mom.''

''Evan's right. It *is* okay. I'm happy to meet you, Mrs. Holden.''

''Marsha, please,'' Evan's mother said, reaching out to grab Vanessa's free hand briefly. She laughed nervously and blinked back the hint of moisture in her eyes.

''Evan called to say this is where you'd both be for Thanksgiving. It got his mother and me thinking,'' Stuart Holden said. ''Evan, we brought those pies your mother made at the beginning of the month. We'd like you to share them with your friends here. There's a box in the back of the Jeep outside.''

Evan grinned at his parents. ''That's really nice of you. I hope you didn't bring them all. I hope you kept a few for your guests tonight.''

''Well—'' the Holdens exchanged hesitant glances ''—actually, we canceled dinner,'' Mrs. Holden confessed.

''Why?'' Evan asked in surprise.

''We talked about it and . . . I think maybe we forgot all the reasons we should be celebrating,'' she said softly, shrugging. ''Thanksgiving is for sharing. With everyone.'' Her gaze swung to Vanessa.

''Then stay and have dinner here with us,'' Vanessa suggested. ''There's more than enough food, and more than enough room for everyone.''

"Thank you. We'd like that very much." Stuart Holden nodded, putting an arm around his wife's shoulders.

The pastor chose that moment to announce the start of the service. Evan drew his parents forward into the gathering of people, introducing them quickly to the Jacksons and Katherine Moran. Vanessa's concern that her mother and Evan's parents would have some sort of parental face-off was completely groundless. The three greeted one another with a sincere graciousness, and Vanessa exhaled the tension that had pumped her adrenaline. Finally everyone was seated, and Pastor Hitchcock began.

All through the brief service Vanessa and Evan held hands. She felt an intense satisfaction and serenity for how things had worked out—which was not to say she and Evan were completely in the clear now. There was merely the promise that no matter what came up in their lives, in their relationship, it could be handled with patience and sympathy.

Vanessa felt a reverence for the occasion and, in particular, a sense of wonder. What had seemed so complicated had turned out to be so simple. All it had taken was a little willingness not to hurt, but to heal. Not to feel disappointed but hopeful. Not to act with suspicion, but faith.

When the service ended Vanessa returned to the kitchen to supervise the dinner. Everyone lined up to be served buffet-style, then took their plates to find places at the tables. Mrs. Holden offered to help, and Vanessa put her next to her, behind the serving counter. Mr. Holden was recruited to carve the turkey, and Mrs. Moran made sure that everyone had a glass of apple cider with dinner.

There was one table left for Evan and Vanessa, their parents, the Jacksons and Terry. With laden plates they stood around the table considering who should sit where.

"Vanessa, if you don't mind I'm going to sit next to you," Mr. Holden said to get things started. "It'll give us a chance to become acquainted."

"Great idea." Vanessa nodded, taking her place.

"Can I sit by you, too?" Terry asked, and sat on Vanessa's other side.

Evan was flanked by Mrs. Moran and Gladys. Harry sat next to Terry and Mrs. Moran, and the circle was filled. For a long moment, as the noise and excitement bubbled around them, all gazes at their table moved around from face to face. There was a cementing of humanity, community and family that made them all smile.

"When I was a little girl we'd all hold hands around the table, and my father would say grace," Vanessa said in quiet reflection. She extended her hands to Mr. Holden and Terry. Everyone did likewise until the chain was complete.

Terry spoke up shyly. "I'd like to say grace..."

Heads bowed and eyes closed. All around the table everyone was feeling in their hearts, for their own reasons, what it was they were most thankful for.

"The Lord make us truly thankful," Terry began, "For what we are about to receive..."

VANESSA STOOD in front of the bureau mirror slowly brushing her hair. From the bathroom she could hear Evan whistling some unintelligible tune under his breath. It was a contented sort of sound, unconscious and natural, and made Vanessa feel dreamy and lethargic. Satiated. Was it all that food she'd eaten at Thanksgiving dinner, making her feel as if she never needed to eat again? Or was it simply being happy?

"Van?" Evan called out, and a moment later appeared behind her in the bedroom. He had just had a shower, and the steam still appeared to waft from his damp warm body. He wore a totally inadequate towel around his middle that a good sneeze would have dislodged in a flash.

Vanessa was only a half a head shorter than Evan, but he could still look over the top of hers, as he did now, to meet her gaze in the mirror. He slipped his arms around her middle and eased her against his chest. The moisture from his skin seeped through the back of her kimono. They smiled at one another silently, and what they communicated made Vanessa feel as if she and Evan shared some great secret that the rest of the world hadn't discovered yet.

"So, what do you think?" Evan asked, rubbing his chin in her hair.

"I think I love you very much," she whispered.

Evan arched a brow and squeezed her gently. "Thank you. But that wasn't what I meant."

Vanessa's sigh conveyed peace. "I think everything went very well. I was happy to meet your parents, and I was even happier that my mother came."

"I like your mother," he said, kissing Vanessa's neck. "She's a sharp no-nonsense lady."

"Were you surprised to see her there?" Vanessa asked.

"Were you?" Evan countered.

"I have to say yes. It was iffy right up till the end whether my mother would go away or stay for Thanksgiving. I just never imagined she'd come to the shelter. That was a bonus."

"Well, as for me I think I always believed my parents would come around."

"Do you think it was maybe some sort of clever plot?" Vanessa asked.

Evan turned her to face him and settled her hips against his. "I think it means that our folks see that sooner or later you have to trust that things will work out for the best. And I think they didn't want to lose us." He paused and probed her features. "Were you expecting some great epiphany, as the pastor would say?"

"No. Only that your parents realize they had nothing to fear from me, and my mother would see she was wrong about you."

Evan released Vanessa and, taking the hairbrush from her hand, led her to the bed. "Parents don't understand things like that. They just don't want to see their children hurt. It had nothing to do with whether you and I were happy or whether we loved each other."

She watched as he pulled back the quilt, plumped the pillows and cast aside his towel. "I guess I'm too tired to understand," she said.

He came to her and began peeling away the short robe. He planted a lazy kiss on her lips. The robe joined the towel on the floor and he gathered her in his arms. "We're not going to have all the answers tonight, anyway—and I have a much better use for the next couple of hours."

Vanessa let Evan nibble at her neck and felt his hands gently stroke her back and sides. "What about Saturday?"

"What about it?" Evan asked, clearly not interested in anything but getting them into bed. Once under the covers they curved together, Evan's thigh resting across her slender legs.

"Am I going to be on display at your parents' house? Is this going to be show-and-tell?"

"Maybe. What do *you* hope to get out of the visit?"

She frowned into the dark. She hadn't thought of that. She'd been so busy warding off both imaginary and real attacks, so busy dodging objections, that she'd forgotten this was a turning point. "I want them to understand I'm not trying to take you from them. I just want to share your love."

"That's pretty much what I told your mother when she asked if I was playing fast and loose with your affections," Evan murmured with dry amusement.

"Well? Are you?"

"I'll tell you what I told your mother. My intentions are honorable. How's that?"

Vanessa closed her eyes. "Evan? Who is Christina de Haviland?"

He was silent for a moment and then he sighed. "She was someone my parents hoped I would marry."

Vanessa was afraid to move. A sneaky sliver of insecurity wiggled through her. "Why didn't you marry her?"

"Christina is the daughter of one of my father's professional colleagues. We were in law school together. She's beautiful. Very energetic, smart and ambitious, fun to be with—and ruthless in the pursuit of what she wants, which at one time was me."

"Sounds like someone in pursuit of the all-American dream," Vanessa said with more humor than sarcasm. "What happened?"

Evan drew her closer and she felt his lips begin a foray from her forehead down the side of her face. "It was really very simple, Van. I just didn't love her. No sparks. No chemistry. No mystery...no need. Not like with you and me. My father asked me once why I loved you, and I said I didn't know. Not with words, anyway. But there's this force that seems to link us together. I don't question it—I just accept it. Maybe that's all love is."

"Where does that leave us?" she asked.

Evan shifted his position. He began to kiss her in earnest, with purpose and obvious need. Vanessa began to feel the heat that softened her body and made each touch a separate delight. Evan stretched on top of her and the masculine weight of him made Vanessa feel curiously grounded, anchored, in place...and in love.

"I think we should love each other well. That's our only responsibility. Love will be enough..."

A Note from Sandra Kitt

When I was growing up, Thanksgiving was a celebration and a day of once-a-year rituals. A dozen people from all corners of the family would converge upon our house or my grandmother's. We would dress in Sunday best, and the children would be warned not to get dirty. The men would watch television while the women cooked and prepared the meal.

The kitchen would take on the smells of foods I will forever associate with Thanksgiving. Turkey, of course, but sometimes a glazed baked ham, turnips and sweet potatoes, celery stalks and olives stuffed with pimiento, chestnuts and raisins and sausage.

It was a day for dazzling white, perfectly ironed tablecloths to replace the daily place mats. Cloth napkins instead of paper. Crystal goblets instead of tumblers. After grace was said, the adults would toast the start of the meal with a glass of sweet port, and the children would have grape juice as a substitute.

All through dinner my mind would drift and be lulled by the adult laughter and stories being retold, as they were each year, around me. I'd feel so safe, cocooned within my family, the ritual never ending.

It was no surprise to learn from my husband that our individual family celebrations of Thanksgiving were very much the same. Except for the fact that his family was white and mine was black, there were still more similarities than differences. The differences were, however, physical attributes and not character traits. We resolutely did not let that wedge itself between my family and his—or ours.

Instead we are thankful that our families raised us to be fair, honest, forgiving; to realize that the love we keep is the love we are willing to share... and that to love is thanks enough.

THE MORE THE MERRIER
Ruth Jean Dale

For wonderful new friends—
Sheryl Lynn, Ruth Wind, Nancy Lawrence,
Janet Greer and Kathleen Broderick—
who make the absence of old friends almost bearable.
And to Hamilton and Apollina, who know why.
Happy Thanksgiving, everybody.

Chapter One

ON THE MONDAY before Thanksgiving, Caroline Chadwick mailed a box of homemade sugar cookies cut in the shape of turkeys to her college-sophomore daughter; chaired a meeting of the Women's Auxiliary at the hospital where her husband practiced general surgery when he wasn't traveling, consulting, teaching or guest lecturing, which seemed to be most of the time; and drove from Del Mar to San Diego in Interstate Highway Five traffic to pick up a custom-made surfboard for her seventeen-year-old son.

Then she went home, checked the mail, telephoned an elderly neighbor suffering from a bout of flu, wrote out a holiday shopping list and rang up her lawyer, who also happened to be her brother-in-law.

"I hope this isn't a professional call," Fred Leggett said with characteristic caution. "I hope you're about to invite us to Thanksgiving dinner. Crissy's a worse cook than your mother, and I'm afraid our kids'll starve if someone doesn't take pity—"

"I'm going to do it," Caroline interrupted before she could lose her nerve. "You told me once that lawyers don't like surprises, so now you won't be."

Fred sputtered a bit. "Caroline, dear, you can't be serious. You do *not* want to divorce Adam."

"I do and I am. I know I've said it before, but this time I mean it."

A brief silence, then, "You've said it to *me,* despite the fact that I'm an insurance attorney, not a divorce lawyer."

"Law is law," Caroline said. "It's hard enough talking to someone I know about this. I'm not about to go to a stranger."

Fred sighed. "Okay, knowing you, I guess I can understand that. But what about Adam? As long as you continue to procrastinate—"

"I'm through with procrastination."

"Oh, really. You've been contemplating divorce for years without giving Adam so much as a clue. Dare I ask when you plan to inform him?"

"Soon," Caroline said, she hoped with confidence. "Very very soon."

"Riiiiight."

"This time I mean it. I'm going to tell him the minute he gets home."

"And when will that be, pray tell?"

"Thanksgiving, that's when. I've got it all worked out. The kids won't be here. Nikki's spending the holidays with her roommate, and Mark's going to his girlfriend's for dinner. Since I'm not inviting the family this year, it'll be just Adam and me. I'll fix his favorite dinner, soften him up and then slip divorce into the conversation."

Fred groaned. "And I suppose you expect him to go along meekly with your plans?"

Caroline gave a bitter little laugh. "Fred, the last time Adam said no to me was at least six years ago when I wanted to sell the Mercedes and buy a Jaguar."

"He was afraid you'd kill yourself," Fred said.

"No, he was afraid I'd get a traffic ticket and mess up his insurance."

"Caroline, that's not true. Adam loves you."

"No, Adam's *used* to me. Adam *loves* golf. Adam *loves* medicine. He even *loves* his children. Me, he takes for granted, and that's not enough anymore. You're darned right I think he'll go along with it. If I bring it up during some boring golf tournament on television, he'll say yes to anything."

"Now, Caroline—"

"Don't speak to me in that lawyer voice, Fred. You of all people know how long I've agonized over this."

When Caroline hung up she sat there for a moment in her sunny yellow kitchen, trembling. *This time,* she promised herself, *I'm going to tell him.*

She'd make sure of it. She'd do something irrevocable.

Jumping to her feet, she dashed upstairs to the large master bedroom, slid open the mirrored door of Adam's closet and began yanking out his clothing. Carrying great armloads to the bed, she dumped them across it and hurried back for more, returning again and again until she was breathless—perhaps from exertion, perhaps from anxiety.

The pile had grown to epic proportions by the time the doorbell sliced through her single-minded concentration. She jumped in guilty reaction, her heart leaping in her breast.

No need for panic; it was only her younger sister, Crissy, looking even more harried and confused than usual. The moment the door opened she rushed inside. "Quick, I need that recipe for spinach soufflé!" she declared. "And your black beaded cocktail dress—you promised to lend it to me, remember?" She headed for the stairs.

Caroline had to run to get in front of her sister and block her path. "Slow down, will you?" She paused for a breath. "You go on to the kitchen and dig out my recipe file. I'll get the dress."

"Oh." Crissy looked flustered but agreeable. "Okay." She turned and galloped toward the kitchen as if her only speed was fast forward.

Heaving a sigh of relief, Caroline climbed the stairs and slipped into the bedroom, wincing at the stack of clothing on the bed. She'd have had a hard time explaining that. Snatching the dress from her closet, she zipped it into a garment bag, then hurried out of the room, closing the bedroom door behind her.

She didn't want the breakup of her marriage known until it was a fait accompli. It was her own personal private business—well, hers and Adam's. She had no intention of justifying or explaining herself to anyone, nor did she intend to expose herself to the scrutiny of others a second longer than was absolutely necessary.

Crissy sat at the breakfast bar, Caroline's recipe file and a diet cola before her. She glanced at the garment bag. "Thanks."

"No problem." Caroline laid the bag over the counter and sat on a stool. "I can't believe you're going to tackle a soufflé, Crissy."

Crissy rolled her eyes. "I can't believe it, either. But Fred raved so much last Thanksgiving when you fixed it that I thought I'd give it a try." She stopped riffling through the pages. "That is, unless you've relented and decided to invite us over again this year."

"Sorry, not a chance." Caroline tried to put on a cheerful face. She'd had the entire family here for Thanksgiving dinner for the past five years, but this holiday was different.

Crissy sighed. "I know. You and Adam and a quiet holiday dinner for two. Boy, am I ever jealous. Married twenty years and still crazy about each other."

Caroline couldn't meet her sister's envious gaze. "Oh, come on," she said uncomfortably.

"No, I mean it." Crissy warmed to her subject. "Mother and I were talking just the other day, and we agreed you've got absolutely the perfect marriage."

Dismayed, Caroline tried to make light of her sister's misinterpretation of the facts. "You leapt to that conclusion on the basis of one dinner for two? Really, Crissy, anybody can do it. You and Fred, for example. I'm sure Mother would take the kids to give the two of you an evening alone."

Crissy stuck out her tongue. "As it happens, I'm ticked off at Fred. It's a good thing we've got kids, because if I cooked a dinner just for Fred, I'd probably poison him."

Caroline's first thought was, *The way you cook, you may anyway.*

Crissy correctly interpreted her older sister's suppressed grin. "I know," she admitted glumly. "I take after Mother in the kitchen. I burn lemonade."

"There's nothing difficult about cooking," Caroline said, glad to get off the subject of marriage.

"How is Mother, by the way? I haven't spoken to her for almost a week."

"She says that's your fault, not hers. She says she's been trying to reach you." Crissy shrugged. "But you know how she is. She refuses to talk to your answering machine."

"Is anything wrong?" Please, surely not. Caroline had all she could handle at the moment without another family crisis.

"Just the usual complaints about Eduardo. You'd think after five marriages, she'd have gotten it right, wouldn't you?" Laughing, Crissy pulled a file card from its plastic sleeve and stuck it in her purse. Then she reached for the garment bag and stood.

"You don't think there's any serious trouble there?" Caroline probed, following her sister to the front door. "She'd be crazy to let Eduardo get away."

"How true." Crissy paused in the doorway. "If it was me, I'd keep him for his looks alone." She arched her eyebrows. "The guy's not only a Ricardo Montalban clone, he sounds like him, too."

"He's a sweetie," Caroline agreed.

"So's Adam. When's he coming home?"

"Thanksgiving morning." Caroline walked outside onto the terraced redwood deck leading down to the driveway. Another beautiful sunshiny November day, and it barely registered with her.

Crissy frowned. "I never did quite understand why he rushed off to Florida when he'd just gotten home from that medical convention. Especially after all the time he spent earlier this year, teaching in Boston and all."

Neither did I, Caroline thought. All she said was, "His father asked him to come."

Crissy groaned. "You're so understanding you make me sick. You also make me look bad in front of Fred. He wanted to play poker the other night with the boys, and I hit the ceiling. I'm sure you'd not only have given Adam your blessing, you'd have made the sandwiches."

"Probably." Caroline waved her sister goodbye. "If I don't see you before Thursday, happy Thanksgiving."

"You, too—and be prepared for Mother!"

Crissy climbed into her minivan and disappeared around the curving driveway. For a moment, Caroline stood with drooping head, thinking about her mother....

Sonja Rogers Hilton Matthews Grant Fisher Garcia was a charmer, no doubt about it. Men flocked around her like... like little boys around a frog pond. She couldn't cook, she couldn't sew, and she definitely couldn't keep a secret, yet everyone adored her.

Reentering the house, Caroline slowly climbed the stairs. The telephone began to ring as she entered the bedroom. Not too surprisingly, it was Sonja.

"I just wanted to find out what you want me to bring on Thursday," she said.

"Nothing, Mother. You and Eduardo are on your own this Thanksgiving. I'm not having the family over this year, remember?"

"You're not? You could have mentioned it sooner!"

Caroline groaned. "I did, about a dozen times. You weren't listening."

Sonja rarely listened; Sonja talked. Cheerfully and unceasingly. To her, no one was a stranger; she'd tell anyone anything. She told the waitress about her fight with her husband, told the mailman about her hot flashes. Even worse, to Caroline's mortification, she sometimes spilled the beans about her daughters.

Sonja's tone grew censorious. "Does Crissy know you've abandoned us? She's not too happy with Fred at the moment, and they'd benefit from being around you and Adam and seeing how a really good marriage works. Your sister and her husband had an awful fight the other day about—"

"Mother, I don't think you should be telling me Crissy's personal business."

"Don't be silly. It's all in the family. Besides, it's not as if I told *secrets* . . ."

Which was true. Sonja never told secrets, because she didn't know what a secret was; nor did she know what "private" meant. This behavior affected her daughters differently. Crissy shrugged it off and over the years had simply become more tolerant, but Caroline withdrew and had become more private. The older she got, the more adept she became at keeping her mouth shut and her feelings to herself.

Until she'd met and fallen in love with Adam. He was different, at least at first. Apparently nothing lasted forever, she thought sadly as she tuned out her mother's recitation of real or imagined crises. Back in the early days of her marriage, Caroline had felt completely secure in Adam's love. Everything had been so wonderful back then. Why couldn't it have lasted?

"...and I said to Crissy, 'Watch Caroline when you go there for Thanksgiving. See how she does it! Why, Caroline is the perfect wife...'"

Perhaps *too* perfect, Caroline thought glumly; too agreeable, too generous. Adam had just entered medical school when they married, and she couldn't have been more patient or understanding about his outrageous hours and inhuman schedule. Of course, the fact that she was crazy about him made it easier. Nor did they have the financial struggles most other young couples in their situation faced.

Adam came from a wealthy medical family; his father was a doctor and his father before him. Adam and Caroline had never had to pinch pennies. They'd lived comfortably with his parents in a big house in San Francisco during Adam's years in medical school and residency.

While Adam learned how to be a doctor, his mother taught Caroline how to be a doctor's wife. Caroline applied herself to those lessons, sure that eventually her husband would reach a point in his career when there'd be time for the two of them.

Silly me, she thought now as her mother prattled on. She should have known their turn would never come, just by looking at Adam's parents. His mother was also a perfect doctor's wife, and his father treated her like a doormat. Although Grace Chadwick never complained, Caroline often wondered how the older woman stood it.

That will never happen to us, Caroline had thought in the beginning. Yet by the time they'd been married for ten years, with two wonderful children and Adam's medical reputation growing, he was busier than ever. That was when the first cracks began to appear in their marriage.

Not that she'd given up without a fight. She'd tried everything she could think of to get his attention, short of meeting him at the door dressed in cellophane and ribbons. Nothing had worked.

Adam was kind and loving, but in an increasingly absent way. He gave her everything she wanted—everything that money could buy. What he didn't give was what she wanted and needed most: himself. After years of soul-searching and despair, she'd concluded that he never would.

"...and I said to her, 'You think you've got troubles? Fred may not be so hot compared to Adam, but he's still easier to live with than Eduardo! You don't hear Caroline complaining because Adam's never home, do you?' I said to her, 'You don't know how good you've got it, Cristine Marie.'"

"Good grief, Mother, it's a wonder Crissy will even speak to me after you shove me down her throat that way," Caroline protested. "I'm no different from anybody else. I've always resented the time Adam spends away from home."

"Really?" Sonja sounded astonished. "Why am I surprised? You've been a secretive little thing right from the cradle. Well, I'm only your mother. You've never confided in me, so how could I know how you feel about anything?"

"Adam does," Caroline said, trying not to sound defensive and knowing she did, anyway. "The last time he was home, I actually asked him to consider taking a sabbatical but—"

"He's much too busy and important to get away," Sonja interrupted. "Eduardo, on the other hand, is underfoot all the time and— Oops, here he comes now. Gotta go."

The line went dead.

Why was every conversation with her mother an exercise in futility? Caroline wondered unhappily. Picking up Adam's favorite old gray sweat suit, she clutched it against her breast. Her mother was right about one thing, though: Adam simply wasn't interested in time away from medicine.

Caroline clamped her lips in a determined line. She was through with subtlety! If he was home now, she'd give him a piece of her mind. She slammed the sweat suit into a box and reached for the cardboard flaps to close the container. If he was home now—

Adam's voice floated up the stairs as if wishing had made it so. "Honey! I'm home!"

Omigod! It couldn't be—he wasn't due for three more days! Casting a wild-eyed glance around the telltale heap of clothes, Caroline felt her stomach clench into a tight little knot of denial.

"Honey, you up there?"

The sound of his footsteps on the stairs spurred her to action. He couldn't come in here, not until she had a chance to prepare him. But she hadn't planned to confront him until Thursday. She wasn't ready! What in the world was she going to do?

"Caroline? Where are you, honey?"

The first thing she had to do was stop him from entering this room. Flinging herself toward the door, she slipped through and slammed it closed. He was already halfway up the stairs by the time she reached the landing. Breathing hard, she looked down into the eyes of the only man she had ever loved.

Adam Roark Chadwick, six one in his stocking feet, looked more like an athlete than a general surgeon. Even a conservative dark suit couldn't conceal the breadth of his shoulders or the lithe body he'd earned skiing, cycling, golfing—all activities that took him away from his nonathletic wife.

Not that she hadn't tried to join him in his various pursuits. She had, but felt that all she'd done was slow him down.

Even so, she realized her fingers itched to wend their way through his dark wavy hair. He had a strong straight nose and a cleft in an equally strong chin. His warm smile deepened the curving lines at each side of his generous mouth.

He was good-looking, all right, but that wasn't what had first attracted her to him. It was his air of utter confidence. Dynamic and decisive, he was a man who went after what he wanted—and got it.

What he currently wanted was evident in the sparkle of his dark eyes when he saw her. Bounding up the final steps two at a time, he swept her into his arms.

"God, I've missed you," he muttered, and kissed her.

She tried to avoid it, she really did, but as always when she was near him, something inside simply melted. Closing her eyes, she slid her arms around his waist and kissed him back. Realizing belatedly what was happening, she tore her lips from his.

"What are you doing here?" she gasped, bracing her forearms against his chest to retain a modicum of control and reason. "You said you'd be back Thursday morning!"

"I got lucky." He nibbled at her chin and walked her back a step. "Aren't you glad to see me?"

"W-why, of course, but..."

What was he doing? She swallowed hard, watching him shrug out of his jacket and drop it carelessly on the floor. He reached for his tie and unknotted it, his grin growing broader and more determined.

Think, Caroline, think! "You must be hungry," she babbled, starting past him toward the stairs. "I'll just see what I can—"

He caught her arm and halted her disorderly retreat. "They fed me on the plane." He lifted her hand and turned it so he could press his lips to her quivering palm.

"Thirsty, then. I always get so dehydrated on an airplane. How about a glass of iced tea and then we can sit down and have a nice long talk."

Adam laughed. "I don't want a nice long talk." He pressed one finger to her lips, gently. "I want—"

"To call the hospital?" Caroline knew what he wanted and she had no intention of giving it to him, not ever again. If only she had time to organize her thoughts, she'd tell him, with calm and rational words, what he needed to know.

His eyes widened with surprise that was obviously phony. "Caroline Chadwick, you *want* me to call the hospital?" He dragged her against his chest, bared by the now-unbuttoned shirt. When had he done that? He dropped a quick kiss on her numb lips. "Nobody knows I'm back, so why don't we just keep it that way for the moment?"

Yes, and she knew which moment: the moment it took him to get her into bed and make love to her. Then he'd jump right back on the treadmill. Delay, stall, *think,* she berated herself. "Your parents!" she gasped, feeling inexorable pressure toward the bedroom door. "You haven't told me... how they're... doing— Oh!"

Still nuzzling her throat, he'd managed to crowd her against the bedroom door, which suddenly swung open behind her. Doomed. Her careful plans were doomed. She closed her eyes and sagged in his arms.

His body tensed, his hands tightening on her upper arms. And then his voice, not angry, not surprised, but bemused. "I just got here. Am I going somewhere so soon?"

Drawing a deep breath, Caroline opened her eyes and surveyed the room, seeing it as he must have: his things all askew, clothing on hangers lying across the bed, tumbling out of boxes. With trepidation, she realized she had no choice now but to reveal all.

"Y-yes, out of here," she said, her voice not nearly as controlled as she'd hoped. "For good. I want a divorce!"

Chapter Two

ADAM WALKED to the center of the room and turned slowly, taking in the disarray. Caroline held her breath, waiting for his reaction.

He tilted his head and looked at her, his face expressionless. "So when did you plan to get around to telling me?" he asked with dangerous softness.

"Th-thanksgiving," she stammered. This was even harder than she'd expected, but at least he didn't seem angry. That realization brought a slight twinge; perhaps he didn't care enough to be angry.

"Thanksgiving," he repeated.

She nodded. "I'm sorry you found out this way," she babbled, "but you said you wouldn't be back until... and I didn't expect... so you really can't blame..."

"Nobody mentioned blame." He tugged his shirttail from the waistband of his trousers. "But to save that kind of news for a holiday..." He shook his head, plainly disappointed. "And Thanksgiving to boot, the day we're all supposed to count our blessings. I'm surprised at you, Caroline."

His shirt hit the floor. She gulped and looked away, trying to ignore his obvious attractions. "Yes, well, I'm sorry about that, but desperate times call for desperate measures." She had to calm down, stop prattling, but she couldn't seem to get hold of herself. "At least everything's out in the open now," she rushed on. "I know how you feel, Adam, but—"

"How *I* feel?" He grimaced, perhaps in anger, perhaps in disbelief. "You have no idea how I feel."

She let out her breath in a nervous explosion. "Then tell me, for heaven's sake. Don't you think I deserve some response?"

"All in good time." Sitting on the upholstered velvet bench at the foot of the bed, he kicked off his shoes. "You'll get a response—on Thanksgiving, just like you wanted. It's your plan, not mine." Rising to his feet, he started toward her, that all-too-familiar gleam reappearing in his eyes.

This she hadn't expected. "Stop!" she commanded, holding up one hand to ward him off. "We'll have no more of *that!*"

"I don't see why not." But he stopped just short of taking her into his arms. Clasping the hand she extended in self-defense, he brought it to his lips and nibbled on her fingertips. "Didn't you miss *that?* Didn't you miss me even a little?"

She jerked her hand free and whirled away, afraid he would read the answer on her face. How could he be so dense? That was what all this was about—what she'd been missing. Even when he resided in the same house, he was never really there for her.

But she wouldn't fall into his arms in gratitude for a little attention, never again. She couldn't afford that particular weakness any longer. "What I did or didn't miss is no longer the issue," she declared, squaring her shoulders and facing him. "We're mature adults and we can act like mature adults if we try. For the children's sake..."

Her words doused the sexy gleam in his eyes. "Do Nikki and Mark know about your plans?" Walking to an open cardboard box, he rummaged around, finally pulling out a knit shirt.

Caroline shook her head. "I thought you had a right to know first."

"Decent of you," he observed dryly.

She ignored the implied criticism. "I thought it would be better for us to tell them together."

"Tell them what, exactly?"

"Why—" she sucked in a shallow breath, wondering why he insisted on belaboring the obvious "—that we have decided—"

"You've decided," he cut in. "I haven't decided a damned thing, except..." He glanced significantly at the bed, then back at her with a devilish grin. "Since nobody knows about this...estrangement, and since we're such mature adults, I don't see why we can't—"

"No way!" She glared at him. "I'm mature, not stupid!"

"Come on, Caroline," he wheedled. "For old time's sake? If you give yourself half a chance, you might even change your mind about all this nonsense."

He called twenty years of marriage down the drain nonsense? His insensitivity stiffened her spine. "I'll move your things across the hall into the guest room until we've worked out the details of the divorce," she said coldly. "Then you can go...wherever it is you want to go."

"Details," he mused. "Unimportant details." His glance locked with hers. "Caroline, why are you doing this? Really."

"As if you don't know!" Unable to withstand his probing gaze for another instant, she snatched a bundle of clothes still on their hangers and carried them across the hall.

Only three days, she thought, trying to bolster her courage as she hung his clothing in the guest-room closet. *He'll be reasonable. He's not as surprised as he wants me to believe. He saw this coming—of course he did.*

All she had to do now was keep everything on an even keel for three little bitty days.

Fortunately the children's rooms were located in a separate wing of the house, so it shouldn't be too difficult to keep Mark from realizing there was a problem—or even that his father wasn't sleeping in his own bed.

Nikki, now... Nikki would have been a major stumbling block, Caroline thought as she made another trip from room to room. Nikki was much more intuitive than her brother and perfectly comfortable rushing in where angels feared to tread.

Caroline entered the hall again, saw Adam and stopped short. He lounged there, drinking a can of soda. He didn't offer to lend a hand, didn't even offer advice. Just watched her scurry back and forth. She might have called his expression baffled if she hadn't known him so well. Adam Chadwick, baffled? He'd learned decisiveness in surgeon's training and applied it to every aspect of his life. He was never uncertain about anything.

The front door slammed below and Caroline started. She darted a frenzied glance at her husband—who merely shrugged.

"Mom, I'm home!"

Adam straightened, a broad grin creasing his attractive face. "Mark," he said with the bone-deep satisfaction of a man who loves his son.

Watching her husband bound down the stairs two at a time, Caroline swallowed back the lump in her throat. Adam adored his children; she would never deny that. His feelings for her, on the other hand, remained in doubt.

He'd acted surprised when she told him she wanted the divorce, but he shouldn't have. Perhaps she'd misinterpreted what she'd seen. Had he been hurt, annoyed? Or was he, deep down, perhaps a little bit relieved?

It wounded her to consider that possibility, because the truth was, Adam was the only man she'd ever loved and the only man she ever *would* love. She just wasn't willing to spend the rest of her life waiting for him to turn to her. With Nikki in her second year of college and Mark about to graduate from high school, it was time for Caroline to think about her own needs, if she ever intended to do so.

She'd be forty years old December 12, she reminded herself as she followed Adam down the stairs. She'd loved this man for two decades, but she was tired of settling for half a loaf. Her home, her children, volunteer work for school, hospital and community were no longer enough.

She'd finally asked Adam for the divorce and she didn't regret it. Well, maybe she did just a little when she saw him put his arms around their son and haul him into a bear hug.

MARK SCOOPED a third slab of meat loaf onto his plate and reached for the mashed potatoes. Much to Caroline's relief, the boy had kept up a running commentary since the three of them had sat down to the evening meal.

"So how's Grandpa doing?" he inquired of his father, once he'd finally run out of personal anecdotes.

Adam shrugged. He'd been attentive to his son but not very forthcoming himself. "You know Grandpa." He poked around at his meat loaf without much interest.

"Yeah." Mark laughed. "And Grandma Grace?"

"Busy."

Caroline gave her husband a sharp glance. Grace Chadwick was always busy—busy doing exactly what her husband wanted her to do. Caroline had always liked her in-laws but found it hard to respect a woman who let her husband walk all over her. Of course, that had been before Caroline decided she was doing the same thing. Now she realized she felt more sympathy than disdain for her mother-in-law.

It had been Grace who'd taught Caroline what a doctor's wife needed to know. In retrospect, she realized it boiled down to one basic dictum: medicine is a noble calling, so you must always put his interests ahead of your own. Caroline had learned the lesson perhaps too well.

Mark drained his glass of milk. "How about you, Dad? You look, I dunno, sorta tired or something."

Adam glanced up from a solemn perusal of a stalk of broccoli. "Yeah, I guess I am a little. It's good to be home, even—" He broke off abruptly, looking at Caroline, his expression thoughtful.

She held her breath. Surely he didn't intend to say anything to Mark about their personal troubles. She couldn't bear it if he betrayed her that way.

He didn't, possibly thanks to Mark's timely interruption.

"One of Mom's great Thanksgiving feasts is just what you need. Turkey and all the trimmings—yum!" Mark licked his lips in anticipation.

Adam nodded. "I think I need the spirit of Thanksgiving more than I need the meal this year," he said softly. "It'll seem a little strange, though, not having the entire family gathered round for the holiday that's supposed to bring us all together."

"Yeah, I guess." Mark obviously had no idea what his father was talking about but, being an agreeable sort, was prepared to go along with anything. "Don't worry, it won't be that strange. Mom'll still get out all the dumb little holiday decorations Nikki and I have been dragging home since kindergarten, and there'll be all the parades on television and—"

The doorbell cut him off midsentence. Before anyone could rise to the summons, the sound of an opening door was followed by Crissy's cheery call. "Caroline? Yoo-hoo, it's us!"

It was indeed. Crissy and Fred and their two kids, eight-year-old Jimmy and eleven-year-old Jennifer, trooped into the kitchen and stopped at the sight of the Chadwicks dining in the attached solarium.

Actually everybody except Fred stopped. Caroline's divorce lawyer, the only one of the new arrivals who was in the know, fell back a couple of steps. His glance swung from his client to her husband.

Mark jumped up from the table. "Sit here, Aunt Crissy," he offered. "I'm finished." Picking up his plate, he carried it into the kitchen.

Crissy accepted without hesitation. "Would you like to make major brownie points with your auntie?" she called after him.

"Sure."

She fished in her pocket and pulled out a five-dollar bill. "Take these kids away and buy 'em an ice cream cone or something before I kill them," she instructed. "Buy yourself one, too. There's a good boy."

Without missing a beat, she swung around toward Adam. "Welcome home, stranger. Nobody expected you until Thanksgiving."

"That's right," Fred agreed, slipping into the fourth chair. His head might have been attached by a swivel, the way he kept looking from Caroline to Adam and back again. "Your wife said—"

Adam interrupted him. "Ah, Caroline, my very own wife." He smiled and reached across the table to pat her hand lovingly.

Too late she realized his intent and forced herself to sit quietly. She must act natural, because Crissy didn't know. Fred didn't know whether Adam knew, Adam didn't know whether either Crissy or Fred knew, and Caroline, who knew everything, anticipated a nervous breakdown at any moment.

Adam squeezed her hand affectionately. "My wife is notoriously closemouthed," he remarked.

Fred mopped his forehead with Mark's discarded napkin. "You can say that again," he muttered.

Crissy picked up a crumb of meat loaf from the platter and popped it into her mouth. "Now that you're home," she said, "maybe you can convince that sister of mine not to be so stingy with her talents."

Adam's eyes widened. "She's stingy with her... talents?"

Crissy nodded, completely out of contact with the currents sweeping around the table. "I know she's been planning this intimate little Thanksgiving dinner for two..."

Caroline all but flinched.

"...and she's planning all kinds of special surprises..."

Fred *did* flinch, then tried to cover up by reaching for a dinner roll and stuffing it into his mouth. Finding Adam here was obviously something Fred hadn't bargained on. Caroline clearly remembered hearing him say, "One thing attorneys don't like is surprises."

"...but now you're home early and all the newness will wear off by Thursday." Crissy looked brightly around the table. "So why can't we have a big family Thanksgiving like we do every year?"

Adam's smile was positively angelic. "I don't know, Crissy," he said. "Perhaps we'd better ask your sister."

Everyone looked at Caroline expectantly.

"Why, because I...that is..." Feeling trapped, Caroline fumbled with the napkin on her lap and managed to drop it. Her reasons were nobody's business!

Fred tried to rescue his beleaguered sister-in-law. "Blast it, Cristine, don't be rude. I told you not to hound Caroline about this."

Caroline blinked in surprise. Although grateful for the support, she'd never heard Fred take that tone with his wife before. He looked extremely irritated.

Crissy's eyes opened wide. "Don't get all worked up, Fred. I would never be rude to Caroline. Besides, she can speak for herself." Her smile was ingratiating. "Can't you, Carrie?"

"Why, I...yes, of course, only—"

"You don't have to answer that!"

Fred's interjection astonished them all.

Crissy laughed. "Gosh, Fred, you sound just like a lawyer," she teased. "Relax, why don't you? You're among friends here, not in court."

"That's right," Adam agreed smoothly. "It's not as if you were *protecting your client* or anything."

Fred's heavy eyebrows bunched together in consternation. Caroline stifled a groan. Oh, Lord, Adam had guessed that she'd gone to Fred for legal advice.

Crissy picked up a spoon and pulled the almost empty dish of mashed potatoes closer. Clueless as usual, she scraped up a bite.

"Didn't you have any dinner?" Caroline inquired, eager to change the subject.

"Sure, but it was lousy," Crissy said. "Now on the subject of a family Thanksgiving—"

"I'm sure Mother and Eduardo would be delighted to have an invitation to *your* house."

Crissy looked crestfallen. "Gosh, Caroline, it isn't like you to be so selfish," she complained, ignoring her husband's glowering gaze.

Caroline lifted her chin. "I suppose it isn't," she agreed, "and I'm sorry, but this year—" she gave Adam a warning glance"—this year, the Chadwicks are dining alone on Thanksgiving." *For the last time,* she thought, but did not say aloud.

Crissy sighed and gave in gracefully. "Never say I'm not a good sport. To tell you the truth, I'm green with envy." She glanced at Fred. "Aren't you green with envy?"

"No," Fred said. "I'm just green. Period."

"FRED KNOWS," Adam said after the Leggetts had departed.

"Yes." Caroline hated to admit it somehow.

"How long has he known—that you want a divorce, I mean?"

"How long?" Caroline pretended to mull this over, unable to lie but reluctant to tell the truth. "A little while actually."

"A week?"

"A little longer than that."

"A month?"

"More. Hey, I think I'll go see if I can find the Thanksgiving decorations. Remember that little *papier-mâché* cornucopia and the—"

"Two months? A year?" He almost shouted the last word but caught himself quickly and calmed down.

"Longer than that," she murmured, then added, "I'll bet that stuff is in the storage closet under the stairs."

"More than a year?" Adam raked his fingers through his hair, leaving it so disheveled that she ached to smooth it. "How long have you been planning that little homecoming surprise?"

"Don't ask." She walked to the kitchen door. "If you'll excuse me—"

"How long?"

"Five years!" She yelled the words at him, whirled and ran out of the room.

He didn't follow her.

Thank heavens, she assured herself when she slipped into the big cold king-size bed that night. But somehow she slept worse with him across the hall than she had when he'd been across the country.

Chapter Three

"YOU LOOK TIRED," Adam announced with almost evil satisfaction the next morning. He regarded her across his coffee cup. "Didn't you sleep well?"

He obviously had, Caroline noted with irritation. He looked terrific, all tall and tan and confident. As usual.

"Fine," she said with appropriate coolness. "Now, about Thanksgiving, I think we should eat early and then we can talk."

"Okay, okay, if you say so." He was even attractive when he frowned. "I'm still trying to get over the way you talked to your sister last night. You *always* have the family over for the holiday."

"And you *always* tell me I should let somebody else take a turn," she reminded him.

He looked innocent as a newborn lamb. "What do I know about it? You were right to ignore me. Why don't you call your mom and your sister and tell them you've changed your mind?"

"Adam!" She forced herself to meet his brilliant gaze without flinching. Why did she let him get her so rattled? She sucked in a deep desperate breath and spoke as calmly as she could. "You and I have too many things to settle to let ourselves be distracted by a crowd. Mom and Crissy and Fred and the kids can survive one holiday on their own. Trust me on that."

"I do trust you, Caroline. Apparently more than you trust me."

That hurt. Really hurt. "Trust isn't the issue here," she said with dignity. "Why are you giving me such a hard time? Do you want to talk about this now, is that it? Because if you do, we don't have to wait until Thursday. In fact, it might be better if we don't."

His expression grew hard. "You said Thanksgiving, so Thanksgiving it is. Come hell or high water, I'll lay my cards on the table—and expect you to do the same. Just remember that you're the one who insisted—"

"Yoo-hoo! Caroline, it's me! I need you, Caroline!"

The hair on the nape of Caroline's neck stood straight up. When had her mother arrived? She hadn't even heard the doorbell.

"It's Sonja," Adam announced unnecessarily. "She sounds—"

The word he never got to say was "hysterical," for at that moment the kitchen door smashed wide to reveal Sonja Garcia. Tears streamed down her cheeks; she cried more prettily than any woman in America, Caroline thought, having grown almost immune to her mother's tears through overexposure.

Sonja paused dramatically in the doorway, drawing herself up to her full five feet three inches. She bit her trembling lower lip for a theatrical moment before speaking.

Then she announced in quivering tones, "Caroline, I've left your stepfather! It's all over between us! May I stay with you and your adorable husband—"

she bestowed a watery smile upon said adorable husband ''—for a few days while I decide what to do with . . . what's left of my life?''

Caroline groaned. The last thing she wanted during this unsettled period in *her* life was the presence of her mother—the very last.

Not that she didn't love Sonja. She did. But if ever there was a person who could demonstrate how *not* to make a marriage work, Sonja was it. After the death of her first husband, the father of her two daughters, she'd married four more times. Truth to tell, Caroline hadn't seen anything wrong with any of her stepfathers.

None of them drank too much; none of them was abusive in any way; all of them were financially independent. But Mother always found something to criticize—frequently and loudly and in great detail. Then she'd divorce them, and before Caroline or Cristine could turn around, suitors would start lining up at the door again.

''Whatever she has,'' Crissy used to say, ''we'd make a fortune if we could bottle it.''

Sonja was a wonderful mother in many ways. Both her daughters adored her, but *one* of her daughters was not in any position to deal with another marital mix-up at the present time.

So, as Caroline hugged and comforted her mother, she suggested desperately, ''Are you sure you wouldn't rather go to Crissy's this time? I know how much you enjoy being around your youngest grandchildren.''

Sonja raised her head from Caroline's shoulder and hiccupped; she did even that with style. ''I'm too distraught to deal with little ones at the moment," she moaned. "I need ... tranquillity. Where better to get it than here, in the midst of all this love and ... loyalty?"

That last word seemed to push her over the edge, and she collapsed back into her daughter's arms.

Adam patted his mother-in-law on the shoulder, his expression overly solicitous. "There, there, Sonja," he soothed in his best bedside manner. "You've come to the right place, dear." He lifted mischievous eyes to Caroline. "Shall I prepare the guest room?"

"No!"

Sonja lifted her head again, her expression wounded. "Why, Caroline, you don't welcome me into your home? Me, your own mother, in my hour of need?"

"No, no, Mom, you misunderstood," Caroline hastened to object. She spared a censorious glance at her husband, who definitely hadn't misunderstood. "I—I'm redoing the guest room and it's a mess. You can stay in Nikki's room, since she won't be home for the holiday."

A trembling smile curved Sonja's lips. "Thank you, my darling," she said wearily. "I knew you wouldn't let me down. I'll enjoy staying in Nikki's room, surrounded by things that remind me of...my own...lost youth."

"Maybe you'd prefer the guest room, after all," Adam inserted hopefully. "Just give me a few minutes and I'll have all those paint cans out of there."

Sonja declined Adam's offer, to Caroline's relief, citing paint fumes as a leading cause of headaches and premature wrinkling. Escorting her mother down the hall toward the children's wing of the house, Caroline tuned out the chatter while she dwelt on Adam's perfidy.

If he thought he was going to worm his way back into the master bedroom, he had another think coming. His ouster from her bed was a fait accompli, the point of no return, the coup de grace to their ailing marriage.

Besides, if he ever worked his way back in, it would be that much harder to get him out again—or to *let* him out, Caroline wasn't entirely sure which.

GETTING HER MOTHER settled was not an easy task, but then, Caroline had done it many times before. She hadn't done it recently, though. Both she and Crissy had thought Sonja's marriage to Eduardo was different. The fact that Sonja had left him was a real worry to her daughters.

"You mean she actually wrote a phony note to throw him off the track?" Crissy marveled when Caroline had broken the bad news by telephone.

"Yes. Told him she was going to Mexico City to think things over. He's got so much family there that Mom expects it'll take him weeks to get away, once he shows his face. She hopes that'll give her time to regroup."

Crissy made sympathetic little noises. "I knew something was going on. So did Mom tell you why she's doing this?"

"Has she told me why? You're kidding, of course. She's told me more about that marriage than I ever wanted to know," Caroline complained.

"Such as?"

"Such as—let's cut to the chase, okay, Crissy? Mom thinks Eduardo is interested in another woman."

"No!"

Crissy's shock and disbelief exactly mirrored Caroline's own feelings. None of Sonja's husbands had *ever* looked at another woman.

"Yes! And she says he's a male chauvinist pig, et cetera, et cetera."

Crissy groaned. "She's in the wrong decade, if you ask me."

"She's in the wrong decade if you ask *her*. All of a sudden she's worried about her age. Crissy, I don't like it."

"Me, either." A pause, then, "Since Mom's already there, does this mean Thanksgiving at your house is on again?"

"Not a chance," Caroline responded grimly. "This is only Tuesday. If she's still here Thanksgiving, I'm sending her over to your house for dinner. I swear to you, Crissy, I'll have her out of here by Thursday or die trying."

Actually she had Sonja out of there half an hour later, but only to go to the drugstore for "a couple of things I need." Drugstores were among Sonja's weaknesses; Caroline knew her mother would come back hours later with bags and bags of cosmetics and gewgaws of every description.

She would also, it was devoutly to be hoped, come back in a mood to discuss this situation rationally.

Standing between Nikki's twin beds, a fresh sheet spread out before her, Caroline paused and sighed. Sonja lived a life of high drama, nearly all of her own making. Caroline, on the other hand, had somehow found herself living a life of quiet desperation.

Which was to be preferred?

A light touch on her shoulder sent quivers of surprised awareness through her. She stiffened, finally turning with reluctance. Adam stood there, so close she had to lean away a little to look into his eyes.

"You startled me," she whispered, throat dry.

"I'm sorry." His mellow voice sent fresh tremors up her spine. "I thought you might like some help making the beds or...something."

Caroline laughed nervously. "You're a doctor, Adam. You don't do beds."

Her attitude seemed to wound him. "Sure I do, honey." Reaching out, he curved one hand along the side of her neck. "You don't really mind having your mother here, do you?"

"I guess not," she said, all too aware of the comfort she took in his touch. "But you've got to admit this isn't exactly a good time for it."

"Is there ever a good time for a marriage to fall apart?"

She bit her lip, knowing he was talking about more than her mother's situation. "No," she conceded, "I suppose there isn't." She pulled away from him. It was either that or lean her cheek against his chest with a sigh of unhappiness, and that she dared not do.

"Caroline?"

She paused, her chin down. "Yes, Adam?"

"I'm trying to understand."

Trying to understand? He should understand perfectly. She gave the barest nod of acknowledgment.

"How upset do you think Nikki and Mark will be when we tell them?"

Her head flew up. "They're not babies. They know the world's not perfect." She licked her lips. "To be perfectly honest, I've tried not to think about that."

"I see." His tone remained noncommittal, as if they were talking about the weather or the price of tea in China. "At best, it'll be a nasty surprise to them."

"D-do you think so?" Dumb thing to say; of course it was going to be hard on them. No one would escape unscathed from what she'd started.

"It was a nasty surprise to me, honey." How gently he said it.

"Please—" she zeroed in on the inconsequential "—don't call me honey anymore, all right?"

He seemed to consider her request. "If you say so," he agreed after a moment. "I'll try, but that's how I think of you. Caroline—" he touched her elbow and guided her gently around until she faced him once more "—my answer Thursday may—"

Past his shoulder, Caroline saw Mark pause in the doorway, a wide grin on his young face. A rush of pride and regret and tenderness swept over her, and she wasn't sure that all of it was for her son alone. Flustered, she stepped away from her husband. "Hi, honey," she said to Mark. "Home early, aren't you?"

Mark walked a few paces into the room. "A little." He glanced at the bed. "Nikki coming home for Thanksgiving, after all?"

Caroline shook her head. "Your grandmother's going to be staying with us for a few days."

"Eduardo, too?"

Mark liked Eduardo. They all did, but his brand of Latin machismo was especially appealing to a seventeen-year-old male.

"Not this time."

Mark frowned. "But he'll be here for Thanksgiving, right?"

Caroline shook her head. "Now, Mark, you know that your father and I want to be alone this Thanksgiving."

Adam wrapped an arm around Caroline's waist and without missing a beat hauled her firmly against his side. "Give us a break, kid," he teased. "I've been gone a couple of months and I've missed your mother."

"A couple of months?" Caroline couldn't believe her ears.

Adam looked startled. "Give or take a week or two."

"Adam, you were gone for six months!"

Glancing at him over her shoulder, she realized that news came as a complete shock to him. Where his work was concerned he was as precise and sharp as ... as a surgeon had to be. But in every other area of his life, he was simply the absentminded professor.

He recovered quickly. "Six months, huh? Guess that's why I missed the family so much. Gotta make up for lost time."

The knowing wink Mark gave his father brought angry color to warm Caroline's cheeks. She waited until the boy had disappeared with a jaunty wave of his hand before turning on Adam.

But he didn't even give her a chance to get started. Leaning over, he dropped a light kiss on the tip of her nose.

"I'm sorry, honey," he said. "Six months, huh? You got me on that one. Let me think about this, okay?"

He left her standing with a sheet in her hand and confusion in her heart.

ADAM LOUNGED in the doorway, watching Caroline scrape carrots for the pot roast she'd be serving for dinner. He'd hung around the house all day, to her surprise and consternation. Where before she'd resented the time he spent away from home, now she found herself resenting the time he spent *in* his home.

He'd even turned down a golf invitation from a neighbor, and he still hadn't called the hospital. Go figure.

"Let's go out to dinner," he said suddenly, "just you and me. Sonja and Mark can keep each other company. They don't need us."

"No, thanks." She rinsed the carrots in a stream of running water before placing them on the chopping block. "Dinner's almost ready."

"So?" He shifted restlessly. "What are you planning to do, hon? Avoid all contact with me until Thanksgiving?"

She glared at him.

"Now what?" He frowned, his forehead drawing into perplexed lines. "Oh, yeah. I'm not supposed to call you honey. I forgot. So sue me."

"I'm going to," she shot back. "For divorce. Remember?"

He gave her an injured look. "That was cold, Caroline. We haven't reached any agreement about that yet."

She picked up a knife and attacked a carrot. "That's why I'm fighting so hard to keep Thanksgiving private."

He shoved his hands into the pockets of his khaki trousers. "Did it ever occur to you that Thanksgiving is not an appropriate time to drop something like this?"

"When is the proper time, Adam?" She paused with the knife poised above a carrot. "I didn't choose the time—you did, when you told me that's when you'd be home. I've hardly seen you for the past six months."

"But you said you'd been thinking about this for years." He shrugged. "It doesn't make sense."

Dropping the knife, Caroline planted her hands on her hips. "Sure it does. Do you remember Nikki's splenectomy?"

"Yes. So?"

"Adam, you weren't there when we needed you! You weren't there when I got the call telling me she'd been in an accident. You weren't there when they said she was in the emergency room. You weren't there—"

"Damn it, Caroline, I was in San Diego for a consultation that day. You knew that."

"Oh, sure, I knew it. But you weren't there when I had to sign the release form to allow surgery, or while I sat in that waiting room alone. . . ."

"I can't believe you've been harboring this resentment all these years," he said slowly. "I got there as soon as I could."

"No, Adam, you got there as soon as it was convenient—after your meeting was over, hours after the fact. When you came strolling in I wanted to strangle you!"

"But I knew she was all right. I'd spoken to her surgeon. Hell, it was routine. She came through beautifully. He told me he'd talked to you."

"I needed to hear it from you!" She was choking on the memories. "I think that's the first and only time I ever lost my cool with you completely. I distinctly remember screaming at you—'I want a divorce!' "

"But you didn't mean it, baby. Everybody understood how upset you were."

"I *did* mean it. But you brushed me off, and after I calmed down I just couldn't bring myself . . . couldn't bring myself . . ." She pressed her fingers over her mouth until she could pull her emotions back into line. After a minute, she went on more calmly, "You know how much I hate confrontations. But since then, every time you pulled one of those doctor things on me, it just built up more and more."

"What doctor things?"

"Doctor things like—"

Sonja swirled through the door. "Oh, here you are, darlings." She stopped short. "Am I interrupting something?"

Chapter Four

CAROLINE, COMPLETELY rattled by the unexpected appearance of her mother, quickly dashed her hands against damp cheeks. "Not at all, Mom. Adam and I were just, uh, discussing the holidays."

"How lovely." Sonja floated across the room, patting Adam on the shoulder in passing. Sliding onto a stool at the breakfast bar, she sighed. "Honestly, I do so envy the two of you."

"Well, don't." Caroline turned back to the carrots.

"But I do. You're so compatible. Not at all like Eduardo and me. Why, even our... most basic drives are mismatched."

"Mother!"

Adam reached past Caroline's shoulders and snatched a carrot. She had just a glimpse of his mischievous grin.

He examined the carrot stick carefully before speaking. "What do you mean exactly when you say 'most basic drives,' Sonja?"

"Why, I mean—"

"Mother, we don't want to hear about your sex life!" Caroline glared at her husband. Apparently he intended to make her pay for what she'd said to him.

Sonja looked confused. "But Adam's a doctor, dear. What could I possibly say that would shock or offend him?"

"Yes, dear," Adam echoed, "what could she possibly say?"

"Stop, both of you." Caroline gathered the carrots into a pile as she tried to gather her wits. "Mother, I'm not worried about Adam being shocked or offended, I'm worried about *me*. I happen to like Eduardo very much, and I'd just as soon you not, you know, say anything to tarnish his image. Then when the two of you get back together we won't have anything to overcome."

"That makes sense," Sonja agreed. "Not that we ever will. Get back together, I mean."

"I don't see why not." Caroline dumped the carrots into the Dutch oven. "As I understand it, all he did was look at another woman. Mom, looking doesn't count. Touching counts."

Sonja bit her lip. "I don't know, Carrie. It really hurt my feelings."

Adam put an arm around his mother-in-law's shoulders. "Even Jimmy Carter lusted in his heart," he reminded her, "but Roslyn didn't throw him out."

"That's true." Sonja managed a weak smile. "I'm so lucky to have you for a son-in-law, Adam. You and my daughter are a perfect match and a shining example to the rest of us."

Caroline groaned. "Don't overdo it, Mother." Suddenly she wondered if this was the time to tell Sonja about the divorce. The strain of keeping the secret was magnified with her in the house. Under the circumstances, perhaps it would be better to just blurt out the truth.

Everything in Caroline shrank from the prospect. Still, it had to be faced sooner or later. She closed her eyes and muttered, "As a matter of fact—"

"Of course, Adam is nothing like Eduardo." Sonja wasn't listening, as usual. "I bet Adam's never once said no to you, Caroline. I wonder if you realize how lucky you are?"

Caroline's nerves snapped. "I wonder if you know—"

"We're both lucky," Adam interjected. "But Caroline's right about Eduardo. He loves you, Sonja. At the very least, you should talk to him face-to-face. A note doesn't cut it."

"But face-to-face, he can talk me out of anything—or into it," Sonja wailed. "Still, if both of you think I should give him another chance..."

"Everyone deserves a second chance," Adam said, looking straight at Caroline.

"I don't know." Sonja continued to sound doubtful. "Second chances are good in theory, but in Eduardo's case...no, it won't work. He'll never change."

"He won't if you don't give him a shot at it," Adam argued, his tone sharper.

Sonja shook her head. "I might as well divorce him and get it over with."

Caroline slammed the lid back on the Dutch oven. "Honestly, Mother, with Thanksgiving coming up and all, don't you think you might put a little extra effort into saving your marriage?"

Adam gaped at Caroline as if he couldn't believe she'd uttered those words. Abashed, she felt an uncomfortably hot tide of color sweep up her neck and into her cheeks. She steeled herself against it. Not only was her mother's marriage worth saving, it was worth saving *before* Thanksgiving—thereby providing Caroline the opportunity to end her own marriage.

Sonja sighed. "I'll think about it," she conceded. "But I must say, if that man cared anything about me, he'd be here."

"But you said you left a note telling him you'd gone to Mexico City!"

"So? If he loved me, he'd see through such an obvious fib. He'd be leaning on the doorbell right now if he really cared. But oh, no, not him, big strong macho hunk. He'll never come after me, never. I guess that shows me where I rate!"

She'd worked herself into another snit. Jumping off her stool, she gave a petulant toss of her silvery head. "Not that it'd do him a bit of good," she declared, tears starting again. "I don't *want* him to come after me. We're finished!"

When her mother had gone to repair her makeup, Caroline turned to Adam. "That's what she wants, apparently—for Eduardo to come after her. Think he will?"

Adam shrugged, his expression thoughtful. "Not if he doesn't know where she is. Maybe we should—"

"Don't, Adam." Alarmed, she shook her head vigorously. "We have no right to interfere."

"She gave us that right when she showed up on our doorstep and cried on our shoulders," he argued. "We earned that right by caring about her. And about Eduardo, too, for that matter."

Caroline met his gaze defiantly. "Whatever happened to privacy? Some things are just too personal to have outsiders sticking their noses in."

Fire flashed in Adam's dark eyes. "That's your philosophy, not Sonja's. But Eduardo's the one I feel for at this point. Poor guy's wandering around Mexico City trying to figure out what the hell's going on. It's almost as if she's . . . testing him, testing his feelings for her." He looked at Caroline through narrowed eyes. "But no mature intelligent woman would pull a stunt like that, would she?"

Caroline hardly thought that warranted a response.

ADAM FOLLOWED HER everywhere she went the rest of the day, his thoughtful gaze always upon her. And when Mark or Sonja were around, Adam did more than look at her. In fact, he showed more public affection than he had since their newlywed days.

He's just trying to fluster me, Caroline reminded herself again and again. Still, her heart ached each time he touched her hand or brushed her cheek with his lips. For so many years, he'd shown his affection primarily in the bedroom. That had been the only place she had his undivided attention.

"Your mom's watching," he whispered, patting Caroline's posterior as she leaned over a basket of towels in the laundry room. "Gotta keep up our image.

"Your mom's watching," he murmured, wrapping his hand around Caroline's ankle in an unexpected caress as she stood on the step stool stretching to reach a vase. "Gotta give her good ideas.

"Your mom's watching," he warned, blocking Caroline's path to the pantry. Before she could protest, he gave her a light kiss that rapidly turned into something else.

Caroline didn't know if her mom was watching or not, but the kiss was a powerful reminder of what she was giving up forever. And she thought it downright rude of Adam to keep reminding her this way!

Especially since he refused to discuss serious matters. "Thanksgiving," he'd say, shaking his head slowly and deliberately. "Your choice, remember?"

Frustration mounting, Caroline counseled herself to be patient. He was right. If they got in the middle of anything personal and Sonja or Mark walked in, it would be a disaster. The one thing Caroline wanted—needed!—was to pick the right time and place to break the news to her doting family.

Doting on *Adam*, not on me, she thought darkly. If she had any doubts on that score, a telephone call from Fred disabused her.

"Well, now," he said with heavy joviality, "I could see last night that you've put all that divorce nonsense behind you."

"You couldn't be more mistaken." Caroline glanced over her shoulder to be sure she was alone. "I've told him the marriage is over."

"Oh, Lord," Fred moaned. "I thought so, but then I didn't ... Damn! How'd he take it?"

"Who knows? He says we'll talk about it Thanksgiving. In the meantime he's in the guest bedroom."

"Does Sonja know?"

"Good heavens, no! If she did, the whole world would be in on it. Adam and I agree we have to be circumspect."

"I thought you just said he hadn't agreed to anything."

"Not in so many words, but he will." Her impatience rose. "As Mother so aptly pointed out, he's never yet said no to me, so why should he start now? My only problem is getting Mom out of here by Thanksgiving, and I figure I can always send her over to spend the holiday with you and Crissy, right? If Adam and I can just get a few hours of privacy I know we can reach an amicable agreement."

ADAM WAS QUIET all through dinner, so quiet it made Caroline nervous. Not that anyone else seemed to notice, with Sonja bemoaning the state of her marriage and Mark talking—when he could get a word in edgewise—about his girlfriend and his grades and his plans for college next fall.

Mark left the table first, in a hurry to meet his buddies and hang out. Sonja followed soon after, declaring herself too upset to be good company.

Caroline faced Adam across the table. "Don't think you're fooling me, because you're not," she announced when the silence became unbearable and she couldn't think of anything else to say to him. Which was a sad commentary, after nearly twenty years of marriage.

He looked startled. "What're you talking about now?"

"All the huggy-feely stuff. I want it to stop, Adam."

He cocked his head and stared at her, not smiling. "It occurs to me you're accustomed to getting what you want. Perhaps it's time I put an end to that."

"Give it up, Adam." She rose and began clearing the table. "It's too late for either of us to change now."

"Then tell me one thing, Caroline. Where did I fail you?" He sounded puzzled. "I'm trying to understand. What did you need that I didn't give you?"

"Yourself, Adam. Just yourself." The truth popped out before she could stop it. "You gave me everything money could buy—cars, houses, clothes. You were generous with the children, a good father—when you were around."

"But it wasn't enough."

"Not...really. Your family was always second best."

"That's not true."

"It is." Leaning forward, she braced her palms against the table. "You want an example? I won't even mention holidays or school events or parties, none of which we ever got through without your damned beeper going off. Let's take vacations as just one horrible instance. Every vacation we ever had was interrupted by some medical emergency or other."

"Not *every* vacation."

She nodded emphatically. "Remember three years ago when I was desperate to go on that cruise? I thought if I could just get you in the middle of an ocean, out of beeper range—"

"Wait a minute, I agreed to that cruise." He crossed his arms over his chest, his jaw thrust out stubbornly.

"Sure you did," she said sweetly, "although your enthusiasm was underwhelming. I booked, I packed, and you canceled—*three times!*"

"Damn!" He looked completely dumbfounded. "That's right, we never did go on that cruise. Wait a minute. When we finally gave up you didn't rave and rant. I distinctly remember how decent you were about it, a real trooper."

"No, I wasn't! Do you remember what I said?"

He frowned. "Something about... Don't tell me, I'll get it. You said something about... some things being more important than others." He gave her a triumphant look. "I really appreciated your understanding."

"Darn you, Adam! What I meant was that your work was obviously more important than your wife, and I was finally conceding defeat. The same day I canceled the cruise I called Fred for the first time— professionally, that is."

"But—" Adam sat down heavily "—why didn't you tell me how you felt?"

She was sorry she'd broached the subject but couldn't stop now. "Don't you think I tried? Every time I'd start a serious conversation you'd get another emergency call. What was I supposed to do, stand between you and sick people? The guilt was horrible. Or you'd..." She came to a trembling halt, biting her lip.

"Or I'd what? Don't hold back now, honey. This is the closest we've come to talking in a helluva long time."

She darted him a hostile glance. "Or you'd do something nice. Then I'd feel selfish because I wanted more of *you*, and guilty because I couldn't stop thinking about divorce."

He looked amazed. "It's hard to believe, I suppose, but I swear to God, I didn't have an inkling. Surely you could have gotten my attention—hit me over the head with a two-by-four, hidden my car keys, something. Damn it, Caroline, why do you always have to be so subtle?"

"Subtle! Well, I like that." But he'd struck too close to home. She grabbed a handful of silverware and headed for the kitchen. He followed. "Other things got in the way, too. Crissy would call, or Mom would have another crisis, or one of the kids would walk into the room and—"

"Mom, Dad! It's me, Nikki!"

He uttered an oath. "Like that?"

"Oh, Lord," Caroline moaned, staggered by déjà vu. "It's happening again. I don't believe this!"

"... and I've brought a couple of friends with me for Thanksgiving," the cheery voice of nineteen-year-old Nikki Chadwick continued. "We'll be one, big, happy family!"

NIKKI HAD INDEED brought friends home for the holidays. She positively beamed as she introduced a slender red-haired girl with a shy smile and a glowing complexion, and a handsome dark-skinned, dark-haired boy with faintly Oriental features.

"Catherine's an exchange student from England and she didn't have anyplace to go for Thanksgiving so I knew you wouldn't want me to leave her practically alone in the dorm," Nikki gushed.

"Please, call me Kitty," the young woman said in a delightful British accent. She extended a slim hand.

"She picked it herself, Mom," said Nikki. "Poor kid's never had a nickname." She made one of her infectious gurgles of laughter, then winked, inviting everyone in on the joke. "And this—" she turned to the young man "—is Marty Burilla. He's from the San Joaquin Valley." She looked suddenly shy. "I've been wanting you to meet him for a long time, and this seemed like a good opportunity, since Kitty and I were already coming home for the holiday."

Caroline knew Nikki had been dating the young Filipino student since the start of the semester; her letters had been full of him. But to bring two unexpected guests home without so much as a word of warning seemed a bit much.

The young man stood there with a hesitant smile on his face, his hand stuck out. Before Caroline could respond, Adam reached past her for a hearty handshake.

"Glad to meet you, Marty."

The boy looked relieved. "That's Martin, sir. She's the only one who calls me Marty." He darted Nikki a warning glance, which was defused by his smile. "I apologize for dropping in on you like this, Dr. Chadwick, Mrs. Chadwick. Nikki said it would be all right."

"The more the merrier," Adam said expansively. "That's what Thanksgiving is all about, right? The three F's—family, friends and feasting." He ushered the trio toward the family room.

As they entered, Sonja rose from her seat on the sofa. "Nikki! What a wonderful surprise!"

"Grandma!" Nikki rushed into Sonja's arms for a hug, then stepped back to indicate her friends. "Gram, I want you to meet . . ."

While introductions were being made, Caroline grabbed Adam's elbow in an iron grip and whispered frantically in his ear. "This is turning into the Thanksgiving from hell. What are we going to do?"

His bland expression immediately put her on her guard. "What *can* we do, honey? Our daughter is certainly welcome to come home whenever she chooses. And that sweet kid from England has no place else to go. Surely you don't want to turn her away on Thanksgiving."

"Don't be ridiculous. Of course I don't, only—"

"And aren't you pleased Nikki wants us to get to know her boyfriend? How many girls her age still bring boys home for approval?" He beamed in his daughter's direction.

At that precise moment, Nikki looked up. "You don't mind, do you, Mom?" she entreated. "I know you weren't expecting me. I was all set to go to Ashley's, but she's just come down with mono."

"Mono?" Sonja repeated.

"Mononucleosis. And when I realized Kitty and Marty had no place to go..." Nikki slipped an arm around her two friends and the three very different young people smiled in unison. So perfect was the presentation it almost looked rehearsed.

"It won't be a problem," Nikki rushed on. "Kitty can take the extra bed in my room, Marty can bunk in Mark's room, and Gram can stay in the guest room."

"Who told you your grandmother was staying here?" Caroline asked sharply. Did Nikki know more about the situation than she was letting on? Maybe Mark had talked to her. But then, Mark didn't know anything, unless he'd guessed.

Nikki blinked innocent brown eyes. "It wasn't hard to figure out. Why else would Gram be sitting in the family room in a robe and slippers?"

"Good point," Adam said. "Your grandmother is going to be with us for a few days, but she's not in the guest room, she's in your room."

"What on earth for?" Nikki glanced from one parent to the other.

Kitty spoke diffidently. "I don't wish to be a burden and spoil the holiday. I don't mind returning to campus, truly I don't."

"Hey," Martin said heartily, "no problem. My mom wouldn't like a houseful of uninvited guests dropping in on her like this, either. I mean, she wouldn't if she was alive. I'll just give Kitty a ride back to school." He backed toward the door.

Caroline felt like the wicked witch of Del Mar. How could she deprive all these wonderful young people of the Thanksgiving they deserved? An exchange student and an orphan—what kind of woman was she? Besides, Thanksgiving was her specialty. She could make this a holiday to remember. Just as soon as she figured out where she was going to put everybody. Without thinking, she turned to Adam—who smiled with perfect assurance and took charge.

"Nik, your mother's been painting the guest room, but I can have it cleared out in a matter of minutes," he lied glibly. "Sonja can move in there and the rest of you can scatter as per your plan. Problem solved."

He looked at Caroline for agreement, his brows arching.

"Problem solved," she echoed faintly, adding to herself, *and a new one created*.

But she had no choice really. Either Adam moved back into the master bedroom or the cat would be out of the bag—and in the worst, most humiliating and public manner.

Chapter Five

CAROLINE STOOD in the middle of the master bedroom with her hands on her hips, glaring at Adam. He didn't seem aware of her displeasure as he replaced his clothing in closets and drawers.

A feeling that she'd been outsmarted nagged at her, but she dismissed it. "Just don't think this changes anything," she warned. "Once we get past Thanksgiving, you'll be out of this bedroom and this house so fast—"

"You plan to stuff everyone full of Thanksgiving cheer and then drop your bombshell over dessert and coffee?" He paused in the act of jamming an armful of underwear into a dresser drawer.

She saw the wariness in his posture and leapt to her own defense. "Give me a little credit, Adam. We can at least let them enjoy the holiday."

"When, then?"

"Friday. We'll take the kids aside and tell them first, and then the rest of the family."

Not even a flicker of emotion crossed his face. "All the kids or just our own?"

He looked so calm that Caroline wanted to cry. "Our own, of course."

Adam dumped his armload and reached for another. "You've got this all figured out."

She lifted her chin at the implied criticism. "I've had a lot of time to think about it," she reminded him.

"Yeah, I guess." He tugged at a drawer. Three pairs of socks slid from beneath his elbow and fell around his feet. Bending to retrieve them, he managed to drop several T-shirts.

Swearing, he yanked everything up and snatched open the drawer. Unable to stop herself, she crossed the plush powder-blue carpet to his side and held out her hands.

"You're putting your socks in the underwear drawer," she said. "Let me do that."

He ignored her offer, shoving everything in willy-nilly. "Maybe I like it this way."

"I . . . I was only trying to help."

He folded his arms over his chest, his jaw tight. "Maybe I'm tired of doing things your way. Maybe from now on I'll do things my way."

Then before her very eyes the angry tension seemed to flow out of him, to be replaced by another more dangerous kind of tension. A smile flitted at the corner of his mouth.

"Remember my way, Caroline?"

She knew that look and fell back a step. "Oh, no, you don't, Adam Chadwick." She retreated another step. "Let's get one thing perfectly clear. You are back in this bedroom, but you are *not* back in that bed."

"Oh, yeah?" His hard jaw jutted out. "Where do you think I'm going to sleep? On the floor?"

"Yes! No . . . you can sleep on the chaise longue," she improvised.

He laughed. "Not in your wildest dreams. If anybody sleeps there, it'll be you."

She shook her head. "I'm the aggrieved party. Why should I give up the nice comfortable bed *where I've slept alone for most of the last six months?*"

"You don't have to keep reminding me how long it's been. I'm back. That's my bed, too, and I'm sleeping in it. End of discussion. If you'd care to join me..."

As if of one mind, they looked at the king-size bed, big as an island and inviting as a cloud.

"No!" Caroline shook her head in violent denial. "You're not getting around me that easily."

"Ah, would it really be easy?" Moving so quickly she couldn't avoid him, he caught her by the waist. His voice dropped to a velvet murmur. "You never did give me a proper welcome home."

"I..." She swallowed hard, hooking her hand over his wrist and exerting pressure he didn't seem to feel. "That wasn't an oversight." She closed her eyes against memories of other homecomings.

"You don't know how I was looking forward to it." He tugged her an inch closer. "And to being pampered. It's been a hard couple of months—"

"Six months!"

"Whatever. I was looking forward to returning to the bosom of my family." He looked at her with half-closed eyes. "You always make the holidays so special, honey."

She groaned. Her own eyelids fluttered, then she caught herself and forced them up again. "You haven't gotten through a holiday meal in years with-

out an interruption, so don't try to butter me up.
Please."

He enfolded her in an embrace, kissing her eyelids,
her temple. "It isn't what's on the table that makes it
special, it's—"

A pounding on the door made Caroline start guiltily. She pulled away from him, her breath coming in
shallow little gasps. He had breached her defenses. If
she knew it, he must know it, too.

At the interruption Adam exploded. "What is it?"
he roared.

After a moment's shocked silence, Nikki yelled back
from the other side of the closed door. "Hey, don't
blame me! Didn't you hear the telephone? It's the
hospital. Dr. Warren says he has to talk to you right
now. He says—"

"No!"

"Daddy, he says it's an emergency. He needs you!"
Another pause. "So what do I tell him?"

"Tell him..." Adam clenched his teeth and looked
at Caroline, then at the closed door beyond which
Nikki waited for instructions.

Caroline turned away. "Go," she said, her voice
sounding rusty. "There's nothing to keep you here."

"Caroline..."

He reached for her again but she avoided him.
"Please try not to wake me when you get in."

"Meaning, don't touch you?"

"Meaning that and a whole lot more."

Their glances locked. After a moment he shrugged.
"Well, Caroline," he said, "you are your mother's
daughter, no matter how much you fight it. Sonja's

not giving Eduardo a fair shake, either." Turning, he walked to the door, where he paused with his hand on the knob. "Be careful what you ask for." He walked out and closed the door behind him.

The threat was implicit but it didn't scare her...much.

CAROLINE AWAKENED cautiously Wednesday morning. Sure enough, Adam slept beside her in the big bed. She had no idea when he'd come in the night before. Looking at him now, she knew why.

He lay on his back practically at attention, his broad shoulders square and his arms rigid by his sides. It was as if his final thought before slumber had been, *Don't touch Caroline.*

And he hadn't, although judging from the stubborn set of his jaw even in repose, such restraint came with considerable effort.

Studying her husband's strong features, she wondered sadly what had happened to their vows to love, honor and cherish. What did "forever" mean, after all? *Twenty years...* But she had never intended her marriage to end this way. Although it was sheer agony to keep up a front for the sake of appearances she had to. If only...

Rising quickly and silently from the bed, she began to dress. As if sensing her absence, Adam sighed and rolled over, one arm sliding out to touch the indentation left by her body. For a moment she froze, sure he was waking up. Instead, a sigh softened the firm line of his mouth.

He slept on.

Oh, Adam! She loved him, and it was killing her to take this stand. But surely it would be less lonely to live without him than to go on this way. For too long, she'd been, if not content, at least resigned to living on crumbs. But no more.

No more.

WHEN ADAM CAME downstairs to breakfast everyone was seated at the table in the solarium off the kitchen.

"Hi, Daddy." Nikki patted an empty chair. "We were just about to eat."

Caroline gave her husband an impersonal smile. "What can I fix you, Adam?"

Sliding into his seat, he looked at the impressive array of food on the table. "Looks like you've already got a little of everything here," he said. "How about a cup of coffee while I consider the options?"

Caroline went to fetch him a cup. He was certainly right; she had prepared a little of everything and had enjoyed doing it.

Sonja had her usual dry toast and juice; Mark his favorite waffles and sausage links washed down with chocolate milk. Nikki had opted for cold cereal with a sliced banana and a cup of coffee.

At Nikki's suggestion and over Kitty's embarrassed disclaimers, Caroline had fixed their English guest a platter of sausage—not proper "bangers" but the flat country patties Adam preferred—and bacon with eggs, accompanied by a slice of fried bread and a fried tomato half.

"You should see her eat breakfast at school, Mom," Nikki confided. "She scarfs up everything she can find, as long as it's fried!"

"A proper English breakfast *must* be fried," Kitty admitted with mock solemnity. "But I do wish you wouldn't go to so much bother, Mrs. Chadwick. As long as I have my tea, I'm quite content." Nevertheless, when Caroline presented the huge serving, Kitty's hazel eyes glowed with pleasure.

Caroline set a mug of coffee in front of Adam and he smiled and raised his eyebrows, glancing toward Martin. The boy's breakfast choices were apparently as mystifying to Adam as they'd been to Caroline: a package of Chinese-noodle soup mix topped by a couple of eggs poached in the broth.

"Different strokes for different folks," Martin had cheerfully explained. "You wouldn't have a Chinese soup bowl around and a pair of chopsticks? No, I didn't think so."

He'd watched her prepare the soup as if he itched to take over the cooking chores himself. Noticing her amusement, he'd shrugged whimsically.

"Hey, what can I say?" He'd given her a charming smile, his teeth very white against his dark skin. "I'm Filipino, and Filipino men cook—at least the ones I know." He'd accepted the soup bowl eagerly. "They also eat." He'd dived in with enthusiasm.

Now Caroline returned Adam's smile. "I have another package of soup noodles if that strikes your fancy," she offered, tongue in cheek.

She didn't miss the alertness in his dark eyes. "I'll pass, honey." He patted her on the fanny and she skittered away back to her own seat at the table. "I had a late bite with Tom Warren last night after we got things straightened out at the hospital."

Kitty looked up from her nearly empty plate, her eyes huge with admiration. "Oh, Dr. Chadwick, it must be so gratifying to save lives and heal people. I do so admire physicians and surgeons who ease the pain and suffering of the world. They're all so very—" she searched for the word "—*special.*"

Adam flushed slightly. "Only a few walk on water and most who do are brain surgeons."

Caroline recognized his embarrassment. Despite Adam's deep commitment to healing, he'd never been comfortable with the adulation doctors routinely received.

"I'm a plain old general surgeon," he went on. "We just patch 'em up and put 'em back the way they were." Without giving the girl a chance to pursue the subject further he added quickly, "So tell me, Kitty, what's your major?"

She poured more tea into her cup. "American studies. That's another reason I was so pleased with Nikki's invitation to take part in a real American Thanksgiving."

Mark nodded. "Ma does it up right, too." He wiped up the last drop of syrup with the final fragment of waffle and popped it into his mouth. "Her turkey and cranberry sauce would have made those Pilgrims drool."

"Certainly the cranberry sauce would have," Kitty agreed with a smile. "The Pilgrims had no sugar, so cranberries are a much later addition to the holiday feast."

"No cranberries?" Mark frowned. "Bizarro!" He stood and dropped his napkin beside his plate. "So what'd they eat?"

"Meat, bread and beer, mostly. And corn, thanks to the Indians, but vegetables were hardly in vogue in those days. In fact, potatoes were known only to botanists."

Mark laughed. "Meat, bread and beer. I could handle that." He glanced at his parents. "Gotta jam or I'll be late for school." To the table at large he added, "Later."

Sonja set down her juice glass. "The way that boy talks. It's like a foreign language. Speaking of which, did I tell you Eduardo wants me to learn to speak Spanish? The very idea! And he also wants me to learn how to cook all those strange things he likes to eat— mariachis and—"

Nikki exploded with laughter. "I think that's *machacas,* Gram."

"Whatever. The man wants tortillas every day of the year, Thanksgiving included. Last year he really missed them." She flashed Caroline a quick self-conscious glance. "Oops. No offense intended, dear. The rolls were delicious."

"None taken," Caroline said. "If I'd known, I certainly could have bought a package at the store." She raised one eyebrow; tortillas for Thanksgiving?

Martin leaned forward, his face animated. "At my house, it's rice. Can't get through a day without it. Thanksgiving, Christmas, Easter, doesn't matter."

"Is a day without rice like a day without sunshine to normal people?" Nikki teased.

"Nikki!" Caroline gave her daughter a disapproving frown.

Martin, however, laughed. "You can say that again, Nik. If you think that's strange, let me introduce you to *dinuguan* or *bagaoong* someday. Then there's that ever popular Filipino specialty, *baluts*."

"Which is?" Caroline inquired.

"Don't ask," he advised.

"For me, it's tea," Kitty volunteered. "You can't imagine how much I've missed a proper pot to brew it in." She patted the small ceramic teapot beside her plate. "This is heavenly, Mrs. Chadwick."

"How about you, Dr. Chadwick?" Martin asked. "What can't you do without?"

When Adam hesitated, Caroline answered for him. "Nothing. There's absolutely nothing Adam can't do without."

"Come on, Caroline." He frowned across the table at her. "You make me sound..."

"Self-sufficient?" she supplied innocently. She spoke to Nikki's guests. "Adam's one of those individuals who's so focused that he doesn't even realize what's going on around him half the time. There's a story about an actor so caught up in his part that when his fellow actors served him dog food on stage instead of hash, he ate it and never knew the difference. That's my husband."

They all laughed, though perhaps a bit politely as if unsure how the man of the house would take this evaluation. In fact, he seemed puzzled by it, not annoyed.

"Am I really that bad? If I am—"

The doorbell cut into his words. "I'll get it," Nikki volunteered, jumping up.

"If I am," Adam resumed, "I'm going to have to reassess my...situation."

Like observers at a tennis match, Sonja, Kitty and Martin swiveled toward Caroline for her response.

"You know you are," she said, keeping her tone light. They were skating perilously close to personal revelations unsuitable for public consumption. Still, she couldn't resist adding, "Two months or six months..."

"Will you forget the two months already?" He glanced around irritably. "Who the— Who's leaning on that doorbell?"

Indeed, after the first sedate peal and a second, the sound had escalated into a veritable assault on the eardrums. That noise ceased abruptly, to be replaced by an ominous silence.

Caroline found herself holding her breath. When Eduardo Garcia exploded through the kitchen door with Nikki at his heels, it was almost a relief.

"It's Grandpa Eduardo," Nikki announced, rolling her eyes. "He's looking for Grandma. Sorry, Gram, couldn't stop him—he already knew you were here."

Spotting his wife, the fiery Eduardo burst into a torrent of Spanish. Sonja turned pale. Jumping up, she hurried around the table to stand behind her daughter's chair.

Adam pushed back his own chair and rose, an action placing him squarely between the estranged couple. He darted Caroline a what-do-I-do-now glance and she responded with a helpless who-knows shrug.

"Keep him away from me!" Sonja cried. "He's threatening bodily harm!"

Eduardo's impassioned recitation broke off as if she'd kicked him. His dark aquiline features twisted.

"No, he isn't," Martin declared. His expression said he thought they'd all gone nuts, especially Sonja. "He's saying he missed you, he can't bear to live without you, he thinks you're a..." He licked his lips, obviously searching for the proper word. "He thinks you're a goddess!"

Sonja straightened. "He does?"

"Sí!" Eduardo took a step toward her, his expression haughty. "You are also my wife and—" Another musical outpouring in Spanish erupted, accompanied by sweeping gestures.

"There he goes again!" Sonja covered her face with her hands.

"Oh, wow!" Martin leaned forward, a study in concentration. "He says you're driving him crazy. He says he thought by now you'd have come to your senses and gone home, but since you didn't... since you didn't, he's come to get you and that's that!"

Eduardo slammed one fist into an open palm and Martin mimicked the gesture for emphasis.

"But he..." Sonja began. She drew a deep breath and started over. "Tell him it scares me when he speaks Spanish! I never know what he's saying and..."

Martin began to translate into Spanish. "Your wife says she's—"

"I know what she says!" Eduardo threw up his hands in evident disgust. "I speak English!" He looked at Sonja, his brows lowered over snapping dark eyes. Then the glare turned to liquid remorse. *"Lo siento mucho, mi esposa,"* he murmured in a voice of honeyed sweetness. *"Yo te quiero."*

Martin nodded and turned to Sonja. "He says he's very sorry. He says he—"

Sonja gestured Martin to silence. She looked at her husband with adoration. "I know what he said," she whispered. "Even I know that much Spanish."

"Querida!"

"Sweetheart!"

"Jeez!" Adam stepped aside just in time. The two beautiful senior citizens rushed into each other's arms like young lovers in a shampoo commercial. For a few seconds everyone else sat in stunned silence.

Then they arose as one and tiptoed quietly out of the room. Not that noise would have disturbed the man and woman wrapped in each other's arms.

Chapter Six

"OH, DEAR!"

Kitty's astonished whisper was a most appropriate response. Standing in a cluster in the middle of the living room, everyone began to smile; first Caroline and Adam, then Nikki and Martin and finally Kitty.

Smiles led to laughter, and it seemed the most natural thing in the world for Adam to slip one arm around his wife, the other around his daughter. Nikki caught Martin's hand, and Caroline drew Kitty into the circle.

"But I don't understand," Kitty insisted when the laugher died away. "Who *is* that gentleman?"

"That," Caroline said, "is my stepfather, my mother's husband."

"Her fifth husband," Nikki supplied.

"Oh, dear!" Kitty said again.

Caroline gave her daughter a warning glance, which was duly ignored.

"Gram and Eduardo had a fight or something, and she left him," Nikki said as if blithely unaware of her mother's disapproval. "I guess he just now tracked her down."

"Nikki!" Caroline spoke reprovingly. "That's entirely your grandmother's business, not yours."

"Oh, Mom, get a grip." Nikki gave her mother one of *those* looks. "Gram made no secret of it."

"Gram makes no secret of anything, which doesn't give us the right—"

"Now, honey." Adam tightened his hold on Caroline's waist. "Nikki wasn't criticizing."

"No way," Nikki agreed. "I love Gram."

"Just because we love someone doesn't give us the right to invade their privacy," Caroline insisted, intensely aware of the pleasure still to be had in Adam's embrace. She needed to put distance between them but was loath to call attention to that fact.

"Sure it does." Nikki rolled her eyes at Kitty. "Isn't Eduardo something? What a hunk!" The two girls burst into giggles.

Caroline glanced at Adam. "I expect Eduardo will take Mother home now," she said hopefully.

Adam smiled. "I wouldn't pack her things just yet."

Which turned out to be good advice. When Sonja and Eduardo entered the living room a few minutes later arm in arm, it was to announce they'd decided to remain for Thanksgiving. Instead of Sonja moving out, Eduardo was moving in.

Omigod! Another one? Caroline's frantic glance sought Adam. He raised his brows and shrugged. There was nothing to be done about it, his expression said.

"I'm giving you another chance against my better judgment," Sonja told her beaming spouse. "Adam and Caroline tell me I should, and they know more about making a marriage work than we ever will."

"Whatever you say, my beloved." Eduardo kissed her cheek possessively. "I just happen to have a few things out in the car. I'll go get them."

"What?" Astounded by her stepfather's foresight, Caroline searched the faces around her but found no answers. "Nikki . . . ?"

"Don't look at me. I'm minding my own business just like you told me to." Nikki led her friends in a strategic retreat. "Wish we could stay and chat, Mom, but I called the homeless shelter first thing this morning and promised we'd come down and give them a hand. They need all the help they can get, what with the holiday tomorrow."

Martin grimaced. "And if we have time after that, we may swim out and save a few whales."

"Oh, you!" Nikki took a swat at him.

Caroline frowned. "But—"

"Don't worry, Mom. We'll keep you posted."

"Why is it that the minute she says, 'don't worry,' I *really* start to worry?" Caroline wondered aloud. Turning to Sonja, she asked, "So, what's going on here?"

Sonja looked confused. "You know Nikki, always trying to help the downtrodden."

"Not Nikki. I'm talking about you and Eduardo."

"Oh, that. He just likes big family celebrations, that's all."

Eduardo entered carrying a small flight bag. He gave his stepdaughter a brilliant smile.

Caroline met it with a frown. "Eduardo, Mom said she left you a note that she was going to Mexico City. How did you happen to come looking for her here?"

Eduardo's heavy brows soared. *"Destino,"* he said grandly. "Destiny, my dear daughter."

And that was the only explanation she got.

CAROLINE STOOD in her kitchen, surveying the fruits of her labor with pride. Six pies cooled on the baker's rack in one corner—three pumpkin, three apple. Would it be enough?

Fresh cranberries, mixed with a pungent touch of orange the way Adam liked them, bubbled and popped in a kettle on the stove. On a back burner, simmering turkey giblets added their fragrance to the savory whole.

A twenty-five-pound turkey rested on the counter, waiting for Caroline to clear out space for it on a re-frigerator shelf. She'd gone to every supermarket in town before she found a fresh bird—there was no time to thaw a frozen one—capable of feeding the crowd suddenly gathered beneath her roof.

That was what happened to last-minute shoppers, she supposed. But now that everything was once more under control, she felt considerable pleasure in her ability to rise to the occasion.

All the ingredients for the dressing had been pre-pared, ready to be combined tomorrow just before being stuffed into the turkey: oyster for Adam, sau-sage and apple for the kids. Adam's favorite sweet potatoes, parboiled and stored in the refrigerator in their baking dish, needed only a frosting of marsh-mallow before she popped them into the oven. Shrimp for the appetizer marinated in a plastic bag, while two jugs of apple cider resided on a pantry shelf, ready for mulling.

It's going to be perfect, she told herself with a sad sort of contentment. She lifted the cranberries from the stove. Although her plans for a quiet dinner followed by a carefully prepared I-want-a-divorce speech had gone out the window, there was great joy to be had in the unexpected sharing of a final holiday feast with family and friends.

Standing there in a house redolent with Thanksgiving smells, a bittersweet mixture of regret and nostalgia swept over her. How many Thanksgiving meals had she prepared for Adam?

How many had been interrupted by an emergency?

Adam walked through the door, frowning. "How do you stand all that racket?" He nodded toward the living room, where Eduardo played mariachi music at top volume. Adam had to shout to be heard. "We'll all be deaf if this keeps up!"

"Patience," she counseled. "He only does that when he's in a good mood."

"He does?"

Adam's response was the wrong one to give, for it reminded her all over again how much he had been absent in the year and a half since her mother's latest marriage. "If you were ever around..." she began.

"I know. Six months," Adam said wryly. "I got the message, Caroline."

"In that case..." She tried to shoo him aside so she could reach the refrigerator.

Without success. He gave her the same smile that had been consistently melting her resolve for twenty-plus years. "Honey, let's get out of here for a while."

His coaxing tone alarmed her. "I couldn't possibly. I'm busy, as you can doubtless see."

He caught her hands and held them tight. "All I see is that you have everything under control as always. Come on, let's play hooky—just for a little while."

She was astonished to hear herself inquire cautiously, "What do you have in mind?"

Whatever it was, she knew she'd want no part of it. She was in no mood to go to the shopping mall, and she didn't need anything from the supermarket. She didn't feel up to a bicycle ride—did she ever?—and if he thought he was going to drag her to his health club...

He regarded her warily. "I was thinking about—" his voice grew low and intimate "—the beach. Remember how much we used to enjoy walking along the water's edge, picking up shells, talking?"

Her breath caught. Did she remember? Dropping her gaze, she concentrated on the top button of his blue pullover. They'd spent some of their happiest times together at the beach.

That was where he'd proposed to her and she'd accepted. Now, on the eve of the last day of her marriage, how could she take such an emotional risk? "That's not a good idea," she murmured.

He brushed her cheek lightly with his fingertips. "I... There's something I need to talk to you about," he said. "Not here, though."

"Th-the divorce?" Dread, deep and debilitating, swept through her.

"Not directly."

What in the world did that mean? She forced herself to look at him and was shocked to realize how much he wanted her to go along with him on this. All her reasons to refuse seemed suddenly unimportant. "Just let me put this food away first," she said.

ADAM AND CAROLINE SAT on a pile of boulders at the water's edge, watching surfers far out on the gray Pacific. A light wind made her shiver, and Adam reached over to draw her cardigan more closely around her shoulders.

Although temperatures were in the sixties, the day was not an appealing one. The leaden sky almost exactly matched her mood. She and Adam had barely exchanged a word on the short drive.

He shifted to look at her, his expression unreadable. "I'm sorry about that call from the hospital last night. I told Tom—"

"Don't," she said sharply. "There's no need to go into that. It's too late to worry about it now, Adam."

He stared out over the water again. "And you don't believe me, anyway—that I'm sorry."

"Not really." She leaned down to pick up a scrap of seaweed tossed onto the rocks by the roiling surf. "You are what you are."

"And what might that be?"

She dropped the seaweed and wiped damp fingers on her jeans. "A wonderful doctor. A dedicated surgeon."

"That's all?"

"Oh, Adam . . ." She sighed. "I think that's all you are to yourself, all you want to be."

He seemed to consider her words. After a moment he said, "Maybe you're right. Surgeons are doers, but we're not necessarily great thinkers. I know I express myself better with my hands than with words. That doesn't mean I'm completely insensitive.''

"I never said you were...completely.'' She found it difficult to remain calm and unemotional but knew she must.

"I thought you were happy. Hell, I thought *we* were happy. I also thought you were a helluva good sport.''

She managed a faint laugh. "I'm not. Just because I didn't harangue you night and day doesn't mean I didn't feel slighted.''

"Slighted.'' The word quivered with frustration. "I don't get it.''

"I suppose you don't.'' She had to force herself to go on. "I know how important your work is, but I can't live like this any longer. I can't.'' She shook her head with finality. "All these years I thought things would get better, but they're not going to. This isn't just a passing phase. It's not only the past and present, it's the future. That's what I can't stand. Maybe I can play second fiddle to your patients but not to conferences and teaching and travel and everything else.''

His expression was bleak. "You could have told me before you hit the breaking point.''

Sadness nearly choked her. "Maybe I could have forced myself if I'd honestly thought it would do any good. Just like you could have given your family more of your time if you really wanted to.'' She stared down at her clenched hands. "I thought I could handle it, but...I was wrong.'' She drew a quivering breath and straightened. "You said there was something you wanted to talk to me about.''

"Yeah. My father." Adam leaned over to pick up a small piece of driftwood. He spoke directly to it, not to her. "He's retiring." The driftwood cracked between his hands and he tossed it aside.

She couldn't have been more surprised if he'd announced that Benjamin Chadwick had run away with the head nurse. "I can't believe it!" she exclaimed. "I thought the only way they'd get Ben out of surgery would be to carry him out feet first."

"Me, too." There was an odd note in his voice as if he hadn't come to terms with this yet. "But it seems he had a close call on the golf course a few months ago, and it got him to thinking about his own mortality."

"On a golf course?"

A smile tugged at the corner of his mouth. "That's what's so crazy. Lightning struck a tree he'd been standing under seconds earlier."

"He wasn't hurt?"

"Just scared." He shoved his hands hard into the pockets of his Windbreaker. "It was so random. There was no warning and nothing anyone could do, except be lucky, which he was. But it's made him question everything—his entire life, but especially his future."

She slid her hands beneath her thighs to keep from reaching out to him. He seemed so shaken by his father's sudden turnaround that instinctively she knew there was more to it. "What's upset you so much, Adam? Of course it's a surprise, but there's no reason your father shouldn't retire if he wants to."

He gave her a glance that was half grateful and half resentful. "Yeah, but it was the way he kept talking about the road not taken, all the things not done. If he mentioned one more time how much he regretted not stopping to smell the damned flowers...!'' Adam gave an exasperated sigh. ''Then, the day I left he asked if I ever regretted my decision to become a doctor.''

Ah, so that was what bothered him. ''What did you say?'' Caroline asked, although she was sure she knew.

''Hell, what would I do if I didn't practice medicine?'' Adam shoved both hands through his hair. ''He said he sometimes thought he'd have been happier if he'd been a teacher. Then he apologized. My father *apologized* for any undue pressure he might have put on me to follow in his footsteps.''

''Benjamin?'' She couldn't imagine such a thing.

Neither could Adam, apparently. ''Damn,'' he said, ''it started me thinking. And then I come home and find...''

He didn't have to go on. They both knew what he'd found.

The conversation was becoming too painful. Caroline jumped up, brushing damp sand off the seat of her jeans. ''Mind if we walk?''

He led the way down off the rocks, turning to lend a hand for her safe descent. Once her feet sank into the sand he released her and turned away. She fell into step beside him, wondering what he was thinking.

They walked for several minutes in uncomfortable silence, and then he spoke. ''You're right about one thing. For twenty years, I've taken you for granted. I thought you'd always be there when I needed you, no matter what.''

"So did I." She walked with her head down, staring at the sand beneath her feet. "It's too late to talk about that now."

The children—now there was a safe topic. "By the way," she went on casually, "has Nikki had a chance to tell you her plans to apply for a fellowship in Philadelphia next summer?"

"I haven't had much chance to talk to her."

Ignoring that invitation to criticize, Caroline plunged on. "She thinks she has a fairly good chance...."

As the gray day darkened toward evening, they walked along the beach and talked—about the children, about family and friends, about everything except that which had driven the wedge between them.

Their conversation solved nothing, changed nothing, and yet Caroline found herself reluctant to see their time together end. Adam must have felt the same, for as he unlocked her car door he said suddenly, "Feel up to a movie?"

Relief made her smile. "Sure. Anything special you want to see?" She slid into the car.

Adam leaned down to look into her face. "No. I'm just not ready to go home yet."

Neither was she. Tomorrow was Thanksgiving, but she wasn't too sure what she had to be thankful for this year. Nor was it possible to know what the holiday would bring, except that a crowd would sit down to her usual sumptuous feast. For a little while, she could pretend that everything was as it should be.

BY THE TIME they got back home, they'd managed to stretch a stroll on the beach into an after-midnight adventure complete with movie and late dinner. Quietly they moved upstairs and into the master suite, where Adam switched on a bedside lamp and turned to her.

Now what? she wondered. After an awkward beginning at the beach, they'd relaxed into a cautious camaraderie that told her he'd been trying as hard as she.

But now they were home, back inside this room where they'd spent the most intimate moments of their marriage. Feeling ill at ease, Caroline glanced past him and saw the piece of paper pinned to her pillow.

She groaned. "Don't tell me it's a message from the hospital. Didn't you have your beeper?"

"Yes. Whatever the note is, it's not the hospital." Adam leaned down and picked up the paper. He read aloud, "Mom and Dad, I have to talk to you about the homeless. Please wake me up, no matter what time it is!!! Love, Nikki."

Chapter Seven

NIKKI'S PARENTS, well aware of her penchant for drama, exchanged smiles.

"She's a good kid," Adam said, placing the note on his bedside table.

"Yes." That was Nikki, Caroline thought, always looking out for others. "Should we wake her?"

He shook his head. "But we can check to see if the girls are still up."

They moved quietly through the sleeping house until they reached Nikki's room. Opening the door a crack, they peered inside. Both girls slept peacefully.

Without a word Caroline and Adam withdrew.

"Whatever it is, it'll keep until tomorrow," he whispered, touching her elbow lightly to guide her through the dark and silent house.

Back in their own room, Caroline made a point of keeping the width of the bed between them. A dangerous tension tightened her shoulders and made her breathing shallow. She was sure he'd reach for her at any minute.

When he did, how would she react? Her head told her to keep her distance, but her heart told her something else entirely.

She'd been ruled by her heart too long; she would go with her head. Steeling herself for a real test of character, she lifted her chin and started past him toward her dressing room.

As she expected, he reached out to stop her. She stared straight ahead for a moment, then turned slowly to face him.

"Adam . . ." she began in a warning tone.

He smiled but didn't let her go. "It's been a memorable day," he said. "You've given me a lot to think about." With that he released her arm.

She blinked in surprise and perhaps just a little disappointment. She'd expected him to be more persistent. "That's it?" she demanded.

"Nope. There's this, too." Leaning down, he touched his lips to hers.

She went rigid, a victim of spontaneous combustion—and confusion, too, for the kiss was as light and fleeting as a snowflake. But warmer. Much much warmer.

Adam gave her that potent smile. "Relax, honey," he advised. "As usual, you're going to get exactly what you want—just as soon as I figure out what it is."

The next instant she found herself standing there, foolishly staring at his broad back while he rummaged in a dresser drawer.

Humming—he was humming, a satisfied if tuneless sound that set her nerves on edge. Without another word, she walked into her dressing room and closed the door firmly. She slipped into her nightgown, washed her face, brushed her teeth, all the while trying to keep her mind off the man who'd be there when she finally had to come out.

This wasn't like last night, when she'd been asleep before he came to bed. Tonight he'd be waiting for her. It wouldn't do him any good of course, but Adam had never been the kind of man who stopped short of a goal.

The lights were off when she came back into the bedroom but that didn't fool her into believing he was asleep. Cautiously she eased into bed, stiff and suspicious. Prepared to counter any move he might make, she waited. And waited...

Adam shifted, causing the mattress to sway gently. *Here it comes,* she thought. *He's about to try something.* She was ready for anything.

Anything except the deep slow breathing that told her that her husband was sound asleep. Chastened and a tad humiliated, Caroline relaxed beside him.

Apparently he really did know what she wanted, she thought, disgruntled by this turn of events. That remark had been his way of telling her she could have her divorce, without undue dissension or family scandal.

She should be happy. Well, she was happy of course. Her ordeal was almost over. Just one more day, she kept telling herself. All she had to do was get through one more day.

CAROLINE AROSE bright and early Thanksgiving morning. Filled with fresh resolve, she showered quickly and threw on jeans and a bright red sweatshirt, eager to begin holiday preparations.

To her surprise and dismay Adam was up and dressed when she came out of the bathroom. He met her unhappy frown with a bland smile.

"Good morning," he said politely. "Thought you could use some help stuffing that monster turkey." He tugged a denim shirt over his head without unfastening the buttons.

"What on earth do you know about stuffing turkeys?" she demanded.

He flexed his long supple fingers. "Hey, I'm a surgeon. I can sew that sucker up faster than you can say good-morning."

"Sorry. Good morning." *That gets me off to a great start*, she grumbled to herself while she hurried downstairs. *Now I'm forgetting to be civil.*

She walked into the kitchen and stopped short, sensing instantly that something was wrong. But what?

Everything was clean and neat. Someone had even made the coffee the night before and set the timer; she could smell the enticing aroma of her favorite French roast. She must be imagining things.

A quick cup of coffee, an equally quick perusal of the morning newspaper, and she'd be ready to tackle the turkey.

Adam entered.

"Coffee?" she asked politely.

"Please. And juice, if there is any."

She nodded, opening the refrigerator. The juice sat right there on the middle of a shelf.

An empty shelf. She stared in disbelief. The shelf where the turkey had been.

Caroline gasped and swung around to look again at the countertops. Clean . . . and empty. That was what was wrong with this picture.

"Good Lord!" Her panicked glance sought Adam for confirmation. "We've been robbed!"

"What?" In the middle of a prodigious yawn he yanked himself up and looked around in confusion. "What's missing?"

"Thanksgiving! Somebody's stolen our holiday dinner!" She began opening and closing drawers and cabinets at random, trying to ascertain exactly what had been taken.

Nothing, apparently, except the food she'd planned to serve to her guests. Nothing, except her dreams of going out on a wave of good cheer. Gone. Every last crumb gone. Turkey, pies, shrimp, cranberries, stuffing ingredients, condiments, veggies . . .

"Gone," she moaned, sinking into shock. "All of it gone. Call the police!"

"No, Mom, please, don't do that." Nikki hurried into the kitchen, Kitty and Martin at her heels. The three looked guilty as sin.

"But we've been robbed!" Caroline wrung her hands. "What do you know about this, Nik?"

Nikki swallowed hard and licked her lips. "I know everything about it. Uh . . . didn't you find my note last night?" Her tone turned indignant. "Why didn't you wake me up?"

Adam put a protective arm around Caroline's shoulders. "It was late. We went to your room, but both you and Kitty were sleeping so peacefully there seemed no point in disturbing you."

"There *was* a point, Daddy, and this is it." Nikki appealed to her father. "The food wasn't stolen. We..." She glanced anxiously at her friends, squared her shoulders and declared, "*I* took it!"

"You?" Caroline gaped at her daughter. "But why? What did you do with it?"

Sonja walked through the doorway before Nikki could reply. "Good morning," she said cheerfully. "I thought I might serve Eduardo his coffee in bed this morning." With a complete lack of awareness of the currents surging around her, she strolled to the cabinet, pulled out two cups and poured coffee.

Nobody moved until she'd carried the cups away with a final friendly smile. Then Caroline repeated, slowly and dangerously, "What did you do with our Thanksgiving dinner, Nicole?"

Nikki gulped. "I gave it to the homeless shelter, Mom. If you'd seen all those poor people... Donations were down this year, what with the economy and all, so there wasn't going to be enough to go around. It just broke my heart. I'm too fat anyway," said the 110-pound teenager. "Kitty and Martin don't care what we eat. Peanut butter, anything—"

"Oh, no, not a bit," Kitty put in. "One tends to forget the less fortunate, and we agreed with Nikki entirely—"

And a new voice, Mark's, chimed in, issued from a sleepy face and a body clad only in pajama bottoms, "I'm starved. When do we eat?"

Caroline slumped in Adam's arms. He held her tight and murmured in her ear, "Courage, honey."

Nikki whirled on her brother. "Don't be a geek," she snapped. "It wouldn't hurt you to drop a pound or two."

"Hey, what'd I do?" Mark appealed to the room in general, his blue eyes wide. "Something's going on here, right? What's Nik done now?"

"Shut up, cretin."

"In your dreams, airhead!"

Caroline, wrestling with her own problems, ignored her children. Almost to herself she muttered, "What on earth am I going to do with a houseful of people for Thanksgiving dinner and no food?"

"We'll figure something out," promised Adam, ever the Rock of Gibraltar in a crisis. "We can always go to a restaurant."

"Oh, no!" Caroline appealed to him, digging her fingers into his denim shirt. "We've never eaten a holiday meal in a restaurant, and I don't want anyone to remember our last—"

She stopped short. She hadn't meant to reveal how important this occasion had become to her. Quick tears filled her eyes and she tried to blink them away, but she knew he'd seen them by the way he tightened his grip on her.

"I'm sorry, Mom." Nikki's unhappy voice was accompanied by a tentative pat on Caroline's shoulder. "If I'd known you'd take it this hard I never would have done it. I mean, it's only *food*. Isn't sharing the point of Thanksgiving?"

A bucket of cold water in Caroline's face couldn't have been more effective. Of course sharing was the meaning of Thanksgiving. Of course she was proud of her daughter and Kitty and Martin for thinking of others first. Of course they could go out for dinner—if they could get reservations for such a large party at the last minute.

But that was in the future. Right now, all Caroline wanted to do was give her daughter a great big hug. "Of course you did the right thing," she said sincerely.

Nikki returned the hug. "Told you she'd understand," she boasted to her friends, but her relief was obvious. She added jauntily, "So what are we going to do about Thanksgiving?"

Caroline drew a distraught breath. "I don't know about you," she said, striving for humor, "but I think I'd like to go back to bed and start all over again."

The four young people laughed appreciatively, Kitty and Martin no doubt out of politeness, Nikki and Mark probably because they knew a control freak like their mother would never relinquish command of a holiday meal. Caroline had the uneasy feeling that her children fully expected her to pull off some sort of miracle, maybe shout, "Surprise!" and open the oven door to reveal a succulent roast turkey dinner with all the trimmings.

"Not a bad idea," Adam said suddenly.

"What's not, Dad? Going to a restaurant?" Mark sounded in favor of anything with the potential to fill the empty spot in his middle.

Nikki poked her brother with her elbow. "What're you worried about? Aren't you eating dinner at Amy's?"

Mark grinned and scratched his ribs. "I sorta got caught up in the excitement around here and invited her over, instead. Like Dad says, the more the merrier."

Or another disappointed diner, Caroline thought unhappily.

"No problem," Adam agreed cheerfully. He hesitated for a moment, lips pursed and eyes narrowed as if deep in thought. Then he announced with all the confidence in the world, "Here's what we're going to do. Caroline, you *are* going back to bed and I will serve you breakfast, as in breakfast in bed."

"But..." Nobody was better than Adam in an emergency, medical or otherwise. It was second nature for him to take charge. Only this time he was out of his depth. The man didn't know the first thing about cooking, and certainly not about making a meal for such a crowd out of a few cans, packages and freezer odds and ends. "Then what are you going to do?" she demanded, albeit weakly.

"I don't know," he admitted, his eyes clear and untroubled. "But I promise you, a satisfactory solution to the Thanksgiving dilemma will be found. You can count on me—count on us."

He indicated the four youngsters, and they chorused enthusiastically, "Yeah, Mom—no sweat!... Brilliant! You may depend upon it....Stand back and let me do my thing! ... Did I tell you she's the greatest mom in the world or what?"

Caroline didn't feel like the greatest. She felt like crying. Which was probably why she allowed Adam to lead her out of the kitchen and back up the stairs.

She'd completely lost control of the situation and her life. Would she ever get it back?

In the bedroom Adam massaged her tense shoulders. "You're tight as a bowstring, honey," he said, prodding one particularly tense muscle. "A nice long soak in a hot tub is just what the doctor ordered."

She found herself agreeing. Why not? The day and its events were completely out of her hands, anyway.

So a few minutes later she crawled into her sunken tub of silky bubbles and leaned back with a sigh. This would not only be her last real family Thanksgiving, it was certain to be the strangest. She might as well try to relax and stop fighting fate.

The bathroom door banged open and she bolted upright with a shriek of surprise, then sank back until the bubbles reached her chin. Adam grinned at her over a breakfast tray. Carrying it to the tub, he set it down and whipped the napkin cover aside.

"Kids helped me fix it," he said with satisfaction.

She'd have known without his telling her.

The egg in the crystal egg cup could only be Kitty's doing. No one in the Chadwick family would ever bother with such a detail. The geraniums in the Bugs Bunny jelly jar were Nikki's contribution; the napkin folded into an approximation of a bird had to be Martin's; and the sports section of the morning paper might as well have had Mark's name written on it.

Caroline took a sip of coffee; it was weak. "Mmm," she murmured. "I'd know Mom's coffee anywhere." She poked at two pieces of slightly singed bread slathered with darkly fragrant topping and hazarded a guess. "Cinnamon toast?"

Adam looked pleased. "I made it," he said, sounding as proud as if he'd announced the first successful brain transplant.

"But you're lost in a kitchen!"

"You underestimate me," he said, "*constantly.* To tell the truth, my college roommate—remember Kev?—had a toaster oven, and that's where I learned to broil cinnamon toast. I haven't had much time to practice for the last twenty years or so, but I never forgot. I've got a mind like a steel trap." He tapped his temple with a forefinger and gave her a hopeful look.

Caroline had never loved Adam Chadwick more than she did at that moment, perhaps because he had never seemed more open. Emotions too near the surface, she swallowed hard. "Then—" she gulped "—everything's under control?"

He waved her worries aside. "Piece of cake," he boasted. "You haven't got a thing—"

The remote telephone on the bathroom vanity rang.

"—to worry about." He picked up the handset and punched the access button. "Yes?"

She knew from his expression that it was the hospital. Appetite gone, she slumped deeper into the big tub. Any minute he would turn to her apologetically, announce a medical emergency and say goodbye. Perhaps he'd ask that they all meet him at a restaurant later in the day or week or month or year, whenever he could get away.

She closed her eyes. *Don't do this to yourself,* she moaned. *You don't have to anymore.*

After the longest pause, he spoke. But he only said one word. "No."

Caroline straightened in the tub and her eyes flew open. Whatever he'd been told obviously hadn't distressed him in the least. He looked calm and composed.

He listened for another minute. "Look," he said then, "I'm not even officially back until Monday. Find somebody else, because I'm spending Thanksgiving with my family." Another pause, and then he grinned. "What do you mean, why? Because *I really want to.*"

Was she dreaming? She knew she wasn't when he added a final cheerful, "Unless I'm the last surgeon left on the West Coast, that's how it is," and hung up.

Turning to her with a smile that could melt steel, he nodded toward the tray. "What else can I do for you?"

"Not a thing." She knew she was staring at him in wide-eyed wonder.

"Okay." He turned toward the door. "If there's anything you want, call on the intercom. But don't come down until I tell you to. We...want to surprise you."

"You've already surprised me," Caroline admitted. He arched his brows and she hastily indicated the breakfast tray. "Thank the kids for me, will you?"

He nodded.

"And Adam..."

He waited for her to go on, his shoulders braced as if for criticism.

"Thank *you,* most of all. I promise I won't worry about Thanksgiving."

"That's good," he said gruffly, and was gone.

HELL, NO, SHE DIDN'T NEED to worry. He was plenty worried for both of them, Adam thought as he walked into the kitchen. Two mature and five youthful faces—Mark's girlfriend Amy, had arrived—turned toward him for guidance.

Thanksgiving was all his.

Chapter Eight

"SO, WHAT'S THE PLAN, Dr. Chadwick?" Martin rubbed his hands together gleefully. He was the only one who seemed completely delighted with the events of the morning. "Where do we start?"

Adam looked at all the eager faces turned toward him—him, a man to whom a decent cheese sandwich was a major undertaking. He thought fast.

"When I was a kid," he said, "I wanted to plant a garden, but I didn't know where to start. My parents' gardener gave me a piece of advice I've never forgotten."

Sonja nodded. "I've got a brown thumb," she announced. "I used to plant tons of veggies every year, but the only thing I could grow was zucchini. And geraniums, of course—can you imagine, even here in California? You're supposed to be able to grow anything here, and all I could grow was zucchini and geraniums—"

Eduardo, slick as a pickpocket, clapped a gentle hand over his wife's mouth. Her blue eyes went wide, but he ignored her astonishment. "And what did your parents' *jardinero* say to you, Adán?" he asked politely in his accented English.

"That I should find out what I could grow, and then grow lots of it," Adam said. "That's all we have to do.

Each of us figure out what we can cook, and then cook lots of it."

WHEN CAROLINE COULDN'T stand the inactivity any longer, she climbed out of the tub and toweled dry. Wrapped in a flowered silk robe Adam had given her for Christmas a couple of years ago, she stretched out on the chaise longue and turned on the television.

She was resigned to whatever was going on downstairs, she assured herself as she flipped through the channels on the television. Finally settling on a holiday parade, she leaned back on the cushions with a sigh.

She wasn't going to worry. She really wasn't going to worry. She absolutely *refused* to worry....

After she'd repeated that mantra about a thousand times, she found to her surprise that she really wasn't worried. No one, after all, would starve.

Nevertheless, by noon she was watching the clock. By half-past she admitted that if she saw another float she'd throw pillows at the television screen. By one o'clock she couldn't stand the suspense any longer.

Dressing for the second time that day, she crept down the stairs. All kinds of noises issued from the kitchen: tuneless whistling, laughter, occasional words in a multitude of accents.

Puzzled, she halted outside the closed door. Everyone in the household must be in there. And unless her ears deceived her, they weren't at all depressed about losing their holiday feast; they were having *fun*.

Compelled by curiosity, she pushed open the door and stepped inside.

And couldn't believe her eyes.

So intent were the cooks that at first no one noticed her standing there. That gave her a real chance to watch what was going on in her kitchen.

Instead of spoiling the broth, "too many cooks" worked happily side by side. True, her compulsively neat kitchen was a mess, but for once it didn't bother her in the slightest.

They were indeed all there, except... Where was Adam? As if answering a subliminal summons, his strong arms closed around her, and he nuzzled the back of her neck. "You're supposed to be lolling around in a bubble bath," he murmured.

She gulped and gave in to the desire to snuggle closer. "If I were still in that tub I'd be wrinkled as a prune. Adam, this—" she indicated the scene before them "—is wonderful. Thank you."

"For a messy kitchen?" he teased.

"For brand-new reasons to feel thankful on Thanksgiving."

"Such as?" he asked in the same intimate voice.

Caroline sighed. She wanted to tell him that she was thankful they hadn't yet come to an irrevocable parting of the ways. She wanted to tell him that Thanksgiving was the perfect day to put the past behind them and start over. She wanted to tell him how thankful she was he hadn't taken her demand for a divorce at face value.

"Come on, honey," he urged. "What are you thankful for this year?"

Surrounded by all these people, she couldn't get into anything so personal, so she said, "That I'm not the only one who can cook a meal around here."

He laughed. She felt his warm breath on her ear and shivered.

"No," he conceded, "but you may be the only one who can cook a *good* meal around here." He straightened and said in a voice that included them all, "Hey, we've got company!"

Caroline's appearance was greeted with enthusiasm, which she returned with pleasure. "Will you tell me what you're doing if I promise not to interfere?" she asked humbly.

"Go ahead, Mom, interfere," Nikki teased. "Be yourself!"

"No one would dare to interfere with me," Eduardo said fiercely. He stood at a counter, rolling out balls of dough into thin, perfectly round tortillas. A blender containing his famous salsa stood at his elbow.

Kitty, passing by, stopped to admire his dexterity with the rolling pin. "I never saw anyone do that before," she said, her voice filled with admiration. "I thought you had to buy tortillas in the store."

"Those store-bought things are barely fit to eat," Eduardo declared, his nostrils flaring with distaste. "Even Sonja's are better than that, but mine are superb."

Sonja, reading the instructions on a box of macaroni-and-cheese dinner as if she hadn't already cooked at least 10,000 such boxes in her lifetime, gave her husband an indulgent smile.

"You and your old tortillas," she teased, dismissing his food preferences out of hand. She rattled her box of macaroni in Kitty's direction. "Now here's something you'll really like. It's my specialty. I practically raised my two girls on it."

"Practically?" Caroline laughed. To her mother, macaroni-and-cheese from a box was haute cuisine.

"I believe I tried that once," Kitty said politely, her careful expression giving nothing away. "I found it quite...orange."

"It can be," Sonja conceded, "but mine's so good you wouldn't care if it had polka dots. You see, I have a secret ingredient. I put in a can of tuna fish!"

"Sounds...lovely," Kitty said faintly.

Adam, his arms still looped around Caroline's waist, rested his chin on her shoulder. She felt a little quiver of pleasure ripple through her. She'd never expected to feel this comfortable and happy in his embrace again.

"Check out the kid," he whispered, indicating their son. "He's just about as talented in the kitchen as his father."

Mark stood at another counter chopping vegetables, Amy at his side. "What's your specialty?" he asked Kitty.

"It's quite complicated," she said, suppressing a smile. "I open this tin of baked beans." She held up a can.

"Yuck." Mark popped a zucchini stick into his mouth. "That's it?"

"Hardly," Kitty sniffed with mock hauteur. "After I open it, I put the beans over toast. It's quite good."

"Yuck," Mark repeated. "Not much of a cook, are you?"

Kitty laughed. "Look who's talking. What are you doing with the courgettes?"

"The what?"

"The courgettes. Those white-and-green things you're mutilating."

Mark waved one. "Man, this isn't a cour—what you said. It's zucchini. You know, zucchini—the potato of Del Mar. And if you think that's a crack about Del Mar, you're right."

Blond beach babe Amy poked Mark in the ribs. "Like, quit eating the veggies," she ordered. "Save some for my dip." She indicated a carton of yogurt. "I mean, like, this is seeeew good for you."

Nikki dismissed her brother and his girlfriend with a condescending glance. "Ignore them, parentals," she instructed. "*I* gave away the food so *I* have saved the day." She opened the oven door and peered inside. "Yep, tiny turkeys are lookin' good."

"Tiny turkeys, my...eye," her brother harassed her. "I know Rock Cornish game hens when I see the suckers."

"Shut up, Mark." She gave him the sibling evil eye.

Mark offered his mother a jicama stick, which she accepted. The Mexican root vegetable still seemed slightly exotic to her, but she liked the crisp sweet flavor.

Mark grinned. "You should've seen Pop getting us organized, Mom. All except ol' Marty there." He nodded toward Martin, standing at the stove in the cooking island in the center of the room. "I think he was a fry cook in another life. So what's on the menu, my man?"

Martin, Caroline realized, had somehow unearthed the wok Adam had given her for Christmas at least five years ago. She'd never even pulled it out of the box. In one hand Martin expertly wielded long wooden chopsticks that must have come with the set; in the other he flourished a metal spatula.

Caroline looked at his T-shirt and smiled. "TGIF," it read, and beneath that in smaller letters the explanation "Thank God I'm Filipino."

Adam's laughter vibrated through her shoulder blades where they pressed against his chest. "Anybody who can handle spaghetti with chopsticks has to know what he's doing," he said.

Caroline was quick to agree. The boy was obviously a pearl beyond price in a kitchen. "So, what are you cooking?" she asked him.

"Pea chop suey." Martin indicated the pot on the back of the stove.

Nikki peered over his shoulder, frowning. "We gave all the peas away to the shelter."

"That's the beauty of it. I used green beans. And this masterpiece—" he pointed to the wok where he was stir-frying spaghetti "—is Turkey Surprise à la Filipino. The surprise is—"

"Yeah, yeah, we know," Mark interrupted. "The surprise is, there ain't no turkey."

Caroline knew she was going to get all teary-eyed if she didn't get out of there quick. Oh, how she loved every single one of them, but most especially the man in whose embrace she stood. Thank heaven no one else knew she'd planned to end her marriage. Thank heaven she still had time to make things right with him.

Thank heaven they had guests for Thanksgiving!

THEY SAT DOWN in midafternoon to the strangest Thanksgiving dinner Caroline had ever seen. They'd just settled into their places when the doorbell rang. Adam, at the head of the table, gestured for everyone to remain seated.

"I'll handle this," he announced. "The rest of you feel free to admire the feast until I get back."

Caroline, for one, was pleased to do just that. Everything looked wonderful to her, though her state of mind might have influenced that judgment.

Certainly she'd never seen such a menu: Cornish game hens, neatly halved by Adam-the-surgeon and roasted by Nikki; tortillas and salsa from Eduardo; baked beans on toast à la Kitty; raw vegetables and yogurt dip offered by Mark and Amy; macaroni and cheese with tuna from Sonja.

Martin had confessed that his Turkey Surprise was really a favorite Filipino dish called *pancit*, improvised with spaghetti noodles since more authentic noodles weren't available. Pea chop suey was his family's name for *sarciado,* he explained, a savory combination of vegetables with a bit of leftover roast pork in a tomato sauce.

He'd even found a package of short-grained rice Caroline had bought by mistake and tossed on a pantry shelf. A fortuitous accident, judging by the pleasure Martin took in washing and steaming the rice.

Everything looked and smelled delicious to Caroline, who was beginning to feel so maudlin that she wondered if she'd be able to get through the meal without humiliating herself with a flood of tears.

Adam appeared in the dining room doorway. "Look who's here," he said.

In came Crissy, Fred and their two kids, hopeful expressions on all four faces. Crissy held out two pumpkin pies like a peace offering.

Two really pathetic pumpkin pies, the crusts cracked and crumbling, the filling cratered and crisscrossed by deep fissures.

"Is there room at the Thanksgiving table for a few more?" she asked plaintively. "I swear, this wasn't my idea, Caroline!"

"Your idea?" Caroline was suddenly overcome with guilt. How could she have forgotten to invite Crissy and family after plans for a quiet holiday dinner went by the wayside?

Fred glanced from Caroline to Adam and back again. "We were going to bring a turkey," he said defensively. "She put it in the oven at the crack of dawn. Unfortunately it was still frozen and she forgot to turn on the oven."

Eduardo regarded Crissy with awe. He said something in Spanish.

Martin translated. "Like mother, like daughter."

Adam gave Fred a friendly thump on the shoulder. "No problem," he said. "The more the merrier. Pull up some chairs. Make room, everybody." His gaze connected with Caroline's. "I have a feeling this is going to be a memorable Thanksgiving in more ways than one."

For Caroline, it was the last wonderful straw. Hugging her sister, she welcomed the newcomers with all her heart. Everyone scooted their chairs close together to make room, and soon they were all packed around the table.

Young Jimmy pointed to the *sarciado*. "What's that?" he whispered suspiciously.

"Shh," his mother hissed. "Be thankful you've got food to eat and kind people to eat it with."

Jimmy subsided.

Adam, seated at the head of the table, stood and lifted his wine goblet. Obediently everyone turned toward him, faces expectant.

He spoke. "Friends and loved ones, thank you for accepting my invitation to share Thanksgiving with us."

Caroline frowned, sure she had misunderstood until she realized a lot of sheepish glances were aimed her way. What was going on? Was Adam really responsible for the full table? What on earth was he up to?

Adam continued calmly. "I thought you should all be present so I'd only have to say this once and no one could be accused of gossiping. Caroline has asked me for a divorce."

A gasp of disbelief swept the length of the table, along with muttered comments. "You're kidding!... Is he kidding?... He's kidding, isn't he?"

Caroline's heart stopped beating. Now was the time for the floor to open and swallow her whole. This was her worst nightmare come true, all her dirty linen waving out there in public for family, friends and strangers alike to view.

Not only that, Adam's pronouncement wrote finis to a marriage she now admitted she wanted to keep. She'd never really wanted a divorce; she simply wanted the man she'd fallen in love with and married.

She wanted her dreams back. Now that could never be.

Adam held up his hands for order, his expression composed. "But I knew she didn't really want a divorce," he continued. "She wanted to get my attention. Well, she got it in a major way."

Nervous laughter greeted this pronouncement. Caroline sat frozen to the spot, anxious only to get this over with so she could find some private place to grieve. *Be careful what you wish for....*

"I told her I'd give her my answer Thanksgiving Day, so here it is."

Caroline braced herself.

"*No,*" Adam announced explosively. "Never. I've loved this woman my entire adult life, so consider this official—*no.* Is that plain enough for you, Caroline? *There will be no divorce.*"

Relieved laughter and a smattering of applause greeted his announcement, but Adam didn't pay the slightest attention. Caroline knew he was now speaking directly to her.

"It took me a while, but I think I've finally seen your point of view, honey. I really have been too wrapped up in my work."

"Oh, Adam." Heart bursting with love, Caroline bit her lip to control its trembling.

He glanced down the length of the crowded table. "In the last few days I've come to realize what's really important—friends and family of course, but most of all my wife."

He lifted his wineglass in a salute to her, his eyes warm and caring. "A toast to the woman I love and cherish more than anything or anybody on this earth. To Caroline."

"To Caroline! Here, here!" Wineglasses and water glasses rose in agreement.

Caroline smiled through her tears. "Do you, Adam? Do you love me still?"

His lips shaped a single word just for her—*Yes*. Then he spoke to them all. "Thanksgiving is traditionally the time to count our blessings. The greatest blessing of all is to share what we have, no matter how much or how little, with those we love. It's not what's on the table—" a smile tugged at his lips "—as fantastic as that may be, but what's in our hearts."

Drawing Caroline to her feet, he tilted her chin so he could look into her eyes. Her pride warred with embarrassment, and for once, pride won. He really *did* love her. Let everyone share in the moment; she had nothing to fear.

"I'm sorry I neglected you," he said. "I love you more now than I did twenty years ago when I asked you to marry me." He faced their guests with his wife in his arms. "Here, in front of God and this company, I promise I'll never neglect you that way again."

"I'll hold you to that," she whispered.

"You won't have to. Caroline, I've already applied for that sabbatical. We'll use it to find a common ground from which to launch our next twenty years."

Caroline's final reservation melted away. How could she match his generosity? What could she give him to equal what he'd just given her?

Suddenly she knew. "And I promise..." She sucked in a deep breath to give her courage and went on in a rush. "I promise the next time I get mad at you I'll say so and not brood about it for five years!"

Turning in his arms, she pressed her cheek against his chest. "After this," she said around the lump in her throat, "Thanksgiving will be even more special to me."

Over her shoulder she looked at the smiling faces of family and friends. "Thank you all for caring," she said softly, "and for being here to share this really... really... *strange* holiday with us."

Strange, yes, she thought, smiling through tears of happiness as applause swept around the table. But also so very very wonderful....

A Note from Ruth Jean Dale

When it comes to holidays, my heart is filled with clichés. On New Year's Eve I make resolutions. On Christmas I truly believe it's better to give than to receive.

And on Thanksgiving, I count my blessings. Among those is the joy of sharing the holiday with family and friends, new and old. "The More the Merrier" is not just the title of my Thanksgiving story. It's my life.

I was fortunate to grow up in the midst of a very large, very close family in the Ozarks. Holidays brought everyone together. As a child, it wasn't the turkey or the pumpkin pie I anticipated, it was Aunt Lyla's chocolate cake with fudge frosting, Aunt Daisy's special macaroni and cheese and Aunt Patty's ice tea, syrup-sweet with sugar inches deep at the bottom of the pitcher. Most of all, I loved running wild "up hill and down dale" with my dozens of cousins.

In the natural order of things, I grew up, moved away and got married. But, oh, how I missed all that togetherness when holidays rolled around!

Fortunately, there were compensations in marriage to a military man. My husband would fill our house on holidays with homesick young Marines. The Corps always provided elaborate holiday meals but couldn't match our home-away-from-home ambiance.

As our children grew, we never knew who they'd invite home next. One particular year, three exchange students from England, college classmates of our youngest, arrived unannounced on our doorstep Christmas day—literally as we pulled the roast beef from the oven.

The *much-too-small* roast beef.

With our own brood and three hungry strangers to feed, my husband rose to the challenge. Have I mentioned he's one of the world's great amateur chefs? He proved it that day, improvising a menu that included *pancit* (fried noodles, Filipino-style), *adobo* (chicken and pork cooked in vinegar, another Filipino favorite), and *shio yaki* (Japanese-style salt-broiled salmon).

And rice. In our house, a day without rice truly is like a day without sunshine.

What a wonderful holiday that was! I still smile remembering how much we enjoyed getting to know Bunni, Chip and Bob—really Marie, Kevin and Simon, who chose their own American nicknames and pronounced them with that delightful British difference ("Bob" came out something like "Baub").

Typical? Perhaps not, but so very, very special—and the incident upon which I drew to write this story. As Adam says in "The More the Merrier," "It's not what's on the table, it's what's in our hearts."

Amen.